Hornet Heaven

Volume 3

Olly Wicken

Hornet Heaven is the paradise where Watford fans go in the afterlife. It turns out we're not just Watford 'til we die, we're Watford for all eternity.

In Hornet Heaven, you can watch all Watford's matches for the rest of time. You can also re-visit any Watford match in history, time and time again.

It's to die for.

The Hornet Heaven stories are dedicated to everyone who has ever loved Watford Football Club.

CONTENTS

ACKNOWLEDGEMENTS

Warm thanks to the Watford fans who helped bring the Hornet Heaven stories into being. In particular:

Watford fans Colin Mace and Jon Moonie whose voice and radio production talents turned the stories into an award-winning podcast.

Watford fan Andy Barker who created the logo.

Watford fans Geoff Wicken and David Harrison who helped improve each story.

Watford fan Lionel Birnie who commissioned the original Hornet Heaven story 'Only Till I Die?' for Volume 2 of the Tales From The Vicarage series of books.

Watford fans Oliver Phillips and Trefor Jones who assembled the historical facts on which the stories are built.

Watford fans Alan and Margaret Wicken who first took me to Vicarage Road on September 7th 1968.

You Horns.

Olly Wicken
October 2018

1

THE OVERLAPPING FULL-BACK

EARTH SEASON 2017/18

On Christmas morning 2017, Bill Mainwood — Hornet Heaven's Head of Programmes — strolled down Occupation Road towards the ancient turnstile.

The 92-year-old was on his way to find out whether Christmas Day and Boxing Day were going to be as troublesome as in 2016 — when Hornet Heaven collided with Luton's equivalent, Hatter Heaven, causing the two separate afterlives to overlap at historic festive matches between the rival teams.

When he arrived at the ancient turnstile in the slick black wall of the stadium, Bill stopped. Someone was standing on the far side, calling out to him.

'You've got to let me into your heaven! My club's a shambles! A disgrace! I'm sick of it! You've got to let me in! I'm begging you!'

'Oh,' Bill said. 'So the heavens definitely have collided a second time.'

'We're out of the title race by Christmas again! Wenger should have left years ago! He's destroying our club! It's doing my nut in!'

'Wenger? You mean you're a Gooner? Are you saying we've collided with Arsenal's heaven instead of Luton's?'

'A club with our history should be walking the league every year. But we're gutless. Spineless. No cojones. I'm done with it. Done. I want to support Watford instead. You've got to let me in. Please let me in. Please!'

* * *

Bill Mainwood was a compassionate man. Perhaps too compassionate. Either way, he allowed the Arsenal fan through the ancient turnstile, and led the stocky 64-year-old up Occupation Road to Hornet Heaven's golden atrium on the junction with Vicarage Road.

Once inside the atrium, Bill looked for Henry Grover — the man who founded Watford Rovers in 1881. He found The Father Of The Club sitting on a yellow leather sofa beneath a huge Christmas tree that had been decorated with yellow tinsel and red baubles.

Bill said: 'Henry! You've changed the baubles! Where are the ones I put up?'

'Really, Bill!' Henry scoffed. 'Black baubles! What were you thinking? Christmas tree baubles should always be red. Just like Watford's shorts.'

'Bah! Honestly, Henry. Switching the baubles behind my back is so petty.'

'Well, I'm afraid it matters, Bill.'

'The colour of baubles matters?'

'No, pettiness matters. It makes the whole red versus black debate so much more fun! Anyway, my good chap, what did you discover on your reconnaissance trip? Has there been a collision of heavens again this year?'

'Yes, there has, Henry.'

'Excellent! Another chance to show those Bedfordshire scuzzballs who's boss! Although, I must admit, Bill — sometimes I think the wretched oiks from up the road are too useless for our rivalry to be fun any more.'

'In that case, you may be glad to hear that, this year, the overlap isn't with Hatter Heaven. It's with a club more at our level.'

'Really? Golly. You don't mean with Bournemouth, do you?'

'I said "with a club more at our level", Henry. If I'd meant "with the tinpot plaything of a Russian robber baron", I would have said "with the tinpot plaything of a Russian robber baron". So, no. Not Bournemouth. We've collided with Arsenal. This chap with me is an Arsenal fan. He wants to come and live in our heaven.'

'Well, I'm not surprised. Actually, I am surprised. Surprised he's the only one. I hope you left someone guarding the ancient turnstile, Bill, or there'll be thousands of whining Gooners in here, bleating on and on about how unfair it is that other teams try to stop them strolling to all the trophies they deserve by some kind of birthright. It's ridiculous, Bill. Arsenal fans seem to think the Premier League title is a hereditary title.'

Henry stood up to introduce himself to the Arsenal fan. He looked the man up and down and tutted disapprovingly at the unfashionable cut of the man's 1970s suit. Then, as he noticed the man's deep-set eyes, slicked-back hair and broad meaty chin, he gasped: 'Good Lord!'

'What, Henry? What's wrong?' Bill asked.

'Nothing! In fact, this is wonderful! We're honoured by this man's presence!'

'Why? As an Arsenal fan, he probably *thinks* we should be honoured by his presence, but—'

'Don't you recognise him, Bill? This man is a former Watford manager! No wonder he wants to support us from now on!'

Bill stared at the man. Eventually the name came to him. He murmured: 'Eddie Hapgood! Watford manager from 1948 to 1950!'

'Exactly!' Henry said. 'Welcome, Mr Hapgood! Welcome to Hornet Heaven! I wish you'd been here all along!'

Eddie Hapgood replied in his Bristol accent: 'Cheers. That were hardly likely after I'd played more than four hundred games for the Gunners. But I definitely wish I'd been here since 2006 when we moved to the Emirates.' Eddie couldn't help moaning again. 'The whole thing's fallen apart! We should never have left Highbury! The mismanagement has been a disgrace! It's unacceptable!'

'Ah,' Henry observed. 'The usual whining and bleating. Perhaps it's good you *haven't* been here.'

'To be fair, Mr Hapgood,' Bill said, 'if you're going to be a Watford fan from now on, you'll have to behave like one. We're a very positive bunch, you see.'

'Fair enough,' Eddie said. 'I can be positive. It's been a few years, though, so… Let me see… um… Hold on, I'm a bit of out of practice…. Alright. I've got it… Look, this Christmas tree is nice. Lovely and… tall.'

'Well, I suppose you have to start somewhere,' Henry said. 'Well done. And, of course, you're correct. To my eye, this tree is as tall as Ross Jenkins, George Reilly, John McClelland and Steve Sherwood all standing on each other's shoulders.'

'Eh? Who?' Eddie asked.

'Ah. Oh dear. What if I said Heurelho Gomes on top of Christian Kabasele on top of Sebastian Prödl on top of —'

'Looks like I've got some name-learning to do,' Eddie said.

'Never mind. I'm sure Bill can help you fill in the gaps in your knowledge. In fact — I say, Bill. How about taking Mr Hapgood on one of your Magical History Tours to get him up to speed nice and quickly?'

'To be honest, Henry, it's not the knowledge I'm worried about. It's the totally new attitude any Arsenal fan would need.'

'Ah, yes. Fewer tantrums, you mean. Less spitting out the dummy. Less wailing like a baby that needs its nappy changing.'

'Exactly, Henry. And I think I know exactly how to help him develop the right attitude. Come on, Mr Hapgood. Let's go and turn you into a Watford fan.'

* * *

Bill fetched a couple of programmes from the shelves in the atrium and immediately took Eddie Hapgood through the ancient turnstile.

He said: 'I thought we'd go and watch a match from when you were our manager, Mr Hapgood. It should re-kindle any feelings you already have for the club.'

'I hope the feelings are good ones,' Eddie said. 'I didn't much enjoy getting the sack.'

They arrived at an FA Cup 4th Round tie at home to Manchester United in January 1950 — and joined the biggest crowd in Watford's history at the time. It was a cold, overcast afternoon, but the place was heaving. The Main Stand and the Shrodells Stand were full and — somehow — another 27,000 people had crammed themselves onto the uncovered terraces and banking that surrounded the mud-bath that passed for a pitch. It was proper.

Bill said to Eddie: 'As you'll recall, we were in Division Three South, whereas United had been runners-up in the top division for the last 3 seasons. We were David, aiming to bring down Goliath.' Bill paused and added: 'Goodness. Occasions like this still give me goosebumps. You too?'

Eddie replied: 'I'm, er, working on it.'

Eddie Hapgood had never really known what it was like to be a David. He'd always been a Goliath. As a player — a hard-tackling full-back — he'd never played outside the top division. He'd won 5 league championship medals. He'd also lifted 3 FA Cups and broken the record for England caps when England were regarded as the best footballing nation in the world.

After that, as an Arsenal supporter, he hadn't been used to cheering on a David. Throughout his life and afterlife, the Gunners had lined up as the superior side in the majority of their matches. (Or, at least, they'd thought they were the superior side.) As a fan, it required a completely different mentality to accept that your players weren't as good as your opponents — and get behind the team. It was a mentality that Eddie Hapgood and thousands of other Arsenal fans in 2017 just couldn't seem to adopt. All they could do was vent their anger at Arsene Wenger.

Bill said: 'An underdog mentality is still part and parcel of being a Watford fan. We never feel entitled to win football matches. It's a mindset that was bred into us for decades while we were in the lower leagues. And we still take it into games against the big clubs in 2017.'

He climbed over the wire fence surrounding the boggy playing area and said: 'Come on, Mr Hapgood. Follow me. I want to show you something.'

Bill led Eddie to the goal at the Vicarage Road end. They both stood on the goal-line behind United's goal-keeper who, as a real-world player in the game, remained oblivious to their presence.

'Do you remember what's going to happen, Mr Hapgood?'

'I do. Watford fans called it "The Goal That Never Was".'

'That's right. We'd tasted so little success or glory

by 1950 that this incident kept us talking for years afterwards.'

'Meanwhile, Arsenal won the whole competition in 1950. And it only kept fans talking for three years — when we won the League again.'

Bill reckoned this summed up pretty well the difference between being an Arsenal fan and being a Watford fan in the past. He also noticed Eddie was still referring to Arsenal as 'we'.

In the 36th minute of the game, "The Goal That Never Was" arrived. Watford's 39-year-old Welsh winger, Taffy Davies, eased past United's legendary captain Johnny Carey with a subtle change of stride before lobbing the ball over the keeper.

Bill and Eddie watched the ball cross the goal line before it was headed away by United's full-back John Aston. The huge home crowd roared to greet the goal. But the referee waved play on.

Eddie shouted: 'That were in! By a mile! On the day, I weren't sure, but now I know for definite! That were a total injustice!'

'And how do you feel about it?' Bill asked.

'I'm furious! That's just big-club bias!'

Bill smiled and said: 'Excellent. If you're angry

about big-club bias, you're already coming along nicely as a Watford fan.'

* * *

Bill and Eddie emerged from the ancient turnstile back onto Occupation Road. Eddie was feeling good about himself and his potential to become a true Watford fan.

Suddenly, though, he felt a hand on his shoulder. A voice with a Welsh accent said: 'I heard you was here, Hapgood. You've got a ruddy nerve!'

Bill Mainwood tried to intervene but was pushed to the ground.

Eddie Hapgood turned round and found himself looking into the much-aged face of the man whose disallowed goal he'd just witnessed. 87-year-old Taffy Davies said: 'Pretending to love Watford! You need to clear off!'

Taffy and Eddie famously hadn't got on as team-player and manager when their paths had crossed nearly 70 years ago. But now that they were meeting again in an eternal afterlife paradise, Eddie thought he'd better try to be friendly. He said: 'Nice to see you, Taffy. It's been a while.'

'It should have been for eternity,' Taffy replied. 'You don't belong here, Hapgood. You're not Watford. You never were and you never will be.'

Eddie said defiantly: 'I'm switching allegiances, as it goes.'

'No, you're not. Can't be done, see. Everyone knows that. Fans can't switch clubs. They can't ever truly love a different team.'

'I can. I reckon I were always a latent Watford fan. I mean, I had some good times here as manager. People talked about "the defence that Eddie built". In 1949 we kept 8 clean sheets in a row in the league.'

Bill called out as he lay on the tarmac: 'In point of fact, Taffy, he still holds the club record for that.'

'Shut your gob, Mainwood!' Taffy shouted back.

Taffy, the former Watford winger, grabbed Hapgood, the former Arsenal and England full-back, by the lapels of his 1970s suit. He growled: 'It's too late, Hapgood. You died an Arsenal fan. You can't suddenly become a Watford fan. You can't be fickle when you're dead.'

Eddie felt there was a certain amount of truth in this last statement. But he wasn't ready to concede.

'Honestly, Taffy, mate,' he said. 'There ain't no

harm in my being here.'

'Yes, there is. You're the enemy. You need to stay out of Hornet Heaven'

'I don't know why you're being so territorial—'

'Because we're Watford. This is our paradise. You'll stay here over my dead body!'

This didn't really work as a threat in the afterlife, Taffy quickly realised. It threw him slightly.

He continued: 'I mean, how do I know you're not here to take revenge on me?'

Eddie frowned. He didn't remember ever wanting revenge on one of his players. He thought for a moment. Then he suddenly realised what Taffy was talking about. In 1950, he recalled, there had been rumours that the Welsh winger had plotted with directors of the club to get him sacked.

The memory incensed Eddie. Now he grabbed the lapels of Taffy's suit. He said: 'So you're finally admitting you got me booted out of Watford.'

'You had it coming. You dropped me from the team for half a season.'

'I were the manager. It were my job to pick who I wanted.'

'Twenty seasons I played for Watford, and you

totally ruined the last one. It was your fault I didn't reach 300 career League appearances for this club.'

'Ha! You're blaming *me*? You should be blaming Adolf Hitler for starting a war that took seven seasons out of your League career!'

Taffy sneered and said: 'Frankly I don't see much difference between the two of you.'

Bill got up off the tarmac to try and stop the argument. 'Gentlemen! Gentlemen!' he said. 'You may have your differences, but—'

Taffy shoved Bill to the ground again.

Bill's head bumped against the black stadium wall. Dazed, he watched Taffy Davies pull two programmes out of his pocket. Then the Welshman bundled Eddie Hapgood through the ancient turnstile.

Taffy said: 'I'm putting you back where you belong, Hapgood! And you ain't never coming back!'

* * *

'Are you alright, sir? You look as knocked for six as Watford against Manchester City this season, sir.'

Back in the atrium, Bill was greeted by his 13-year-old programme assistant Derek Garston.

14

Bill replied: 'I'm afraid there's all kinds of trouble going on, young man. There's been a collision of the heavens and—'

'Crikey, sir. With our usual hapless rivals from the town that dare not speak its name? With those unloveable cockwombles, sir?'

'Derek! No, I mean with Arsenal's heaven, young man.'

'Really, sir? Super, sir. That's much more like it: a much better class of rival, sir. It proves we're definitely going up in the world, sir.'

Bill thought about this for a moment. 'I see what you mean, my boy. If clubs can be defined by who their rivals are, then it's probably best for us to keep a good distance from, ahem, cockwomblery.'

'And does the overlap of the heavens occur at historic Christmas matches like last time, sir?'

'I expect so. And that's where I need your help, my boy. When have we played Arsenal over the festive period?'

Derek's encyclopaedic knowledge of Watford facts and statistics meant he could answer instantly: 'Boxing Day 2006 is the only time, sir. A 2-1 home defeat, sir. Tommy Smith scored, sir.'

'Right. Well, that's the game I need to visit. Fetch me a programme, please, my boy. Actually, make it two. I'd better take Lamper with me.'

'Aha! Craving a bit of festive fisticuffs, are you, sir? Want some, do you, sir?'

'No! Of course not! This is a peace mission, young man. A Christmas peace mission. I need Lamper for my own protection.'

'From Arsenal thugs, sir? From a Gooner squad?'

'Goodness, no, my boy! It's Taffy Davies I'm frightened of. Now, run along and fetch me those programmes.'

* * *

'And we will fight for evermore because of Boxing Day!'

Hornet Heaven's Chief Steward — Lamper, a former hooligan — followed Bill through the ancient turnstile to Watford's Boxing Day 2006 game at home to Arsenal. He said: 'If they bring it, I'm going to do them. Big-time.'

Bill stood in the old Main Stand and looked around the stadium.

He said: 'I expect Taffy will try to force Eddie Hapgood back into the main part of Arsenal's heaven — Arsenal Arcadia, or whatever the place is called. We need to find the gateway. But where would it be?'

A voice squeaked: 'I know, sir!'

Bill turned and saw his young assistant. He said: 'Derek! You weren't meant to come too!'

'But this is so exciting, sir! And 13-year-olds are especially good at hide-and-seek, sir.'

'Then where should we be looking?'

'Well, Arsenal are a posh old club, sir, so I reckon we should look in the Directors' Box. Come on, sir!'

Derek skipped past Bill and hopped over the low dividing wall into the Directors Box. He called out: 'Hurry up, sir! Last year, the heavens separated at midnight on Boxing Day, so we've only got today and tomorrow, sir!'

Bill paused. In all the excitement, he'd forgotten about the time limit on the overlap of the heavens. Perhaps this meant that Eddie Hapgood wouldn't be able to make a permanent transfer to Hornet Heaven after all. Or would different rules apply if Eddie was on the other side of the ancient turnstile when the deadline came? He didn't know.

'Come on, sir! Move it!'

Bill and Lamper followed Derek into the Directors Box and down a short staircase inside.

Suddenly Derek came to a halt, awestruck. He said: 'Look, sir and Mr Lamper, sir! Arsenal Arcadia!'

Bill and Lamper stared. Ahead of them was a wide marble staircase leading upwards. On the walls of the staircase, above polished wooden bannisters, were art deco lamps. Etched into the marble of each of the steps was a small red icon — a cannon.

'Blinking flip!' Lamper said. 'This is well swanky. Not like Luton. Last year, when I was chasing scummers back through their gateway, the entrance to Hatter Heaven was a toilet. Hadn't even been properly flushed.'

Standing on the bottom step of the staircase was a uniformed commissionaire. He didn't exactly look overworked: the staircase was empty and silent. Lamper asked: 'Is this a library?'

The commissionaire politely doffed his cap. Bill, Lamper and Derek climbed the stairs.

At the top, they found themselves in a huge marble lobby. It was very impressive. The floor was white marble with red geometric edging and an old-style red AFC crest tiled into the centre. Less impressive was the noise. The place was full of Arsenal fans complaining.

One said: 'It's an embarrassment that we're in the Europa League! All the pride's gone from this club!'

Another said: 'Troy Deeney was spot on! Wenger's built a squad of fairies!'

A third said: 'This club used to be a class act, but it ain't no more. We need to spend more money! Loadsamoney!'

Bill, Lamper and Derek wanted to cover their ears. They fully understood why Eddie Hapgood had had enough of this place.

They started searching the lobby, looking for Eddie and Taffy in between the groups of moaning Gunners.

Before long, Bill spotted the two men in front of a bronze bust of Herbert Chapman. Bill didn't like what he saw. Taffy Davies was still grappling his former manager. The Welshman had his 1950 nemesis in a bear-hug — squeezing the breath out of him.

Bill, Lamper and Derek rushed over to separate them. But when they arrived, no separation was necessary. Taffy let Eddie go. The two men smiled at each other. There didn't seem to be any animosity between them at all.

Eddie said: 'Taffy's got quite the man-hug on him, Bill.'

'You mean you've made up with each other?' Bill said. 'Thank goodness. I was expecting more trouble.'

Lamper couldn't hide his disappointment: 'This is no good. Let me start some more trouble. I mean, look at all these miserable Gooners. Why don't I give them a good Christmas kicking to cheer them up?'

Eddie explained to Bill: 'Taffy's taken pity on me — now he's seen what Arsenal's heaven is like. Haven't you, mate?'

Taffy said: 'I wouldn't wish this place on my worst enemy. Seriously. I'm not being funny or anything, because Eddie Hapgood is actually my worst enemy.'

Taffy shook his head in disbelief at the state of the Gooners around him. Then he led Eddie towards the wide marble staircase so that Watford's former manager could make his way back to Hornet Heaven and spend the rest of eternity in a happier place. Bill, Derek and Lamper followed them.

At the bottom of the staircase, the commissionaire respectfully doffed his cap again as they all left Arsenal Arcadia. Lamper booted him up the bum.

* * *

For the next day and a half, Bill Mainwood continued Eddie Hapgood's Hornet education. He took Eddie to a selection of old matches that would shape his new friend as a Watford fan in the way that all long-standing Watford fans are shaped by the past.

He took Eddie to see Watford losing at Darlington to drop into 92nd place in the Football League in August 1975.

Then they went to watch Watford win at Old Trafford, three years later, with two Luther Blissett headers.

Next they went to the 3-0 home defeat to Yeovil in 2013, followed by the 3-0 home win over Liverpool two seasons later, with two strikes from Odion Ighalo.

Bill said: 'No matter where our ambition takes us, our past helps us keep perspective.'

On their various trips to the old games, Bill and Eddie thoroughly enjoyed each other's company. Eddie was taking to being a Watford fan like a duck to water. When he mentioned that, in his playing days, he'd been known as "The Prince of Full Backs", Bill took him to watch Albert McClenaghan — 'The Dunce of Full Backs'. Eddie thought this was hilarious. He was starting to forget that he'd ever been an Arsenal fan at all.

* * *

Late on Boxing Day evening, after they'd been to that day's 2017 home game against Leicester, Bill reckoned Eddie was ready for the acid test of whether the newcomer had put his feelings for Arsenal behind him.

He took Eddie down Occupation Road and through the ancient turnstile to Watford's most recent game against Arsenal — the spectacular comeback win in mid-October.

They settled into the Rookery End in seats behind the goal.

When Per Mertesacker put Arsenal ahead from a corner just before half-time, Bill watched Eddie closely. Eddie swore. But not at the opposition.

'Zonal marking!' he seethed. 'I hate it!'

Then he added: 'Decent delivery, though, you have to admit.'

Bill began to worry that Eddie might be failing the test. It seemed as though the former Arsenal stalwart might still have an affinity with his old team.

But he was reassured when the game turned in the second half. When Troy Deeney came on as a substitute and banged home a penalty, Eddie sang: 'Co-jones! Whoa-oa-oh! Co-jones! Whoa-oa-oh!'

After that, for the final 20 minutes of the game, it was all Watford — they bullied the Gunners. Every Watford fan could sense the real possibility of David beating Goliath. The noise in the stadium grew and grew.

Eddie said to Bill: 'It's funny. When you lot won at Highbury in January, I were livid you'd stolen our points…'

Bill noticed Eddie had said 'you lot'.

Eddie continued: '…But this is brilliant. I'm a total convert.'

They watched a deflected Etienne Capoue shot send Petr Cech the wrong way. Hapgood leapt to his feet. The ball bounced onto the post and out.

Hapgood sat down and said: 'I love the spirit of this team. The desire, the drive. The togetherness. I'm going to have no problem watching this for the rest of eternity.'

Watford kept attacking. In added time, Holebas

shot from outside the box. Deeney challenged Cech. The ball came back to Capoue. Capoue's shot was blocked. The ball fell for Tom Cleverley 10 yards from goal.

Bill turned to watch Eddie. Eddie was already out of his seat. The former Watford manager screamed with joy as Cleverley blasted the ball into the roof of the net. The whole stadium shook with noise. Eddie was leaping up and down, punching the air. Bill couldn't stop himself joining in. They grabbed each other, hugged each other, and bounced and bounced. Bill was totally elated that the joy of supporting Watford had entered the heart of another football fan.

But as they bounced, Bill felt his grip around his new friend loosening. Suddenly the stocky former full-back wasn't feeling as solid to the touch.

They stopped bouncing.

Eddie said: 'What's happening, Bill? You're fading! Everything's fading!'

Bill realised it must be midnight on Boxing Day night. The Watford and Arsenal heavens were separating after their Christmas overlap — just as Derek had warned.

Bill let go of Eddie and said: 'Oh, Eddie. I'm so sorry.'

'What's happening?'

'You're going back to Arsenal's heaven.'

'But I don't want to go back!'

Bill watched Eddie Hapgood continue to fade away.

'Goodbye, Eddie,' Bill said sadly. 'We've had a lovely two days.'

Eddie was barely visible now. He cried: 'I don't want to be an Arsenal fan for eternity! Please! Bill! Do something! I want to be a Watford fan!'

As Eddie finally disappeared, Bill heard Eddie's fading voice one final time: 'I want to be a Watford fan!'

Bill looked around. Every Watford fan in the stadium was still bouncing and shouting — enjoying one of the best David and Goliath moments they'd ever known. But Bill sniffed back a tear and headed back to the ancient turnstile.

*   *   *

The next day, in the atrium, Bill sat with Henry Grover and Derek Garston on the yellow sofas beneath the Christmas tree. Bill was still feeling sad that Eddie Hapgood hadn't been able to stay in Hornet Heaven.

Henry said: 'I say. Cheer up, old chap. You really can't justify being down as a Watford fan at the moment. We've had some great times so far this season — especially against the big beasts of the Premier League.'

Derek tried to lift his boss's spirits: 'Look, sir. Have you noticed the baubles on the tree, sir?'

Bill saw that his young assistant had replaced Henry's red baubles with black baubles again. Bill half-smiled, and thanked the boy, but he still felt an overwhelming sense of loss over Eddie Hapgood.

Taffy Davies came up. He sat down next to Bill and said: 'Now, I'm not being funny or anything, Bill, but snap the hell out of it. It's like I said, see. Fans can't switch clubs. They can't ever truly love a different team.'

Bill sighed and said: 'I guess I just wanted more people to know the joy of supporting Watford.'

'You're too kind-hearted, Bill,' Taffy said. 'Arsenal fans have made their bed, so now they've got to lie in it. And how can you be sure that Hapgood would have stuck around anyway? He's a manager — and you only have to look at Marco Silva to know what managers are like. If Marco was up here, he'd probably want to bugger off to Everton's heaven.'

Derek piped up: 'I bet it's called Toffee Utopia, Mr Davies, sir. It would be great fun to overlap with them next year. Though, maybe the overlap is only ever with our rivals, Mr Davies, sir. And perhaps the level we've reached as a club means our rivalry will always be with Arsenal from now on.'

'Maybe,' Taffy said. 'Until it's with Barcelona!'

Henry wasn't so sure. He said: 'I see what you mean, Derek, but personally I think I'd prefer it if we collided with Hatter Heaven again next year. To my mind, Luton are our traditional rivals — and Christmas is all about tradition.'

Derek said: 'But they're a horrible Christmas tradition, Mr Grover, sir. They're like Brussels Sprouts, Mr Grover, sir!'

At last, a smile came to Bill Mainwood's face. Young Derek was right. Luton Town were definitely the Brussels Sprouts of football teams: disgusting, but at certain times you just had to accept their existence. His smile became a giggle. His giggle became a chuckle. His chuckle became a chortle.

Henry, Taffy and Derek watched Bill chortling and felt pleased for him. The Head Of Programmes had regained his happiness — just like all Watford fans had done in the second half of 2017.

With the year drawing to an end, the four of them sat together on the yellow sofas feeling good — feeling ready for even more happiness in 2018.

They were in their heaven, and all was right with the world.

THE END

2

THE OFFICIAL STORY

EARTH SEASON 2017/18

In late December 2017, Frank Gammon, the angriest man in Hornet Heaven, entered the atrium. He noticed that the Head Of Programmes, Bill Mainwood, was giving an orientation session to a new arrival on the yellow leather sofas.

Frank wasn't happy. He went over to Bill and growled: 'What's he doing here?'

Frank pointed tetchily at the new arrival — a squat, middle-aged man with milk-bottle glasses.

Bill replied: 'Now now, Frank. You should never judge a man by appearances. He's wearing the clothes he died in and —'

'Those clothes tell me all I need to know. He's a total—'

'Frank! Don't swear at the man! He'll have had enough of that back down on earth!'

Frank glowered at the new arrival. The man was wearing a black shirt, black shorts, and black and white socks. There was a whistle on a string around his neck.

Frank seethed: 'Referees don't support Watford, they hate Watford. Get him out. His sort ain't welcome in Hornet Heaven.'

*   *   *

The man in the milk-bottle glasses and refereeing kit was upset — understandably. Dying hadn't been a great start to the day.

And after that — thanks to Frank Gammon goading the crowd in the atrium — he'd found himself being widely booed and jeered in the place where he was to spend the rest of eternity.

The volume of the abuse he'd received couldn't have been louder — and the new arrival felt this wasn't really fair. As a Watford fan himself, he was of the firm opinion that the crowd should have held back their very loudest abuse in case Rob Styles somehow ever set foot in Hornet Heaven.

The referee felt better, though, when Bill Mainwood took pity on him and led him down Occupation Road to the seclusion of the Bill Mainwood Programme Hut — to finish the orientation session.

The previous summer, the hut had been converted into the Bill Mainwood Man Cave. Now, inside the small cosy space, the referee relaxed into one of the yellow and black striped deckchairs, surrounded by nostalgic Hornet memorabilia. It was a place that would make any Watford fan feel safe and happy.

The referee watched 92-year-old Bill ease himself into the other deckchair. The Head Of Programmes said: 'Well, I really must apologise for the rude reception you received earlier.'

Suddenly, the door to the Man Cave burst open. In walked Bill's 13-year-old assistant, Derek Garston. He said: 'Hello, sir, I was just… Oh. Who's the wanker in the black, sir?'

'Derek!' Bill cried. 'Get out! Now!'

Derek left. Bill apologised a second time.

But the referee was upset again: the lack of respect had been so instinctive, so casual — and from a child, no less. He adjusted his glasses and said: 'By heck! The lip never seems to stop, up here.'

'Oh dear,' Bill said. 'I'm afraid young Derek can be a bit—'

'I mean, I don't believe all fans in Hornet Heaven actually hate referees, but something about seeing a man in a black kit just seems to raise their hackles. It's like I symbolise their broken dreams, or something.'

'Yes, you may be right. Just looking at you, I'm thinking back to the 1950 FA Cup tie against Manchester United and the clear goal the referee ruled out. I want to blame you. In fact, I think I do.'

'But I've done nothing wrong to Watford fans. I'm a Watford fan myself. I'm one of the Watford family. People forget that every referee is a human being underneath.'

'Is that strictly true? I mean, *you're* not a human being, obviously. Not now you're dead.' Bill paused. Then he apologized. 'Oh dear. Sorry. That was possibly a little harsh. After all, you don't seem quite as inhuman as many of the referees that are scarred into my memory. I'm thinking of Roger Milford, Stuart Attwell, Alan Seville, John Hunting…'

The referee waited while Bill finished reciting a

list of referees responsible for crimes against the Hornets.

Several minutes later, Bill said: '…And, of course, Lee Probert.'

The referee couldn't believe he'd been mentioned in the same breath as such evil men guilty of such terrible wrongdoing. He complained: 'That's not fair. You can't tar me with the same brush as that lot. I weren't a *professional* referee. I only officiated in local football. I didn't ref at the highest level because I didn't have the necessary personality deficiencies.'

'Really? Many fans would argue that all referees are sociopaths.'

'Well I'm not. If anything, it's the fans who are sociopaths — for projecting their frustrations onto me. The truth is that I'm just an ordinary Watford fan who loves football and wanted to give back to the game at grassroots level in my spare time.'

'Oh. Well, when you put it like that, you seem like a good man.'

'Thank you,' the referee said. 'Wow. No-one's ever said that to me when I've been wearing this kit.'

'Ah, you're cheering up now,' Bill observed. 'Good. You should keep seeing the positives. I mean, wearing that kit for the rest of infinity means that, mathematically, there's a small chance that someone else might possibly, at some point, say something nice to you.'

Bill hadn't meant it as a withering put-down, but it had that effect. The referee peered down through his glasses and contemplated wearing his refereeing kit for the rest of all time. He shook his head sadly and said: 'Back on earth, players and fans wished I were dead. And now I'm here, everyone wishes I *weren't* dead. I can't win.'

He was exaggerating a little, but so far Hornet Heaven definitely didn't look like being a paradise as far as he was concerned.

Bill said: 'Well, I'm here to help. What we need is a way of getting people up here to accept the presence of a referee among us. Have you got any ideas?'

Suddenly, the referee felt more optimistic. He wanted to be accepted. He thought for a moment. Then he looked up with a new light in his eyes. He said: 'I know. You could put me in charge.'

'Ha! Put a referee in charge? Give free rein to a deep-seated psychotic need to boss everyone around? That would be one of the worst ever decisions seen at

Vicarage Road. And that's saying something, I can tell you.'

The referee sank back into his deckchair in disappointment.

But then Bill said rather more sympathetically: 'No. We need a far better solution than that. Let's go and see the man who's actually in charge up here. He might have some ideas on how to make a referee in Hornet Heaven acceptable. Come on.'

The referee shrugged. He supposed there couldn't be any harm in getting up out of his deckchair and following Bill out of the Man Cave. Surely things could only look up from here.

* * *

The referee went with Bill Mainwood to the swanky Gallery restaurant in the south west corner of the stadium. This was where, Bill said, they'd find Henry Grover — the man who founded Watford Rovers in 1881, The Father Of The Club. The referee was confident that a man of such great esteem would surely set an example to everyone else in Hornet Heaven by having due respect for officialdom.

When he stepped inside the restaurant, the referee dithered momentarily. He wasn't sure he was properly dressed for such a swanky restaurant. Suddenly he heard a loud voice say: 'Oh! Look, Johnny! Ha ha! Look at the absolute state of this fellow!'

Henry Grover was sitting in one of the restaurant's semi-circular booths with Johnny Allgood — the man who, in 1903, had become Watford's first-ever manager.

Henry's exclamation made the referee feel even less confident that he was suitably attired. He hesitated by the door.

Henry got to his feet and pointed at the referee. He chanted: 'You don't know what you're doing! You don't know what you're doing!'

The referee's heart sank.

Over at the table, Johnny Allgood — an intelligent man who'd commanded respect throughout the entire footballing world in the Victorian era — said reproachfully: 'Now now, Henry. I think we can do better than that!'

Henry took Johnny's point on board. He said: 'Ah. Quite right, Johnny. OK. How about...' He began another chant: 'Who's your father, who's your father, who's your father, referee? You ain't got one, you're a bastard, you're a bastard, referee!'

Things weren't going the way the referee had hoped. The mere sight of him seemed to have made him the scapegoat for all of The Father Of The Club's disappointments since 1881. He actually felt close to tears as he finally made his way over to the booth with Bill.

When they'd sat down, Bill said: 'Anyway, Henry, I thought that, as The Father Of The Club, you might have some ideas on how we could make the presence of a referee more acceptable to fellow residents.'

Henry immediately made a suggestion: 'Ah. I know. Do we have any medieval stocks in Hornet Heaven, Bill? I'd love to throw a putrid tomato or two at a referee. I mean, look at this man's officious sneer. Wouldn't it be wonderful to see it wiped from his face by a slowly descending veil of rancid custard.'

The referee felt this was definitely unfair. Down on earth, in his bedroom, he'd often practiced pointing and whistling in the mirror — and he hadn't thought he'd looked officious at all. In fact, he reckoned that in Hornet Heaven he was pretty much indistinguishable from any other Watford fan — apart from his refereeing kit. That, and the sadness in his eyes at the constant vilification he was receiving.

He heard Johnny Allgood say: 'I don't think locking the man up was quite the kind of thing Bill meant, Henry.'

'Oh. Ah,' Henry replied. 'In that case, perhaps we should release him, give him a slight head start, and give chase. Les Simmonds knows where the pitchforks are kept. I do love a good angry mob.'

'That's just vindictive, Henry. If anything, we should be looking for a positive way of harnessing this man's talent.'

Henry murmured to himself: 'Talent... Referee... Talent... Referee... No, Johnny, I simply can't compute what you're saying.'

'Honestly, man,' Johnny said. 'Show him some respect. This is a man who knows the Laws of the Game and how they should be applied.'

'Ha! Applied to penalise Watford unfairly, you mean, old thing. That's what all referees do. I bet he thinks Tony Coton really did bring down Ian Rush in the 1986 FA Cup Quarter Final Replay.'

The referee, despite his distress at Henry's overplayed prejudice, saw the chance to assert his Watford-supporting credentials. He said: 'As a matter of fact, I watched that game. I were on the Family Terrace as a young lad. Mind you, I can't claim I saw the incident clearly.'

'In which case,' Henry replied, 'you should definitely go through the ancient turnstile to watch Coton's challenge again. It was never a penalty. It was a typical example of the kind of injustice that your sort has invariably handed out to Watford over the years. You're all monsters. Monsters! The lot of you!'

The referee stared at Henry Grover despondently. He couldn't take this any more. He shouldn't take it. He needed to stand up for himself. He said defiantly: 'Well, if I did go and look at it again, at least I'd be able to make an expert judgement. I'm more qualified than you. More qualified than anyone else up here, probably.'

The referee suddenly felt Bill's hand on his arm.

Bill gasped: 'Golly! That's it! That's how we could get you respected by fans in Hornet Heaven! We could make you a guide on one of my Magical History Tours. As a qualified referee, you'd provide a second opinion on controversial refereeing decisions that went against the Horns.'

As soon as he heard this idea, the referee's eyes filled with delight at the prospect. 'Now we're talking,' he said. 'I could give you the official story. Wow. I'd be... I'd be like Graham Poll in the BT Sport truck!'

Next to him, Johnny Allgood grimaced at the realisation he was in the presence of a man who wanted to be like Graham Poll.

Johnny warned: 'You know, gentlemen, I don't think this is a good idea.'

But Henry interrupted: 'Nonsense, Johnny! This is a great idea! Imagine it — we'd have verification from an official source that Andy Gray headed the ball out of Steve Sherwood's secure grasp! We'd have authentication that Reading's ghost goal was a heinous wrong inflicted on our club! After all these years we'd have closure!'

Henry leaned over and planted a big kiss on the referee's forehead. He said: 'You're welcome here! Everyone in Hornet Heaven is going to love you!'

* * *

The referee, feeling newly confident, went back to the atrium with Bill. They found Frank Gammon still there. Frank didn't seem at all pleased to see the referee again. He screamed a string of swearwords so foul that he'd only ever shouted them at Luton fans before.

The referee's eyes watered behind his milk-bottle glasses. Some of Frank's swearwords were based on parts of the body so rude that the referee had never heard of them.

He heard Bill say: 'Now, now, Frank. I was thinking you might like to join us on a Magical History Tour — in the interests of eternal harmony. Our friend here could—'

'Friend?' Frank said. 'The only referee that's a friend is Kevin Friend. And he's a—'

Frank used a word that made the referee's eyes water again.

Bill said: 'That's not very nice, Frank. My idea was that this man could give us his expert verdict when we revisit a match where a referee did us wrong. You know, where a referee completely—'

Frank interrupted Bill. He supplied a particularly disgusting verb.

Bill said: 'Well, yes. I suppose you could put it that way, Frank. Where a referee did... er... *that* to Watford.'

With watering eyes, the referee told himself to look for the positives in Frank's attitude towards match officials. The only thing he could think of was that it was expanding his vocabulary. But then Hornet Heaven's angriest man seemed to engage with Bill's idea a little.

'But how would you choose which game to go back to?' Frank asked. 'There's been dozens of criminal decisions this season alone. Troy's red at home to Huddersfield. Zeegelaar's at Burnley. Gah! That one still makes me livid! Lee Probert is the worst of the lot. He's a complete—'

The word Frank used to describe Lee Probert caused the referee to take off his glasses and dab at his eyes for several seconds.

As he dabbed, he began to think that perhaps Bill's plan wasn't going to work after all. Maybe he had to face the fact that Watford fans would never accept a referee in their midst. Not for the rest of eternity.

But then he remembered the inspiration he'd felt when he'd first heard Bill's idea in The Gallery restaurant: he remembered how much he really, really wanted to be like Graham Poll.

He pulled himself together and said: 'If that's how you feel about Lee Probert, Frank, we should check that you're justified.'

'Oh, I'm justified alright. He's an utter —'

'Now, now. That's just name-calling. As a qualified official, I could give you an expert assessment of his performance.'

'It'll only tell me that Lee Probert's an even bigger—'

'No! We need to review his decision-making properly. Come on. I've got a particular incident in mind. It were down at Bournemouth on Friday 30th January 2015. I'll fetch the programmes.'

* * *

The referee took Bill and Frank through the ancient turnstile. They arrived at the Goldsands Stadium, Bournemouth. They only had to wait 25 seconds before the abomination occurred. Gabriele Angella, with Craig Cathcart covering him, tripped the Bournemouth striker Callum Wilson thirty yards out from Watford's goal. Referee Lee Probert produced a red card.

Watching the incident again from Hornet Heaven, the new arrival felt exactly the same sensations that all Watford fans felt the first time around. For a few moments he felt hollow with disbelief. Then anger poured into the void — a boiling anger that wanted to explode out of him. His mind felt like it was bending with fury.

But he managed to keep just enough control of himself to say with calm conviction, from his official perspective: 'That's categorically not a red card. Lee Probert has got that wrong. He's made a mistake there.'

Bill said: 'Golly. I feel quite a bit better for you saying that, ref. The Horns have still been wronged, but I feel better for knowing for sure that we've been wronged. It takes the edge off my rage.'

The referee asked: 'And how's it working for you, Frank?'

Frank sounded surprised and pleased. 'Yeah… Feels good.'

The referee was delighted.

Bill said: 'I guess there's nothing like a little bit of vindication to improve the mood of a football fan. In Hornet Heaven, you see, we miss out on that. For example, we never get to hear the media giving their verdicts on refereeing decisions.'

'Blimey,' Frank said. 'I'd never thought about that before, but it's true. At home to Spurs this season, I would have felt a lot better afterwards if I could have heard a studio pundit saying he reckoned Erik Dier's handball was a "stonewall penalty".'

'Quite,' Bill agreed. 'We never had that satisfaction.'

Frank continued: 'And after we lost 4-1 at home to Huddersfield it wouldn't have hurt nearly as much if I'd got to hear someone on telly say their first goal was offside "all day long". Any old washed-up ex-pro could have said it — I wouldn't have minded. As long as it got said.'

'Exactly, Frank,' Bill said. 'Normally, up here, we never receive confirmation of the injustice. But now, with this man here among us, we'll have proper verification.'

The referee enjoyed hearing this conversation. At last he began to feel he'd be welcome in Hornet Heaven. He couldn't stop fans feeling aggrieved by decisions, but he could make them feel more agreeably aggrieved.

Frank said to him: 'Right. I like this feeling. I want you to come with me, ref. We'll go back and watch every injustice ever. You can tell me I'm officially right to feel wronged.'

The referee grinned. He liked being appointed to pass judgement. It appealed to something inside him — something deep and innate.

Suddenly, though, he heard Frank grunt: 'Hang on a minute. That'll only sort out the old games. We'll need something for the new games too — in real time, as the atrocities are happening.'

The referee hadn't thought about this.

Bill said: 'How do you mean, Frank: a kind of VAR to check decisions during the game?'

Frank jumped on the suggestion: 'That's it! We need VAR!'

Bill started to scratch his head. He said: 'Well, I don't quite know how we'd do that.'

But the referee knew. He stepped in and took control. He had an even bigger grin on his face as he said: 'I've got the answer. *I'll* be the VAR — the Validating Afterlife Referee. Leave it to me. I'll come up with a system and run the whole thing.'

* * *

A few days later, on December 30th, VAR was in place in Hornet Heaven for Watford's Premier League home game against Swansea City.

The referee had devised a very straightforward system: he simply followed the real-world match referee,

Martin Atkinson, all over the pitch. Every time Atkinson made a decision, Hornet Heaven's Validating Afterlife Referee, in his milk-bottle glasses and baggy black shorts, would thrust his hand up into the air with either a thumbs up or a thumbs down.

'Good decision, Martin,' he'd call out. Or, 'Oh dear, Martin — you've dropped a clanger there.'

He was so pleased with what he was doing that each time he provided his instant second opinion, he couldn't help providing a smug smile too. The crowd cheered and booed his verdicts — like a raucous pantomime audience. A few people shouted out that VAR had turned the spectacle into a farce, but he just shouted back: 'If you want correct decisions, there's a price to pay.'

He was most pleased, though, when the key moment of the match arrived with four minutes left on his watch. Watford were one-up when Andre Gray failed to accept a gilt-edged chance at the Rookery End. Sixty seconds later, at the other end, Swansea swung in a cross from their right wing. Their substitute centre-forward rose at the far post and headed the ball back across goal. Jordan Ayew, totally alone in the six yard box, turned it into Watford's net. In the land of the living, Martin

Atkinson signalled a goal and the linesman ran away up the touchline with his flag at his side. But in Hornet Heaven, the Validating Afterlife Referee stood in the Watford goalmouth with his arm raised. He turned his thumb down. He announced: 'Offside! Pure and simple!'

The Hornet Heaven crowd roared its approval. The referee, beaming with pride, drew a rectangle in the air with his hands, and signalled for an indirect free-kick to Watford. It didn't matter — he told himself — that, in the real world, the game was re-starting with the score at 1-1. In Hornet Heaven, fans who'd been feeling robbed by shipping a late goal to the bottom team would now have the consolation of official verification of that feeling.

He had the power to heal their pain.

As he ran off after Martin Atkinson again, he allowed himself a punch of the air in jubilation. His VAR system had been a triumph. He finally felt accepted in Hornet Heaven.

*   *   *

After the match, the referee walked up Occupation Road. He was holding his head high. Swansea had gone on to score a second goal — a perfectly good last-minute winner — but no referee in heaven or earth would ever have ruled that one out. He reflected that he'd been a crowd-pleaser for Swansea's first goal, and kept his integrity for their second. Watford fans everywhere may have been plunged into a gloom that couldn't be tempered by a sense of injustice, but personally he'd done a great job. No-one could criticise him.

He was approaching The Hornets Shop, feeling good, when, suddenly, Frank Gammon came up to him and jabbed an angry finger into his chest.

'Oi!' Frank said. 'Swansea's second goal was offside too! But you stuck your bloody thumb up!'

The referee adjusted his glasses and replied calmly: 'Steady on, Frank. I understand you're upset, but the second goal wasn't offside.'

'It bloody was offside — and you know it. You're a bloody cheat too — as well as Atkinson.'

'Now now, Frank. I'm not a cheat. You don't hate me. You're just projecting your frustrations onto me. Can you not see that?'

Frank glared at the referee with renewed fury. He said: 'Projecting my frustrations onto you? Shut your bloody psychobabble!'

Then he began a chant, pointing viciously at the referee: 'You're not fit to referee! You're not fit to referee!'

A number of other fans heard Frank and saw the referee. Watford had lost and they weren't happy. The referee was right there in front of them — the perfect place to bear the brunt of their anger.

Soon, about a hundred other fans had joined in with Frank's chant.

The referee ran away.

*　*　*

The referee hid in the atrium. In his baggy shorts, he sat cross-legged on the floor between the shelves that housed programmes from the earliest games in Watford's history.

He felt safe from people like Frank there because, he reasoned, if you were a fan who went back to watch matches from the start of the 20th century, you probably weren't the type to complain about officials. Back then, the men who were appointed referees commanded respect. If you knew Major Weatherington had killed forty men in the Boer War, you didn't give him any backchat.

After some hours, the referee looked up and saw a face he knew. It was Johnny Allgood — the man he'd met in The Gallery restaurant with Henry. The former manager was browsing programmes from his own era.

'Ach, well I never,' Johnny said. 'It's Graham Poll.'

The referee had been thinking long and hard about his own behaviour. He held up his hands and said: 'Yes. Touché. I have to admit I may have let my ego get the better of me.'

He watched the bald, moustachioed 78-year-old sit down on the floor next to him. He thought Johnny looked a sensible man you could have a proper conversation with.

'So,' Johnny asked 'How are you feeling about the VAR shenanigans?'

After his hours of reflection, the referee had changed his mind. He said: 'The whole idea of VAR is daft. Martin Atkinson made a decision. Then I made a decision about his decision. And now the fans have made their own decision on my decision about his decision. It solves nothing.'

'Aye, you're right.'

'People just aren't thinking straight. Frank Gammon hates referees, but apparently he wants *more* referees. It doesn't make sense.'

'Aye, you're right.'

'It's madness to change an officiating system that has worked for more than a century just because fans get upset when something goes against them. Fans are passionate. They'll be upset however a decision's arrived at. And they'll still need to find someone to blame. I mean, you've seen it for yourself: ever since I set foot in Hornet Heaven, I've been abused just because of what I happen to be wearing. This kit brings out so much pent-up resentment.'

'Well, there's a simple answer to that. Don't wear it.'

'What? You mean, go naked in Hornet Heaven for the rest of eternity? Oh dear, you don't want to see that. Anyone would rather be a referee than see that.'

'I mean, wear something else.'

'But these are my only clothes. I'm stuck with them forever, aren't I?'

'I know a way to get a replica shirt out of The Hornets Shop — if you want to wear one of those instead.'

'Really? You mean I could be an ordinary fan. Not a hate figure?'

'Aye. It's a no-brainer, really.'

The referee fell into silent thought — because it wasn't *quite* a no-brainer. For years, being a referee had been part of his identity. People had also known him as a husband, a father, an accountant, and a Watford fan. But being a referee had given him attention, status, and authority. He'd enjoyed those things. He'd have to sacrifice them.

He tuned back into what Johnny was saying.

'If you give up that kit,' Johnny advised, 'the character assassinations will stop. No-one will be able to accuse you of being a Little Hitler, or an exhibitionist on a power trip.'

'Well, that would be nice.'

'No-one would secretly suspect you're one of those people that seems to get off on being called dirty words. No names, obviously, but…' Johnny whispered: 'Lee Probert.'

Suddenly the dirty word Frank Gammon had used about Lee Probert echoed in the referee's mind. It wasn't something he himself personally got off on. But could he really give up being a referee?

Eventually he said to Johnny: 'No. I'm going to give it one last go. Maybe I can change Frank Gammon's mind about refs.'

'Well, good luck with that. Because I don't believe football fans will ever properly appreciate referees. They only remember the times they think they've been wronged. They forget the times they're helped. There's a reason Bill Mainwood doesn't have a Magical History Tour entitled "Thanks, ref!"'

'Yes, I know what you're saying, but I just feel I should try to change people's views — on behalf of referees everywhere.'

The referee watched as the old man stood up and headed away from the shelves.

A few steps later, Johnny stopped and said: 'Let me know if you do ever want a change of shirt.'

* * *

During the next couple of weeks, the referee thought hard about what Johnny Allgood had said to him — not the thing about getting a new shirt, but the idea of a 'Thanks, ref!' Magical History Tour. He ended up talking to Bill Mainwood about it and together they went ahead and designed a tour to old Watford games where the Horns benefitted from controversial refereeing decisions. Bill then managed to persuade Frank Gammon to join them on the tour — without telling him the tour's title, of course.

First, they went to Watford's first-ever game in the top flight — at home to Everton in August 1982. Pat Rice misdirected a free-kick from in front of the main stand and Everton's keeper, Neville Southall, caught the ball beneath the bar. To most people's amazement, the referee awarded a goal. Watford fans were delirious.

Next they went to the 1987 FA Cup Quarter-Final against Arsenal at Highbury. With two minutes left, the linesman flagged for a foul by Steve Sims in Watford's penalty area. The referee waved play on and Luther Blissett scored. Then the referee consulted the linesman. Every Watford fan expected the ref to disallow Luther's goal and award Arsenal a penalty. But he let the goal stand, and Watford were into the semi-final. Watford fans were delirious again.

Finally, they went to the first game of the 2017/18 Premier League season — at home to Liverpool. In the last minute, Miguel Britos, standing in an offside position on Liverpool's goal-line, bundled the ball home to make it 3-3 and earn a rare point against a Big Six side. The referee let the goal stand. More delirium.

After the tour, the referee walked up Occupation Road with Frank and Bill.

The ref said: 'So. Tell me, Frank. Did you enjoy that?'

'I loved it,' Frank replied. 'Getting the rub of the green like that always feels brilliant.'

'And did you love the refs — for the decisions they made?'

'Love the refs? No chance! I loved fate smiling on us.'

The referee realised the tour hadn't worked. He said: 'Fate? It were the refs! Honestly, Frank, I don't get it. You hate the refs when decisions go against you, so surely you should love the refs when—'

'Listen, mate,' Frank growled. 'I get what you're saying. But I ain't feeling it, alright? You took me to some old games, and I loved the games, not the refs. No-one will ever get me to love refs the way I hate them when they—'

Frank supplied the disgusting verb he'd supplied once before.

Bill said: 'Well, yes. I suppose you could put it

that way again, Frank. When referees do… er… *that* to Watford.'

Through freshly watering eyes, the referee watched Frank walk off. He'd lost all hope that the man's feelings about match officials could ever be changed.

* * *

Later that day — Saturday January 13th 2018 — the referee went to Watford's Premier League home game against Southampton. He still hadn't taken up Johnny Allgood's offer: he was still in his refereeing kit.

The referee watched the game from the Rookery. He noticed that Frank Gammon was there too, a few seats along.

Watford went 2-0 down before half-time. The Horns pulled one back through Andre Gray but, as the final whistle approached, they were heading for a defeat that would drag them into a relegation battle. Watford fans weren't happy.

Then, with a minute to go, Roberto Pereyra chipped the ball into the Southampton penalty area at the Rookery End. Troy Deeney nodded the ball across the face of the goal. Abdoulaye Doucouré ran forward and deflected the ball into the net with his right hand.

Watching from Hornet Heaven, the referee had a perfect view of the incident. It was a clear handball. But very quickly he realised that the real-world referee — Roger East — hadn't spotted it. Roger East was allowing the goal.

He screamed with delight. In his joy, he turned towards Frank Gammon with his arms aloft. He saw Frank bouncing manically, punching the air. Then their eyes met. Suddenly, Frank started pushing past other fans towards the referee. He was waving a clenched fist. From recent experience, the referee thought he'd probably better make a run for it.

But before he could get away, Frank reached him. Frank had a look in his eye that the referee had never seen before. Frank had been overwhelmed by the emotion of the new game, in a way that he hadn't at the old games on the Magical History Tour. The gruff old man suddenly leaned in and kissed the referee on the forehead — exactly the way Henry Grover had done in The Gallery.

Frank said: 'You're welcome here! Everyone in Hornet Heaven is going to love you now!'

* * *

A few minutes later, the referee was sitting on Frank's shoulders, in his milk-bottle glasses and refereeing kit, being chaired up Occupation Road.

Frank shouted: 'Thank God for crap referees!' Then he chanted: 'The referee's a hero!'

The referee had no idea whether this was for fun or for real. Either way, he leaned down and said: 'You're overdoing it, Frank. I'm not really a hero.'

Frank replied dryly: 'What's wrong? I'm just projecting my *delight* onto you.'

The referee would have held up his hands and said 'touché', but he needed them for clinging on to Frank. Instead, he just laughed.

As he headed up the slope on Frank's shoulders, the referee felt happy at last. He finally felt welcome in Hornet Heaven. His previous attempts to become welcome — trying to be Graham Poll, bringing in VAR, and taking Frank Gammon on a "Thanks, Ref!" Magical History Tour — had all failed. But thanks to the ineptitude of Roger East he was riding high — for now, at least. He couldn't imagine a referee in Hornet Heaven ever enjoying a better moment than this.

They drew level with The Hornets Shop. Generations of relieved Hornets, in replica shirts from many eras, were swarming across the junction. The referee watched them. He felt a connection with them. And he came to a decision. He'd always been a Watford fan, but since he'd been in Hornet Heaven he'd stood out as different. It was time to take up Johnny Allgood's offer. He wanted to be at one with everyone else. He jumped down off Frank's shoulders, shook Frank's hand, and thanked him.

He went over and looked at the window display of clothing. He reckoned he quite fancied wearing an away shirt. So he was grateful the away kit was red this season, not black: he never wanted to wear black again. It was a part of his identity he wanted to shed.

From now on, the only part of his identity that he wanted to express was the one that mattered to him most — the same one that bonded every resident in Hornet Heaven for eternity.

He entered the shop, 100% a Hornet.

THE END

3

THE LOST COWBOY

EARTH SEASON 2017/18

A middle-aged man in an extra large Dallas Cowboys jersey stood in the half-light on Occupation Road. He was confused. He'd suddenly found himself standing in front of a row of disintegrating garages and decaying fences.

He said to himself: 'Well, this ain't Texas!'

It took a while for him to recognise where he was. He hadn't set foot on Occupation Road since the summer of 1977 — when his parents had taken him to live in America. Soon, though, in the gloom, it dawned on him.

'Jeez,' he drawled. 'I remember this place… But

how the hell did I get here?'

With his back to the stadium, he gazed through the twilight at the brambles and nettles. The back gardens of these houses were as run-down as they had been when his grandad had brought him to matches here as a boy.

For a moment he felt himself becoming sentimental. He told himself off. All of that had been years ago. He'd moved on. He'd been a die-hard Dallas Cowboys fan for his entire adult life. Soccer hadn't featured since. This wasn't the time to be remembering the past. Right now, he needed to focus on the main question: how had he suddenly found himself here?

He saw a boy walking up the slope towards him. He called out: 'Hey, kid!'

The nine-year-old was wearing a yellow Adidas Watford shirt. The boy saw him and froze.

The man in the Dallas Cowboys jersey approached the boy and said: 'Kid, I need you to help me out here. I'm kinda confused. A moment ago I was back home in the States and now, somehow, I'm in Watford.'

The boy took two steps backwards. He said: 'You're another one! Leave me alone!'

The boy ran in panic to a gate in the wooden fence.

'What do you mean?' the Texan called out. 'I'm another what? Another Cowboys fan? Hey, we ain't so bad!'

The boy started pulling on the handle but couldn't open the gate. He shouted: 'Go away! Go away!'

The man couldn't work out why the boy was acting so scared. 'You ain't a Washington Redskins fan, are ya?' he asked. 'I know we're rivals, but it's kind of a friendly rivalry.'

In the half-light, the boy carried on rattling the handle. 'You don't belong here!' he cried.

At last the boy managed to open the gate. He ran through and disappeared into the garden beyond the fence. He called out: 'Go away! And never come back to Watford!'

The man stood on his own in the twilight. He felt offended — wronged. Sure, he was a Cowboys fan, but he'd been born in Watford. He may not have been back for decades — or even thought about the place — but he had every right to be here.

The kid needed setting straight, he decided. He tugged down on his jersey, ready for the argument, and went through the gate.

* * *

The garden behind the gate was just as shrouded in gloom as Occupation Road. The man looked for the kid but there was no sign.

He made his way to the back door of the house. Through the window, he saw the boy slumped over the kitchen table, sobbing.

The man found himself affected by the scene. The small kitchen reminded him of his grandad's house. And the boy's tears reminded him of his own reaction, in 1977, to the news that he'd be emigrating to America. He'd totally forgotten how upset he'd been to leave Watford.

The man couldn't help feeling sorry for the kid. He stood on the step and said: 'Hey, I'm sorry if I scared you or something just now. Are you OK?'

The boy looked up through wet eyes.

The Texan said gently: 'I mean, if you're this upset, you probably got all kinds of problems I don't even know about.'

The boy nodded.

'Is that so?' the man said. 'Well, I guess I can lend an ear, if it helps. My name's Malcolm. What's yours?'

'Cole,' the boy replied.

Malcolm stepped into the kitchen. The gloom from outside was inside the house too. It was weird. Cautiously, he pulled out a chair and sat down at the table.

He said nothing for a while, hoping Cole would open up. But Cole just stared down at the table, occasionally glancing at Malcolm.

They sat like this for a long time. Eventually Cole was ready to talk. He said quietly: 'I want to tell you my secret now.'

Malcolm said softly: 'OK.'

The boy seemed terrified. His lips were trembling. He whispered: 'I see dead people.'

Malcolm was shocked. But he made sure his face didn't betray his true reaction. He didn't want to upset the boy more. He asked: 'In your dreams?'

Cole shook his head.

'While you're awake?'

Cole nodded.

'Dead people, like in graves and coffins?'

'Walking round like regular people,' Cole said. 'They don't see each other. They don't know what they are.'

'How often do you see them?'

'All the time,' Cole whispered huskily. 'They're everywhere.'

*　*　*

Malcolm looked carefully at Cole. The boy's problems were more extreme — more abnormal — than he could possibly have imagined.

Cole said: 'You won't tell anyone my secret, right?'

Malcolm nodded solemnly. He had to help the boy. 'I promise,' he said.

Sitting in the strangely murky kitchen, Malcolm felt out of his depth. He was no expert, but it seemed to him that Cole's pathology was severe. The child appeared to be suffering from hallucinations and paranoia — probably schizophrenia too.

Malcolm tried to find a topic that would normalise the conversation and get Cole back on an even keel for now. He looked out of the window and said: 'So you live next to a soccer stadium. Is that good?'

'Good and bad,' Cole replied, still rather subdued. 'The bad is seeing dead people.'

Malcolm didn't get how seeing dead people could possibly be connected to living next to a soccer stadium.

He tried to keep the boy positive. He said: 'Tell me about the good.'

A faint smile fell across Cole's lips as he thought about his answer. He said: 'The buzz on match days. Suddenly thousands of people arrive. They're full of hope and anticipation. I stand at the gate at the end of the garden. I listen to the noise building. I watch the excited faces.'

Cole's description started to stir childhood memories for Malcolm — memories that had long been overwritten by other events and other passions in his life in America. Years ago, he and his grandad had regularly been among those thousands of people arriving with hope and anticipation.

Suddenly he remembered the way his grandad's hand had always tightened around his own as they joined the queue for the turnstile. He remembered the clank of the turnstile getting louder and louder until it was his turn to go through. Thinking back, he could almost smell the aromas of a 1970s English football crowd — tobacco, beer, Old Spice aftershave. He began to develop a sense that something had been missing in his life for a very long time.

But he still felt a disconnect. His rekindled memories of visiting Vicarage Road were sunlit — completely unlike the weather today.

He said: 'Say, do you get weather like this a lot in Watford? It's so grey. I can hardly see you in here without the lights on.'

Cole glanced up at the lights in the kitchen ceiling. They were at full brightness.

The boy said: 'The dead people always complain about that.'

Malcolm cursed silently to himself. He thought he'd distracted the boy from thinking about ghosts. He tried to think up a new topic of conversation.

'So would you like me to tell you about the Dallas Cowboys?' he asked. 'They're a hell of a team.'

Cole looked at him with a half-smile. 'American football?' he said, mischievously. 'You've got to be kidding.'

Malcolm felt slightly offended again, but he was pleased to see Cole was brightening up.

Cole said: 'My dad calls it "egg throwing".'

Malcolm thought it best not to argue. He decided to humour the boy. 'Yup,' he said. 'Two armies of 250-

pound men in helmets and body armour, fighting over a big egg.'

Cole grinned at Malcolm, almost as if they were becoming friends.

The boy said: 'Do you want to see my Watford stuff?'

Malcolm wanted to keep Cole focusing on happy things. So he said: 'That's a great idea. What have you got?'

Cole got up from the table and told Malcolm to follow him.

* * *

Cole led Malcolm up the stairs of the terraced house. The boy stopped on the half-landing. There was a window looking out over the stadium. Cole looked out and said: 'The best time is when the floodlights are on.'

Malcolm looked out of the window. He could hardly see the stadium through the gloom.

But Cole's words stirred a visual memory: white light pouring from a pitch-black sky; wet grass shimmering; bright yellow shirts. He had a flashback of a match from years ago. It must have been 1973 or so.

Watford were playing... who was it? A team called Scunthorpe? There was a gangly blond guy playing up front. He'd never looked any good, but that night, out of nowhere, he scored two goals. What was his name? Ross something? That was it. Ross Jenkins. Watford had won 5-1. Grandad had been thrilled. The team had turned a corner, Grandad had said. Of course, they hadn't, and the thrill had turned out to be momentary. But today, for the first time in 40 years, Malcolm was savouring again the excitement of a night under the lights.

His flow of memories was interrupted when Cole said: 'Oh no.'

The boy closed his eyes and bowed his head. 'She's still there,' he said.

Malcolm looked down into the garden and onto Occupation Road. 'Who?' he asked. 'I don't see anyone.'

'That's the way it works. You can't see her, I can.'

'You mean, there's a dead person out there? By the stadium?'

'I don't think she'll ever go away. I've tried to help her.'

'Where is she?'

'I think she's stuck between worlds. She hasn't

found her true self.'

Malcolm wanted to move the conversation away from the boy's hallucinations. But he couldn't resist asking:

'What worlds do you mean?'

'There's a world that exists for dead people, I think. Dead Watford people.'

Malcolm didn't know what to make of this. It was the craziest idea he'd ever heard.

He set off up the rest of the stairs and said: 'Come on. Show me these Watford things of yours.'

*   *   *

Cole's bedroom was like a shrine to Watford Football Club. The cathedral-like gloom in the room only added to the feeling of sanctity.

On the near wall were photographs of modern-day players in yellow shirts. Malcolm had no idea who they were.

On another wall were hung various old replica shirts. Malcolm noticed that the designs varied much more than American football jersey designs did. Some of them were awful. One shirt seemed to have red and black tractor-tyre marks across the chest. Another had black horizontal lines like a television on the blink. But one of them he recognised. It was yellow with two vertical black stripes down the left front and a cartoon hornet, in football boots, on the right breast. All of a sudden, names and faces came flooding back to Malcolm.

'Ken Goodeve! Brian Greenhalgh!' he said. 'Jeez, they were awful!'

A phrase floated into his mind. 'Bonser out! Bonser out!' he chanted quietly.

The phrase seemed to stir something deep within him. He chanted it again, louder. 'Bonser out! Bonser out!'

He was starting to feel this. He said: 'It's all coming back, Cole. I remember us being relegated. 1975 or something. It hurt so bad. But only because I cared so much.'

'Did you stop caring?'

'Not deliberately. Life took me someplace else: Dallas, Texas.'

Malcolm gazed around the room. On another wall, there was a series of photos that seemed to span about 25 years. The same man was in all of them. He had dark hair. It looked like he was the team manager. Above the photos was a paper print-out with the phrase #ThankYouGT. Malcolm asked: 'Did I miss much while I was away?'

Malcolm went back to the first wall and looked at one of the player photos. He struggled with the name. 'Rich-ar-li-son,' he said. 'Is he any better than Brian Greenhalgh was? When I emigrated, we were only heading in one direction — and it wasn't up. What division are we in now?'

He didn't pause to get an answer. The deluge of recollections was too distracting. 'It would be amazing if we were still in the league — or maybe up in Division Three. As a kid, I had dreams of Watford getting promoted. I had dreams we'd play in Europe. But that's all they were ever going to be. Dreams.'

Malcolm was feeling a little overwhelmed by the emotion of everything he was remembering. A few moments passed.

Cole asked: 'And what happened to your grandad? Did he go to America with you?'

'He died,' Malcolm replied quietly. His voice began to crack slightly as he continued: 'In June 1977. Two weeks before we emigrated. That hurt much more than getting relegated had. I loved grandad. Those times we had together at the soccer were… so special.'

Malcolm took a few moments to gather himself.

The he went on: 'I don't know, in Dallas I threw myself into supporting the Cowboys. But maybe the real reason I took no interest in soccer after that was because it would have reminded me of the times with grandad that I'd never get back.'

Malcolm paused and looked around the walls again. He couldn't feel upset for too long in a room like this. It was totally inspiring.

'But now I *am* interested again,' he said. 'It's as if my love for Watford Football Club never actually left me. I feel like I'm rediscovering what I always was. What I truly am.'

Malcolm sat down on Cole's bed.

He said: 'Kid, I'd like it very much if you could tell me everything I've missed since 1977.'

* * *

In the bright bedroom, Cole sat down on the floor opposite the man in the Dallas Cowboys jersey. He was excited at the prospect of telling the man all about the club's recent history. He'd told it to several of the others he'd met on Occupation Road. It always worked. It made them go away.

But this time, with Malcolm, he didn't get the chance. Before he could say anything, Malcolm started fading. The man had already recognised, deep down, what he was. He'd found himself.

Cole watched as Malcolm slowly vanished.

The boy smiled.

He'd liked Malcolm and would have happily spent more time with him.

But he always preferred it when he couldn't see dead people.

* * *

Malcolm was looking up at one of the photos of the manager with the dark hair. The manager was holding up a trophy with yellow and red ribbons. It looked like Wembley stadium in the background, but in the gloom of the room Malcolm guessed he must be mistaken. Watford winning at Wembley? Surely that was too amazing to be true. He turned back to Cole, impatient to hear the story of the last few decades. But the boy wasn't there.

'Cole?' he said.

Malcolm got up off the bed and left the bedroom. He called out: 'Cole? Where did you go?'

He went down the stairs. He stopped to look out of the window on the half-landing. He couldn't see Cole. But he noticed that, at the top of Occupation Road, beyond the twilight, there was some kind of golden glow.

He went down into the kitchen.

'Cole? Cole! You were going to tell me the story of the last 40 years! I want to hear it!'

Confused, he went back out into the garden. There was still no sign of the boy. He didn't know what to do.

He guessed he didn't actually need to worry about Cole: the boy had been in his own house; he wouldn't be in danger.

Malcolm shrugged and went through the gate back onto Occupation Road.

* * *

Back on the tarmac, Malcolm peered up the slope through the murk. Now he could see what had been creating the glow he'd just observed from the window: there was a huge golden building at the junction with Vicarage Road. He didn't remember it being there when he'd left in the summer of 1977. He made his way towards it, intrigued.

As he walked, he noticed the gloom beginning to clear. Now he could see more clearly. The stadium had slick black walls with bright yellow panels over the turnstiles. It was very different from the rough brick wall he remembered from when he was last here. He couldn't wait to find out everything that had happened in the intervening years. All the excitement he'd felt on a match day, as a kid, was flooding back. He broke into a run.

Soon he was in bright sunshine. He found himself in a crowd of people milling about. Many of them were in modern replica shirts but some of the men, he noticed, were wearing 1930s suits; there was even a woman in a long Victorian dress. Malcolm looked around in amazement as he ran. No matter what they were wearing, everyone seemed comfortable mixing in this environment. And so did he. Despite his Dallas Cowboys jersey, he was already feeling a profound connection with the people here. A sense of community.

He kept going and arrived at the junction with Vicarage Road. He slowed to a stop in front of the huge golden building he'd seen from down the slope. It was where he remembered the Red Lion pub had been when he was young.

He gazed up at its futuristic glass and steel curves. Then he noticed there was a sign above the entrance. It was a sign that explained everything. It said 'Hornet Heaven'.

It explained where he was. It explained who he was.

Malcolm felt a sudden wave of happiness pass through his body. It was the kind someone might get from a homecoming when they hadn't been home for 40 years.

He smiled.

And then — as he saw a man in a 1970s suit coming out of the golden building — his eyes filled with tears.

He called out: 'Grandad!'

THE END

4

THE LONG GOODBYE

EARTH SEASON 2017/18

'Alright, mate. Just arrived, have you?'

'You are steward? Explain to me. I was at meeting. But now — sudden — at this moment I am here. Is not normal. You must explain.'

'Ooh. Nice. I like a bossy boots. They always need knocking down a peg or two.'

'How is I am outside stadium? Why is so grey, this light? Explain.'

'Pushy, ain't ya? Come on, then. Give *me* a push. See what happens.'

'No, no, no. I am not fighting. I am man who is important. '

'Oh yeah? Try telling that to my boot when it's stamping on your face.'

'Is enough. Is bad situation. Very bad. I am not wanting be here.'

'Ha! What, mate? Say that again?'

'I am not wanting be here.'

'Ha ha ha! Well, that ain't a surprise, mate! Ha ha ha!'

'Hey, why is you laugh at me?'

'Because everyone knows you never liked Watford from the start, mate! Ha ha ha! I mean, honestly! What the hell is Marco Silva doing in Hornet Heaven?'

* * *

It was the morning of Sunday 21st January 2018 — the day after Watford's 2-0 Premier League defeat at Leicester City.

Lamper — Hornet Heaven's chief steward, a former hooligan — led Marco Silva through the gloomy twilight of the lower reaches of Occupation Road.

'Just so you know,' Lamper said, 'I'm the top boy round here. I would have said you're too handsome to join my firm — I like ugly ruckers, you see — but I know plenty of Watford fans who'll be very happy to fix that face of yours.'

They walked up the slope and emerged into eternal sunshine. Lamper took Marco into the atrium — a futuristic building on the site of Red Lion pub. There, Lamper left the former Head Coach with a 92-year-old who introduced himself as Bill Mainwood — the Head Of Programmes, and the man who gave orientations to new arrivals.

Bill said: 'Well, Mr Silva, this is a bit of a shock. It's only yesterday that we all saw you in our technical area during the defeat at Leicester. What happened?'

Marco looked down his nose and sneered as if he didn't care: 'Gino Pozzo terminate me.'

Bill gasped. He was aware Watford's owner had a reputation for being ruthless with head coaches, but as far as he knew none of the previous gaffers had ended up dead.

'Golly. I see,' Bill said. 'Well, welcome to Hornet Heaven. This is the afterlife paradise reserved exclusively for Watford fans after they pass away.'

'Wait. I am not passing away. I live.'

'Ah. Yes. A lot of people struggle with this. I'm

sorry to have to break it to you, but—'

'No. I am Marco Silva. I not die.'

Bill frowned. He'd always sensed Marco Silva was an arrogant fellow. But he hadn't realised the man had delusions of immortality.

Bill tried to carry on with his orientation. He said: 'Anyway, once you're here in Hornet Heaven you stay for the rest of eternity.'

'No. Is not possible. I insist on break clause.'

'I'm sorry, but that's not how it works up here.'

'Then I walk. I walk away now.'

Bill sighed, exasperated. He said: 'Well, honestly! You haven't been here for one game yet. At least on earth you waited nine games before you tried to clear off to Everton.'

'Is very bad situation,' Marco grumbled. 'I call my agent.'

Bill looked at Marco Silva. He felt sorry for the former Head Coach. The standard conditions of entry to Hornet Heaven meant all new arrivals must love Watford deep down. In which case, here was a man who simply wasn't aware of his love for the club.

So Bill decided to try and help. He reckoned that if he could settle Marco in — and make the former head coach realise what a wonderful club Watford was — then the man's commitment issues would evaporate. Marco would finally attach himself to Watford emotionally, and be happy for the rest of all time.

Bill said: 'Right, Mr Silva. I'm taking you to meet a few people.'

*　*　*

In the Captain's Bar, Neil McBain — who'd managed Watford in both the 1930s and 1950s — glared at Marco Silva from behind his thick glasses. He said: 'What the hell's *he* doing in Hornet Heaven?'

Bill Mainwood had been pretty confident of finding McBain down here beneath the Graham Taylor stand. Down on earth, while he was manager, McBain had never been far from a bar.

Bill replied: 'Sadly, Mr Silva has passed away and—

'Wait,' McBain interrupted. 'It's not sad at all. The fact he's croaked means the team might actually win some games now.'

'Well, yes, there is that, but—'

'And think of the severance package Gino won't

have to pay.'

Marco Silva scowled at McBain: 'I already say. I not die.'

Bill rolled his eyes at the coach's misplaced self-belief. Then he explained why he'd brought about this meeting.

'The thing is, Marco,' he said, 'I wanted you to meet McBain because he's a good example of someone who loves Watford even though, as a manager, there must have been times that he thought he didn't.'

McBain frowned. He said: 'What are you talking about, Mainwood? What times?'

'Well, when you were sacked in 1937, for example.'

'Ach, shut up about that!'

'And when you were sacked again in 1959.'

'Ach, shut up about that too!'

'And in between — when, probably out of spite, you went to manage that filthy lot from up the road.'

McBain clutched his head. 'For God's sake! OK! I managed Luton! Will no-one ever let it lie?'

McBain stormed out of the Captain's Bar.

Bill said to Marco: 'Hmm. That hasn't gone so well. Maybe I can find you another former manager who'll be an inspiration to you in a different way.'

Bill's first thought was that Watford's first-ever manager, Johnny Allgood, might be a good candidate. In his first season, Johnny had managed Watford to a championship, undefeated. And even when he wasn't so successful later, and lost his job, he carried on living in the town and helping the club out.

But then Bill thought of someone even better to advise Marco Silva.

He said. 'Ah. Yes. I know just the man. Follow me.'

* * *

Bill led Marco down Occupation Road. They arrived at a gate beside an old brick garage that had mint green paint clinging to its wooden doors.

Behind this gate, the previous summer, Bill himself had received a pep-talk from a former manager — from Watford's greatest ever manager. Bill opened the gate and ushered Marco through.

Marco was astonished. Suddenly they weren't anywhere near Occupation Road. They were in a park.

Bill led Marco across a wide expanse of grass to a

brown wooden bench surrounded by recently planted trees. There was a plaque on the back of the bench. Bill already knew what it said, but he took the trouble to read it again — to feel it again.

The plaque said: IN LOVING MEMORY OF FRIEND GRAHAM TAYLOR. MUCH LOVED. ELTON.

Bill's eyes misted a little.

As they cleared, Marco said: 'Why are you bringing me?'

'Sorry,' Bill replied. 'It seems the man I wanted you to meet isn't here at the moment.'

'Is bad,' Marco said. 'I have more important place to be. Better place. Bigger place.'

'Ha! Typical Marco Silva!' Bill laughed to himself under his breath.

But what wasn't funny, he felt, was that the man had this attitude in a place Bill regarded as sacred.

Bill said: 'You need to spend time here. Absorb the vibe. Just reading the plaque on the bench will give you a sense of the depth of feeling that The Great Man generated in everyone who—'

Marco huffed. He glanced impatiently at the huge watch on his wrist.

Bill glowered. He'd always thought Marco's watch was ridiculously big. The next size up would have been the Watford Observer clock.

Bill realised he'd made a mistake coming here. He took Marco by the arm and led him back across the grass.

He said: 'You know, maybe it's best that The Great Man doesn't meet you.'

* * *

Bill felt he needed moral support. He left Marco in the atrium and went to find Henry Grover, the man who founded Watford Rovers in 1881.

Henry was in his usual booth in the swanky Gallery restaurant in the south west corner of the stadium. Bill joined him and explained the difficulties he was having in trying to help the former head coach.

'Marco Silva's not an easy man,' Bill said. 'I've noticed he always avoids eye-contact. He seems unsettled... restless.'

'Ah. Yes. Indeed,' Henry said. 'Actually, I think the word is "shifty".'

'But I haven't given up hope yet,' Bill continued.

'I think I need to take a different tack to get him to appreciate what Watford Football Club is all about. He's too focused on himself. He needs to learn that Watford is all about community.'

'Absolutely, old chap. The man is all about his own personal ambition. He doesn't understand that the greatest joy in football comes from sharing success. Sharing always multiplies the joy that any one person feels.'

'But do you think he can change, Henry? Or are we asking a leopard to change his spots.'

'Aha. Excellent metaphor, old thing. But a leopard doesn't feel the right animal for Marco Silva somehow. Have you got a metaphor that involves a snake?'

'I just want him to see that Watford is about the collective, not the individual — that there's a huge group of people who absolutely treasure the away wins he got us at Bournemouth and Southampton. We treasure them far more than his CV benefitted from them.'

'Oh, well. Don't stress yourself, old son. If you can't teach him, maybe he'll learn in his next job.'

'But he's not going to get another job, Henry.'

'Really? Golly. Are you saying that future employers will be put off by his utter lack of commitment to our club? Put off by his Machiavellian machinations in trying to jump ship? Put off by a display of sulking to which even Matej Vydra could only aspire?'

'No, Henry. I'm saying he won't get another job because he's dead.'

'Oh. Ha! Ha ha ha! You are a silly billy, Bill. Marco Silva's not dead.'

'What? But he's here. In Hornet Heaven. He must be dead.'

'But that's where you're wrong, Bill. You see, Hornet Heaven reveals itself to certain people while they're still alive.'

Bill was amazed.

'Really?' he said. 'I never knew. Who gets that privilege?'

'Oh, it's not a privilege, old chap. It's a punishment. It happens to people who are leaving the club and never loved the place — players and managers who want away. I remember seeing David Connolly up here. And Patrick Blondeau. Brendan Rodgers too. Their souls were temporarily transported to Hornet Heaven to show them what they were going to miss by not having Watford in their hearts. Now it's happened to Marco

Silva.'

'Golly. I see. But isn't that rather cruel? It's bit like that TV show Bullseye where, as soon as a contestant lost, Jim Bowen immediately said "Let's see what you would have won". Except that, in this case, the star prize Marco missed out on was eternal bliss supporting the most wonderful club in the world.'

'Well, it's not the only cruelty he can expect, Bill — if the temporary visits to Hornet Heaven of David Connolly, Patrick Blondeau and Brendan Rodgers are anything to go by. At the end of their visits, as their souls faded back to the real world, hundreds of Watford fans up here were waving them off, chanting "Cheerio, cheerio, cheerio!"'

Bill took a few moments to picture these scenes. Given how he felt about Connolly, Blondeau and Rodgers, what he pictured rather tickled him. He giggled and giggled.

'Steady, old son,' Henry said. 'It wasn't *that* funny.'

'Sorry, Henry. I'd moved onto laughing about something else.'

'Really? Splendid. Do tell.'

'I was remembering how Marco told me that Gino

had 'terminated' him. I thought he meant Gino had killed him.'

'Oh! Ah! Ha ha ha!'

Now it was Henry's turn to giggle and giggle.

Eventually, Henry patted Bill on the shoulder and said: 'Dear, oh dear, Bill. You're a good man, trying to help everyone be happy. And I'm not saying Marco Silva isn't a good man. But he should definitely be more concerned with other people's happiness — not just his own. Forget about him, Bill. Because I'm sure everyone else up here will — very quickly.'

* * *

In the atrium, Marco Silva ignored the shocked stares of the deceased Watford fans who couldn't believe he was in Hornet Heaven. He made his way to the programme shelves.

He'd been told that one of the benefits of this paradise was that he could go to watch any Watford game in history by taking the programme from that game through an ancient turnstile on Occupation Road. So he decided to go and watch his first win — away at Bournemouth in August 2017. He wanted to watch himself in victory.

At the Vitality Stadium he stood in the away section with the Watford fans. But he didn't watch the game. He had eyes only for his real-world self in the technical area. As he watched himself, he was pleased with how he'd come across. He'd maintained a high level of moodiness throughout the game. And the way he was always rubbing his stubble had created an aura of being both rugged and thoughtful. He reckoned the chairmen of other clubs must have been extremely impressed.

He particularly liked what he saw at the final whistle. The Watford fans around him were leaping around, totally delirious at finally beating the south coast upstarts on their own patch. But, on the touchline, the mean, moody and magnificent Head Coach was behaving as if achieving a cracking result for a mid-table club was beneath him. It was exactly the look he'd been trying to carry off.

Next, he re-visited his second win — in the following away match, at Southampton. This time he noticed how the Watford fans around him in the away section were falling in love with what they were watching: the style of play, the adventure, and — most of all — the team unity. He could see it in their faces. He was surprised how much it seemed to mean to them. After all, a Watford side that all pulled together wasn't going to benefit each fan personally. Unlike him, none of them were going to be able to buy a bigger watch.

After that, he went to the home win over Arsenal in October — his greatest triumph as head coach of Watford. He watched from the Sir Elton John Stand, behind the dug-outs. When Tom Cleverly smashed home the late winner, Marco saw himself losing the studied cool he'd been trying to maintain on the touchline: the real world version of himself ran into a mad embrace with his coaching staff. As Marco watched again from Hornet Heaven, he allowed himself a smile. He remembered the elation that had been coursing through his body.

But now, as he looked at the fans around him, he could see the same elation coursing through the bodies of every single person in the Sir Elton John stand. It was as if a powerful electricity was connecting everyone who wanted Watford to win. It made him realise something. The first time around, he'd regarded the brilliant comeback victory mainly as an advertisement for himself. But now he could see it was more than that. It was something that was entering the hearts and minds of generations of people, and would stay in their hearts and minds for the rest of their lives — and beyond, apparently.

Marco stared at the communal jubilation around him. For the first time, he felt guilt for the self-centred way he'd approached the job at Watford. He realised he'd shut the fans' feelings out of his thinking. He'd never looked the community in the eye and engaged with them emotionally. He'd been shifty.

He made his way back towards the ancient turnstile — full of regret. He wished he'd had this insight about collective happiness sooner. If he had, he'd have wanted to stay at Watford as long as he could — to build something wonderful for everyone to share. Suddenly he liked the idea of creating a success that every Watford fan would feel belonged to them. But it was too late now.

He exited the ancient turnstile. As he emerged onto Occupation Road, he saw a crowd of Watford fans standing on the slope in the eternal sunshine. They hadn't been there before. He wondered why they'd gathered.

He stopped on the pavement. It struck him that this

was an opportunity to say sorry to Watford fans. He could go up to them, shake their hands, and apologise to each fan in turn for how he'd behaved as head coach.

He decided he would do it. He took a deep breath. He stepped forward.

But before he'd left the pavement, something odd started happening. Everyone started fading. The whole of Occupation Road started fading.

Marco wasn't sure what was going on. It felt as though he was disappearing from Hornet Heaven.

If this was the case, he realised, he wouldn't have time to speak to people individually. So he called out to the crowd: 'I am sorry. Sorry for how I was.'

The crowd waved to him. They seemed to be bidding him a friendly goodbye. He was pleased. He hoped he was forgiven.

But now, as the crowd faded from view, and a white mist swirled, he could hear that everyone was chanting.

He could just about make it out: 'Cheerio, cheerio, cheerio!'

A moment later, Marco was enveloped by the white mist. In the silence, riven with remorse, he repeated: 'I am sorry. Sorry for how I was.'

* * *

Soon the mist cleared. Marco recognised where he was. He was back in the meeting he'd been in before he'd found himself in Hornet Heaven — the meeting in which he'd been fired as head coach.

Marco Silva looked at Gino Pozzo in the chair opposite.

Marco closed his eyes and, with deep regret, repeated his words one more time.

'I am sorry. Sorry for how I was.'

Then he got up out of his seat and left Watford forever.

THE END

5

THE RESTORATION

EARTH SEASON 2017/18

Towards the end of the 2017/8 season, Hornet Heaven was holding one of its regular quiz nights in the Captain's Bar beneath the Graham Taylor Stand. Henry Grover, the man who founded Watford Rovers in 1881, was watching the proceedings with an old friend.

Henry loved these evenings — when the residents of Hornet Heaven immersed themselves in the rich history of the club he'd originated. He was especially pleased to see that, tonight, there was a younger crowd than normal in the room.

'Right,' squeaked the question-master. 'Here's the next question. Who's the most famous footballer ever to take the field for Watford?'

Derek Garston, a fact-loving schoolboy who died at the age of 13 in 1921, looked expectantly around the room for answers.

A fan called out: 'John Barnes!'

Another called out: 'Pat Jennings!'

Henry Grover knew these answers weren't quite correct. So he was pleased when young Derek said: 'No. Those two reached the height of their fame *after* they played for Watford. I want the name of the man who was the most nationally pre-eminent at the time he played.'

Henry looked around the room. Everyone appeared stumped.

Henry knew the answer, though. He was sitting next to the answer. He said to his bald, moustachioed, 78-year-old companion: 'Go on, old son. Stand up and tell everyone it's you.'

'Ach, no. I don't want to draw attention to myself.'

'You deserve the attention,' Henry insisted. 'You were a household name in the Victorian era before you joined us. You were the Stanley Matthews or George Best of your day.'

'Maybe I was, Henry, but that's ancient history.'

Derek called out: 'Last chance, people. Has anyone got the answer? The most famous footballer to have played for Watford.'

Henry said: 'Go on, old fruit. Most people here were born years and years after us. They should be made aware how well-known you were. It's only right.'

'Fame is a curse. I wouldn't wish it on anyone.'

'What? Every football fan in the land admired you. How can that have been a curse? Look. If you won't speak up, I will. I'll tell everyone exactly how renowned you used to be throughout the entire country. How people said you were one of the grandest players ever to take to the football field.'

The bald moustachioed man got up.

'Please don't, Henry,' he said — and made his way silently out of the Captain's Bar, unnoticed by everyone else.

Derek said: 'Oh well, if no-one knows, I reckon I'll save the answer for a future quiz.'

Henry Grover watched with a heavy heart as his companion left the room. He felt it was wrong that a man who'd been so celebrated in his playing days no longer received any recognition at all.

He wished someone would do something about it.

* * *

Henry caught up with the bald moustachioed man in Hornet Heaven's golden atrium on the junction of Vicarage Road and Occupation Road.

Henry said: 'Look. I'm sorry, old boy, but I'm not going to let this go. It's not right that so few people know how famous you once were. You're Johnny Goodall. *The* Johnny Goodall. One of the Old Invincibles who did the Double with Preston. Captain of England. Football's first superstar.'

Johnny said: 'Fame comes and goes, Henry. For me, it receded as swiftly as my hairline.'

'But this isn't only about fame. In fact, forget the fame thing. What I really mean is that it's not right how few people know how great you were as a player. Greatness doesn't come and go.'

'Ach, Henry. It's irrelevant now how great I might once have been. It's the current Watford stars who should be in the spotlight.'

'But our current stars aren't sporting greats like you were. Not yet, anyway. I mean, there's so much hype in football these days. Fans are led to expect that any old 12.5 million pound signing must be a world-beater — especially if his surname is Success. But then it turns out that he can't actually get in the team!'

'Ach, I'm old news, Henry. The current players are the ones creating the new stories. They're the ones writing the modern history of the club week by week.'

'But your story stood out. Johnny. You were the greatest player in England before the media put every player on a pedestal. You achieved it without a publicist, without an Instagram account. Your story wasn't an "Instastory". You were the real deal.'

'People don't want to know, Henry. All Watford fans really care about is each new game as it comes.'

'No. I'm sorry, Johnny, but you're wrong. Recognition of greatness is essential to any football club. It creates values. It sets standards. If a club doesn't celebrate greatness, it allows mediocrity to prevail. And, as you well know, we weren't short of mediocrity at Watford for several decades after you left the club.'

'But there's no mediocrity now. Our 2018 squad is full of internationals. They're all outstanding players.'

'Not in the way you were, Johnny. You were the era's finest centre forward. Arguably the first world-class number nine.'

'Nonsense. We didn't have numbers on our shirts in those days.'

'Stop quibbling. In terms of pedigree and prior reputation, you're still Watford's biggest ever signing. Still. In 2018.'

'Henry, take a look around you. If I really was one of the game's greats, people wouldn't have forgotten me. Has anyone ever had my name printed on the back of their replica shirt?'

'Right, Johnny. I'm simply not having this. You've clearly forgotten what a giant you were.'

Henry marched over to the shelves on the far side of the atrium. He brought back two copies of the programme for the final game of the 1903/04 season.

'Come on,' he said. 'Follow me.'

*   *   *

Henry led Johnny Goodall — or 'Johnny Allgood' as he was widely known because of his prowess and sportsmanship — through the ancient turnstile on Occupation Road. They arrived in a West London park on Saturday 23rd April 1904. Two thousand people in Edwardian clothing were clustered around a football pitch to watch Southall FC host Watford FC in Southern League Division 2.

Henry and Johnny passed through the crowd and stood on the touchline on the halfway line. The match started. They overheard a Southall fan say: 'I'm only here to watch the great Johnny Goodall play. It's something I'll be able to tell my grandchildren.'

As Henry looked for the 1904 version of Johnny among the yellow, red and green jerseys of the Watford team, he heard a Watford fan offer up a familiar shout using the team's nickname at the time: 'Come on you Wa-asps!'

Soon Henry spotted Johnny — the player-manager — receive the ball and glide past two heavy challenges.

'Look,' Henry said. 'There you are, Johnny. You were still a world-beater — even at the age of 40.'

'Rubbish, Henry. Southall hadn't even turned professional. They were literally amateurs. They're just making me look good here. I only scored 4 league goals all season, whereas Harry Barton and Bertie Banks scored more than 100 between them in all competitions. Most matches, they were drunk. If I was really one of the game's greats, I'd have outscored a pair of boozed-up bozos.'

'But you *were* one of the game's greats. I don't understand why you won't admit it.'

After fifteen minutes, Watford scored. The winger Jimmy Tennant cut inside and shot against the bar. The ball rebounded to Harry Barton — who also hit the bar. It came back to Goodall — who volleyed home.

Henry sighed and said: 'Now, you have to admit it — that finish was pure class, Johnny. And you know what they say about class: it's permanent. In fact, it's more than that. In Hornet Heaven, it's eternal.'

'Ach, forget it, Henry. No-one in 2018 is interested in all this old stuff.'

'Well, they should be. This was your first season as a manager and you led us to the club's first ever championship. And not just that. When the whistle blows at the end of this game, the team will have gone undefeated all season. You made a Watford team invincible, Johnny. You weren't just a great player, you were a great manager too.'

'Well, that's where you're definitely wrong. I couldn't sustain it. After we were promoted, I was manager for six more seasons and I never got us higher than ninth.'

'And because of that you think we should ignore

such an incredible achievement as going a whole season unbeaten?'

'Well, I ignored it. So I don't mind if everyone else does too.'

'You ignored it? How do you mean?'

'Right. It's your turn to follow me. We're going to another game — about fifteen years later. Come on.'

* * *

After a quick trip back to the atrium to collect two programmes, Johnny took Henry through the ancient turnstile again. This time they arrived at Cassio Road — Watford's home ground before Vicarage Road. It was September 4th 1920. Watford, in black and white stripes now, were playing Queens Park Rangers.

Henry looked around the ground. On the western side of the pitch, the ten rows of seats in front of the pavilion were packed. So were the two stands at the northern end of the pitch. Further round, fans stood behind ropes all the way along the eastern touchline and behind the southern goal. The crowd of 10,466 was a new record for the West Herts sports ground.

Henry said with excitement: 'Golly, I remember

this. It was our first home match in our first-ever season in the Football League. We reckoned we'd finally made the big time!'

Henry looked at Johnny's face and saw no excitement.

'Well,' Henry back-tracked, 'obviously it was only Division Three South. It wasn't quite like your own first season in the Football League — when you did the Double with Preston North End and became nationally renowned. But we were little old Watford, and we were very proud of ourselves.'

'Quite rightly so,' Johnny said. 'And let's be very clear: it wasn't due to any greatness on my part. By 1920 I'd long since stopped playing or managing.'

'So you had. Then why have you brought me here?'

'I'll show you.'

Johnny led Henry to the pavilion. By the pavilion gate, Henry saw a bald moustachioed man in his late 50s. He seemed to be some kind of steward. Henry recognised the man. It was Johnny.

Henry was amazed. He hadn't known Johnny in the land of the living, and Johnny had never talked about how he spent his later years.

'You were the gateman in 1920? You? Johnny Goodall? But you'd been a star player. You'd been an invincible manager. Why did you take such a… I'm sorry, but I have to say it… such a lowly role?'

'Actually, I wasn't just a gateman.'

'Ah, good. Perhaps you were just filling in on the day. Did you also have a more executive or chairman-like role — something more appropriate to your legendary status?'

'I was a groundsman too.'

'Ah. Oh dear…. But why?'

'It's simple. I wasn't great any more.'

* * *

Back in the atrium, Johnny and Henry sat down on the yellow leather sofas. Johnny told Henry the story of his final years.

'For the rest of my time on earth,' Johnny said, 'I lived a simple life in the town. I lived in a modest place on Longspring. I ran a caged bird shop on Market Street. I grew vegetables on an allotment near Gammons Lane. And I walked my pet foxes.'

'I beg your pardon?'

'I kept pet foxes.'

'You? One of football's greatest ever players? Shuffling around Watford with a fox on a lead?'

'I'd had my day. People had other heroes.'

'Well, I'm sorry to have to tell you, Johnny, but I think you were in some kind of denial.'

'It's the way things were. I wasn't relevant any more.'

'Ah. I see. Now I get how you were feeling. I had the same thing, in my own way, only last summer. In fact, let me show me you something. You'll see that you aren't the only one who's felt irrelevant. And, more importantly, you'll see that the feeling can be overcome.'

Henry got up. Johnny followed him out of the atrium.

* * *

The Hornet Heaven atrium was on the site of the real-world Red Lion pub. Henry marched out of the building and turned left onto Vicarage Road towards the rows of shops.

Johnny asked: 'Where are we going? To get some

chips?'

Henry led Johnny along the pavement until they were level with the Bridgewater Glass showroom. Then he turned left through black iron gates into Vicarage Road Cemetery.

Johnny stopped. He said with a sudden tremor in his voice: 'No. I'm not going in there.'

'Come on. Don't be a scaredy-cat, Johnny. Death is nothing to be frightened of — as all of us up here know very well indeed.'

'No. I can't go in there.'

'But I want to show you my gravestone. What it says about me. How, in the land of the living, I'm a nothing.'

'I tell you, I can't go in.'

'Come on, Johnny. It'll prove I know what it's like to be forgotten. My headstone makes no reference to my founding the club or anything. My name is tacked onto an existing slab. It just says "Also, Henry William Grover". Come and see.'

Johnny's eyes filled up. He turned his back on Henry — to hide his emotion. He said: 'Well, at least you...'

Johnny couldn't bring himself to say what he had

to say. He bowed his head. Then he shuffled back towards the atrium.

Henry called out after him: 'Johnny? What's wrong? Johnny!'

*   *   *

Henry didn't know what had upset Johnny so much. So he went to see Hornet Heaven's Head Of Programmes, Bill Mainwood, for advice.

Bill was in his office with his young assistant Derek Garston. Henry explained the situation and what had happened at the cemetery

Young Derek piped up: 'Well, I'm not surprised Mr Goodall didn't want to go into the cemetery, Mr Grover, sir. In fact, it was very insensitive of you to take him there.'

'What? Why?' Henry asked.

Derek went over to a shelf. He picked up a book. It was the Official Centenary History of Watford Football Club, published in 1991. He said: 'Because this book told him something he should never have found out, Mr Grover, sir.'

Bill said: 'Derek's right, Henry. On reading this book, Johnny discovered that, when he died, he was buried in Vicarage Road cemetery in an unmarked grave.'

'What?'

'Yes. An unmarked grave. There's no headstone. No memorial of any kind.'

Derek said: 'The book says it's Section G, plot 828, Mr Grover, sir.'

'That's right,' Bill said. 'You can go and see for yourself, Henry. Except, of course, that, er, there's nothing to see.'

Henry protested: 'But Johnny was a true sporting great! How did this ever happen?'

'I don't really know,' Bill said. 'It was the war. There wasn't a lot of money around.'

'Good Lord! I'm aghast,' Henry said. 'This means he's anonymous down there on earth. It's a terrible oversight. It's completely unwarranted. A national giant of football, and his final resting place isn't even marked! No wonder he thinks he's irrelevant. No wonder he thinks he's undeserving of acclaim. No-one even bothered marking his grave!'

Henry thought back to the moment in the summer when he'd learned that he was memorialised only as an afterthought on a gravestone. He'd been devastated.

Now he tried to imagine how it must feel not even to be an afterthought. To merit no thought at all.

'Right,' he said. 'Things are far worse than I imagined. We need to make amends. We need to restore Johnny Goodall to his rightful place in the pantheon of sporting greats. We can't affect anything down there in the land of the living, but at least we can put things right in Hornet Heaven. Ideas, please, Bill! Ideas, please, Derek! And fast!'

* * *

It didn't take long for Henry, Bill and Derek to come up with a plan. Over the next few days, they busied themselves with preparations. Derek did a lot of research — sifting through history books to firm up on his facts and statistics. Bill took a trip to the cemetery to make sure of the latest state of affairs. And Henry went to The Hornets Shop, returning with his arms full, having used a trick Johnny himself had taught him.

Meanwhile, Johnny kept a low profile around Hornet Heaven as always. He carried on going to games both old and new, supporting the club he loved, but he never sought attention. Whenever he saw the way ordinary fans in Hornet Heaven reacted with complete awe to finding themselves in the company of Cliff Holton — The Big Fella — or Graham Taylor — The Great Man — Johnny didn't feel jealous. He just minded his own business. In his quieter moments, he wished his caged birds and pet foxes had loved Watford enough to enter Hornet Heaven and keep him company.

* * *

A few evenings later, Johnny was sitting quietly in a strangely deserted atrium.

Henry went up to him and said: 'Ah, there you are, Johnny. It's quiz night again, old chum. Come on, let's go and watch. I happen to know that young Derek's got something very special lined up for tonight.'

Henry took Johnny to the Captain's Bar. The place was packed. Henry and Johnny sat at the back.

Soon, Derek, as quiz-master, began proceedings. 'Right, ladies and gentlemen,' Derek called out. 'Tonight's quiz is a little more, um, "themed" than usual. So without further ado, here's the first question. Which former Watford player and manager was the Football League's top scorer in its inaugural season of 1888/89?'

Henry glanced at Johnny.

Johnny sighed: 'Henry, I said I didn't want—'

Henry interrupted firmly: 'I bally well don't care what you said, Johnny. Just watch.'

On the other side of the Captain's Bar, Skilly Williams —Watford's goalkeeper from 1913 to 1926 — stood up. Skilly took off his huge flat cap. Then he took off his woollen jumper. Underneath he was wearing a yellow adidas Watford shirt. On the back was the number nine. Above the number nine was the name 'Goodall'.

Johnny saw his name on the shirt. He felt a surge of… he didn't know what. He wasn't sure whether he was about to laugh or cry.

Derek called out: 'Correct answer, Skilly. Second question. Which former Watford player and manager scored 12 goals for England and — thirty years later — was still regarded so highly that he was named in an all-time England XI?'

This time, two people stood up. Tommy Barnett and Arthur Woodward — one-club men with 874 Watford appearances between them — peeled off their jackets to reveal 2018 replica shirts with the number nine and the name Goodall.

Johnny stared. He still didn't quite know what he was feeling.

'Correct answer, gentlemen,' Derek called out. 'Third question. Which former Watford player and manager was such an all-round sporting great that he not only captained England at football, but also played first-class cricket for Derbyshire, played bowls for England, and finished second in the Great Britain Curling Championships?'

This time two more people stood up. Everyone turned. The Big Fella and The Great Man were on their feet. An awed hush fell.

The Big Fella took off his blazer. The Great Man took off his 1979 yellow black and red tracksuit top. Underneath, both were wearing yellow adidas Watford shirts. Number nine. Goodall.

Johnny found he was trembling. He still wasn't sure whether he wanted to laugh or cry. But before he could work it out, he found he was both laughing and crying. Especially when every single person in the room stood up. They were all wearing 2018 replica shirts with his name on the back. To a man, they turned round and faced Johnny. They started applauding. They kept it up for a full minute.

Eventually Derek called out: 'Ladies and gentlemen, I have one final question for you. Which former Watford player and manager has the following inscription on his gravestone? It reads: "In 1903, he became Watford's first manager, leading the club to promotion to the Southern League First Division in his first season."'

Johnny stopped laughing. He stopped crying. The boy had got something wrong. The historical fact was correct, but the reference to an inscription was wrong. Painfully wrong. No gravestone existed for John Goodall.

Johnny felt he should stand up and tell everyone. He felt he should set the record straight and tell them that his earthly remains lay in an unmarked grave. But he wasn't sure he could bear the public humiliation.

Before he could decide, though, something odd began to happen in the room. Everyone started heading towards the exit. By the doors, they formed two lines. It looked like a guard of honour.

Henry said: 'Through you go, old son. There's something you need to see. In the cemetery.'

* * *

Johnny arrived at the iron gates of Vicarage Road cemetery, propelled by the applause and cheers of generations of Watford fans lining the road, all wearing shirts with his name on the back.

He hesitated.

Behind him, Henry said quietly: 'You were a champion in your day, Johnny. Be fearless now.'

Johnny steeled himself and entered the graveyard. With Henry a few steps behind him, he made his way towards Section G, plot 828.

As soon as he approached the plot, he saw what Henry had brought him to see. He couldn't miss it. There was a jet-black gravestone topped by a huge yellow, black and red Watford club badge. It stood out from everything around it in the cemetery. Now he saw there were words below the badge. In large yellow lettering, it said: "Here lies John Goodall, 1863-1942."

Johnny arrived at the gravestone. Tears filled his eyes. He fell to his knees. He stretched out a hand and ran a finger down the smooth stone.

Henry said: 'Oh, it's real, alright. It's down there in the land of the living for all to see.'

Johnny gazed at the gravestone. He could see there

were about a dozen lines of yellow lettering beneath his name, but his eyes were too full of tears to read what it said.

He whispered: 'Henry… Could you…?'

Henry knelt beside Johnny and read aloud the inscription that — 76 years after he died — finally honoured Johnny Goodall's life and achievements. Johnny wept openly. He simply hadn't realised how much the recognition would mean to him.

When Henry had finished reading, he put an arm around Johnny's shoulders.

Henry said: 'They've finally done the right thing down there, old chap. It's like I said before. Recognition of greatness is essential to any football club. It creates values. It sets standards. But it's also essential for the person concerned. You can't deny it anymore, John Goodall. You were a true great. And you will be for all time. In heaven and on earth.'

Johnny Goodall, kneeling at his own grave, nodded. He closed his eyes and finally, after decades of denial, started to allow memories to flood back into his mind. He recalled lifting the FA Cup in 1889; writing one of the first ever books on football in 1898; arriving in a small Hertfordshire town in 1903 and making their football team unbeatable.

A smile broke across his face and lifted his moustache. He opened his eyes and got to his feet.

Henry got up too. He asked how Johnny was feeling.

For years, the man known to everyone as Johnny Allgood hadn't had enough self-esteem to accept the high regard in which he'd been held. But now he answered: 'I'm all good, Henry. I'm all good.'

THE END

6

A SAD, SAD SITUATION

EARTH SEASON 1976/77

In May 1977, in Hornet Heaven, a despondent Henry Grover stepped off Occupation Road and traipsed down the stairs that led into the dingy Supporters Club Bar.

He sang quietly to himself: 'Going down, going down, going down.'

The Supporters Club Bar was a dismal place — perfectly matching the state of Watford Football Club at the time. Two years earlier, Watford had slumped into Division Four. Now Henry slumped into a seat next to one of his old Watford Rovers team-mates and sighed: 'The 1970s are getting worse and worse, Freddie. Strikes and power-cuts were bad enough, but now we're having to put up with Arthur Horsfield playing at centre-half. It's a whole new level of misery.'

The man next to Henry was Freddie Sargent, the cantankerous inside-forward from the 1880s and 1890s. Freddie said: 'Stop moaning, Grover.'

But Henry continued. He said: 'What's more, it's Friday the 13th today — which means something terrible's bound to happen. And yet it's hard to imagine how things could actually get worse for our beloved club.'

'Pull yourself together!' Freddie said. 'You're The Father Of The Club! People in Hornet Heaven take their lead from you. You need to be positive at all times.'

Henry laughed ruefully: 'Ha ha ha! Positive! Ha ha ha!'

In May 1977, things weren't going well for the club Henry had founded nearly a century earlier. Watford were a mid-table side in the bottom division with no sign that they'd ever improve. Home crowds had been dipping below 5,000 in the land of the living — and, in Hornet Heaven, the ancient turnstile wasn't getting much use. In his bleaker moments, Henry had sometimes wondered whether the ancient turnstile might soon rust away through inactivity — and he wasn't too sure he'd care all that much if it did.

'When did you last go to a game?' Freddie asked.

'The FA Cup defeat in January.'

'Ha! Northwich Victoria broke you, did it, you wimp?'

'Like a butterfly on a wheel, Freddie. Like a butterfly on a wheel.'

'Well, things have looked up since then. We sacked the manager a month ago. Mike Keen's finally gone. You should be shouting positive messages from the rooftops — rallying the residents — instead of moping about in here.'

'I don't see any urgency, Freddie. The new Chairman still hasn't hired a new manager yet. He's moving even more slowly than Arthur Horsfield trotting into position for a corner.'

'Right, Grover. This negative attitude isn't good enough. I'm going to—'

Freddie was interrupted by a booming bombastic voice: 'It's alright, Freddie — leave this to me.'

Freddie turned and saw the grand figure of Alderman Ralph Thorpe. The former mayor of Watford, and former Chairman of the club, had entered the bar wearing the chain of office and ceremonial robes that he always wore in Hornet Heaven. The robes were a vivid red, richly trimmed with fur.

The Alderman said to Henry: 'I overheard what you were saying, Henry William. I shall take you to a game to re-enthuse you.'

Freddie protested: 'Oi. I'm handling this, Alderman. You can't just walk in and start lording it over everyone.'

'Stand down, Mr Sargent,' The Alderman ordered. 'As you know, I am widely reputed as "The Prince Of Good Fellows". Watching a match in my company will put a spring in Henry's step and get him looking forward to the future. Come on, Henry William.'

The Alderman got Henry out of his seat and — with his robes flowing behind him — led Henry through the gloom of the bar towards the exit.

Freddie seethed as he watched them go. He didn't like Henry's negativity, but he hated The Alderman's air of superiority even more. Freddie had been awarded an OBE in the land of the living, so he found the self-importance of The Alderman — who only had a JP after his name — utterly infuriating.

He wanted to teach them both a lesson.

And he knew exactly how he'd do it.

* * *

The Alderman took Henry to the wooden programme hut on Occupation Road. He chose two programmes to the previous Saturday's match at Swansea City — a surprising away win — and took Henry through the ancient turnstile. They arrived at the Vetch Field and sat in the Directors Box.

At the final whistle, The Alderman said: 'Well, that should have done you a power of good, Henry William.'

Henry seemed distracted. He mumbled: 'Oh… Um… What? Ah, it's you, Alderman. Hello. Did you say something?'

'This performance should have left you hugely encouraged about how we might do next season. 1977/78 could be wonderful.'

'Oh. Ah. The football. Yes. Sorry. I wasn't paying attention.'

'What? You didn't notice that we won 4-1? Ross Jenkins scored! Keith Mercer scored! Alan Mayes scored two! And Steve Sherwood made some fine saves!'

'Sorry, old thing. I was distracted.'

'Well, that's a poor show, Henry William. To what exactly were you paying attention?'

'Embroidery.'

'I beg your pardon?'

'The embroidery on Elton John's trousers. He was sitting just along the row from us. The way the late afternoon light was playing on the gold-work adorning the seams was simply captivating. Far more exciting than mid-table Fourth Division football.'

Henry Grover had long held two passions: football and aesthetics. When the flamboyantly dressed Elton John had become the chairman of Watford Football Club in May the previous year, Henry had hoped the two passions would be perfectly combined. But the football, under Elton's leadership, had proved unable to sustain Henry's interest.

The Alderman growled. His attempt to re-enthuse Henry by bringing him to a resounding away victory had failed.

'Elton John!' he fumed. 'Don't talk to me about that clown!'

'Oh, he wasn't in a clown costume, Alderman. Not today, anyway. Hopefully he's saving that for another match. Imagine the audacious way he'd pair stripes and polka dots.'

'I'm not interested in Elton John. Nor should you be, Henry William. You should be interested in our football and the future of our club. It's wrong that you're not.'

The accusation hurt Henry. He turned to the friend he'd known for decades. He took a deep breath and said: 'Given the way our club is floundering, Alderman, look me in the eye and tell me that it's fair to blame me.'

* * *

At the same moment, just the other side of the ancient turnstile, Freddie Sargent was looking up and down Occupation Road anxiously — hoping no-one would see what he and his accomplice were up to.

'Hurry up, McBain,' he hissed. 'Why's it taking you so long?'

Beneath the mechanism of the ancient turnstile, Neil McBain was lying on his back with his legs sticking out. It was a pose that wouldn't have surprised anyone familiar with the Scotsman's drinking habits during his second spell as Watford manager in the 1950s.

'Ach, don't hurry me,' McBain moaned.

Freddie had chosen McBain for this job because the Scot had performed labouring tasks around the stadium during his first management spell. In the summer of 1932, he'd dug a stairwell out of the north east corner of the Vicarage Road terrace.

'I've never tampered with high technology before,' McBain called out. 'Digging, though, I was brilliant at.'

'Then why couldn't you dig the club out of Division Four once you'd got us relegated into it in 1958? Hurry up! You're as terrible a workman as you were a manager!'

McBain grunted. 'Right,' he said. 'That should do it.' He slid himself out from under the turnstile and stood up.

Freddie checked to see if the job had been a success.

He nodded at McBain and the two men scuttled away.

* * *

At the Vetch Field, The Alderman and The Father Of

The Club left the Directors Box and headed back towards the ancient turnstile.

'One day this club will rise, Henry William,' The Alderman said. 'Just like it rose when I was in charge.'

Alderman Ralph Thorpe had been Chairman of Watford Football Club between 1903 and 1922. When he'd taken over, Watford had been going out of business as a Southern League Division Two club at Cassio Road. But under his leadership, and with his money, they'd become a Football League club and moved to a brand new stadium at Vicarage Road. For the rest of eternity, Watford Football Club would owe its existence and league status to Alderman Ralph Thorpe's business acumen and financial generosity.

The Alderman continued: 'But my optimism for the future is tempered by one thing, Henry William. Or, more accurately, one man. Elton John. The most important thing at a football club is the owner's vision — and Elton John has none. Vision drives success. What an owner believes, a club achieves.'

'I say, that's a natty phrase, old thing,' Henry said. 'It's almost as natty as the embroidered matching flat cap Elton was wearing with his suit just now.'

'Huh!' The Alderman grunted. 'That's the

problem with you, Henry William. You only see style — not substance. My point is that, as long as this club's Chairman is a jumped-up pop-star wearing preposterous spangly spectacles as big as his face, there'll be no clear vision.'

'Goodness!' Henry protested. 'Elton's spangly spectacles aren't preposterous — they're gorgeous! In fact, his whole wardrobe is an inspiration. I wish I'd had the panache myself — back in the Victorian era — to wear a suit with sequinned flares and platform shoes.'

'He's a show-off, Henry William. That's the only reason he's taken over. He has no ambitions for Watford Football Club. He's just seeking attention.'

Henry glanced at the Alderman's mayoral robes as the portly old man walked back to the ancient turnstile. They were as ostentatious as anything Elton might wear.

The Alderman continued: 'The only thing Elton John inspires in me is fear — that he'll destroy the club I love. I wouldn't ever want to meet him, Henry William, but if I did, I'd say "Don't go breaking my heart — you ridiculous little man".

'Ha! "Don't Go Breaking My Heart." I see what you did there!'

'I beg your pardon?'

'The way you quoted—'

'What are you talking about?'

'Never mind... Anyway, I think you're wrong to knock Elton. He's got pots of money to spend on the club.'

'Huh! Only if he doesn't spend it all on something like gold lamé pantyhose.'

'Good Lord!' Henry gasped. He added dreamily: 'Gold lamé pantyhose! Racy!'

'Oh, for goodness sake, Henry William! Focus on what matters. I'm the greatest benefactor in the club's history and I'm telling you: Elton John is definitely not the man to take Watford on a journey to football stardom.'

The Alderman's chain of office clinked slightly as he carried on shuffling heavily towards the ancient turnstile. When he got there, he pushed at the turnstile — but it wouldn't move.

'What impertinence is this?' he demanded. 'Is it someone's idea of a joke?'

Henry took over the pushing, but the turnstile wouldn't budge.

'Golly,' Henry said, 'this leaves us in a bit of a pickle. The turnstile's stuck.'

'Stuck. Just like Watford Football Club while its Chairman is a pop star. Utterly stuck. I hate 1977.'

'So what are we going to do now?'

With no way out through the turnstile, the two men returned to their seats. The game started again, and they could do nothing but re-watch a meaningless away victory at the end of a second season of drift in Division Four.

Henry and the Alderman felt trapped and powerless — like Watford fans everywhere.

* * *

Not long later, on Occupation Road, Watford's first-ever manager, Johnny Allgood, leaned his weight against the ancient turnstile and shoved.

'Ach, I don't know what's happened here. The ancient turnstile's stuck. I can't shift it.'

Johnny — 78 years old, bald and moustachioed — stepped back. He was with the club's third-ever manager, Fred Pagnam — a white-haired 70-year-old.

Johnny said: 'This is terrible luck, Paggie — on Friday 13th of all days. We could be stuck for the rest of eternity without a single game to go to.'

'That would be a stroke of *good* fortune — the state the club's in,' Paggie said bitterly.

'Don't be so down, Paggie,' Johnny said. 'I know times are bad, but we just need to keep hoping for the best.'

'I *am* hoping for the best. I'm hoping we never have to watch a Watford game ever again! We're a joke of a club — on and off the pitch!'

Johnny Allgood — the greatest footballer in England during the Victorian era before he joined Watford — remained his calm, measured self.

'A jammed turnstile makes our paradise a prison. If we can't go to games, there's nothing for us to do. We'd better inform The Father Of The Club. Do you know where Henry is?'

'I bumped into him earlier. Him and The Alderman were going to last week's game. I don't know why. We've been a laughing stock this season. Do you remember when we lost 4-0 at Cambridge? Our goalkeeper — Peter Gibbs, his name were — were so useless he gave up football straight after!'

'Wait,' Johnny said, alarmed. 'You mean Henry's at a match? But he won't be able to get back!'

'Well, if you ask me, he's a lucky man!'

'This is serious, Paggie. Henry's trapped. This is an emergency.'

Johnny was trying to think what to do when Freddie Sargent appeared as if from nowhere — though it was actually from behind the programme hut just up the slope, where he'd been hiding.

'Afternoon, gents,' Freddie said in a happy, carefree tone. 'Is there a problem?'

Johnny explained that the turnstile was jammed.

'Well, that's unfortunate,' Freddie said. 'I hope no-one's stuck on the other side. That would teach them a lesson.'

'Teach them a lesson? What do you mean?'

'Eh?' Freddie replied. Then he realised his mistake. 'Oh. Nothing, nothing. Look, this ain't the time for chitter-chatter. I'll take charge here and organise the rescue. I'm good at this sort of thing. My organisational abilities on transport committees in the first world war were recognised with an OBE.'

'Hang about,' Paggie said. 'We ain't told you yet that anyone's stuck.'

'There's bound to be people stuck,' Freddie replied. 'Important people, probably. Just leave it to the man with the OBE. I'll sort it all out.'

Johnny and Paggie eyed Freddie suspiciously, but let him get on with it.

* * *

On the other side of the ancient turnstile, the final whistle blew at Swansea — again.

This time, Henry and The Alderman didn't move from their seats. Silently, they each individually reflected on the fact that they were trapped indefinitely behind the ancient turnstile.

As the real-world crowd around them dispersed, Henry became aware of what the tannoy was playing. Henry recognised the tune from previous plays on Radio Hornet at Vicarage Road. It was a hit song by Elton John from the previous autumn — Sorry Seems To Be The Hardest Word. Henry supposed the DJ at Swansea liked the idea of Watford's Chairman apparently apologising for his team's unexpected victory.

As Henry listened to the sad song, he began to feel melancholic. He started to realise what he'd miss if he was stuck here forever and couldn't get back to the main part of Hornet Heaven.

He'd miss watching the ups and downs of the

football team he loved. He'd miss the warmth and camaraderie of the Hornet Heaven community. And he'd miss the way Elton John's outfits boldly blended the contemporary with the antique, and the intricate with the flamboyant. Henry would never see another Watford game, and he'd never see another frilly epaulet.

Over the tannoy, Sorry Seems To Be The Hardest Word was still playing. Henry turned to his companion and saw that he wasn't alone in being upset. He watched as The Alderman shook his head and mumbled: 'It's sad, so sad. It's a sad, sad situation.'

For a split-second, Henry wanted to laugh. But there was a teardrop rolling down the Alderman's cheek. The former Chairman's face was normally formidably stern, but now it looked as if it was about to crumple.

Henry wondered if hearing Elton John's music was softening his old friend's strictly old-fashioned views about the pop star's dress-sense. Perhaps this was a sign that The Alderman would now — like Henry — delight in the fact that the current Chairman chose to dress like a male showgirl.

Henry felt a wave of both sympathy and empathy for his old friend as the Swansea DJ faded the music to silence.

Until, that is, The Alderman revealed the real reason for his gloom. 'A bloody poofter as Chairman!' he growled. 'This club's going nowhere!'

'I say!' Henry protested. 'Good Lord! I say!'

*   *   *

On Occupation Road, a crowd of Watford fans had gathered by the broken ancient turnstile. They were getting agitated that they couldn't go to any games.

A middle-aged man from the 1990s said: 'It's a double whammy. The club's malfunctioning down there, and Hornet Heaven's malfunctioning up here.'

An Edwardian man in a formal suit said: 'I definitely don't want 1976/77 to be the last season I ever see. It'll haunt me forever.'

A woman in a short skirt from the early 1960s said: 'What if 1977/78 is the start of something big? If the turnstile ain't fixed, we'll miss it.'

On the edge of the crowd, Johnny Allgood and Paggie were keeping an eye on Freddie Sargent. Freddie was busy informing everyone he was in charge of the situation — but not actually doing anything to resolve it.

Johnny went up to him and said: 'Freddie, the

turnstile needs fixing urgently. Henry and The Alderman are stuck at a game on the other side.'

'Are they? I had no idea,' Freddie replied archly. 'Why didn't you say?'

Freddie announced to the crowd that he knew how to get the turnstile mended, and that he, Freddie Sargent, would rescue the marooned Father Of The Club and the hapless Alderman. Then he headed off to find his accomplice.

Paggie said to Johnny: 'A rescue sounds more exciting than the football we've seen this season, but that's not saying much. I can't be bothered. I'll see you later.'

Paggie walked up the slope and went into the wooden programme hut that sat on the gravel towards the junction with Vicarage Road. Inside, he saw Neil McBain sitting at a table playing a board game with the young schoolboy who helped organise the programmes in Hornet Heaven — 13-year-old Derek Garston.

Derek — in his school uniform, as always — looked up and said: 'Oh, hello, Mr Pagnam, sir. We're just finishing a game of Soccerama. Apparently it's been very popular down on earth recently.'

McBain said: 'Ach, I don't know why it's so

popular. It's basically just football snakes and ladders, going up through the divisions.'

'But that's what makes it great, Mr McBain, sir. You can reach Division One and get into Europe amazingly quickly. That never happens to a club in real life, Mr McBain, sir.'

'Well, I suppose I like the way that if the dice says you've won a match, you receive money,' McBain conceded.

'Exactly, Mr McBain, sir,' Derek agreed. He said to Paggie: 'Look at all my winnings, Mr Pagnam, sir. Wait… what?… Hey, where's my money gone?'

As well as the drinking, another feature of Neil McBain's tenure as Watford manager had been the misappropriation of other people's money. It had led to his sacking in 1937. He got to his feet. His pockets were bulging with paper notes.

He said: 'Ach, I've had enough of this Soccerama. It's too unrealistic. I got my team up to Division One in about five minutes.'

'Actually, Mr McBain, sir,' Derek replied bitterly, 'I watched you across two spells as Watford manager in the 1930s and 1950s — so the idea of your getting a team promoted is not only unrealistic, it's laughable.

You took Watford Football Club in only one direction, Mr McBain, sir. Down.'

'Why, you cheeky little—'

Suddenly Freddie Sargent walked through the door of the hut. He said: 'McBain, I need to borrow you.'

Freddie calmed McBain down and led him out of the hut.

When they'd gone, Paggie sat himself down at the table. He moaned: 'Everything to do with our club is so miserable, I need distraction. Come on, Derek, lad — show me how to play this Soccerama. Is it fun?'

Derek beamed and said: 'It's brilliant, Mr Pagnam, sir — especially getting into Europe. It makes me realise how much I'd love to see Watford in Europe, Mr Pagnam, sir! Imagine it!'

'McBain were right, then. The game's completely unrealistic.'

'Not totally, Mr Pagnam, sir. It's a dice game, so there's no strategy at all — which reflects exactly the way Watford Football Club is being run at the moment, Mr Pagnam, sir.'

'Oh, God. Don't say that. You're making me think I could play Soccerama for 57 years and find myself no higher up the league system than when I started — just like Watford in real life.'

'Oh dear, Mr Pagnam, sir. You actually sound a bit depressed.'

'Aye. I think I am. It's probably for the best that I won't be able to watch the final game of the season tomorrow.'

'Won't be able to watch?' Derek replied, rather shocked. 'Why not, Mr Pagnam, sir?'

'Haven't you heard? The ancient turnstile's broken.'

'What?'

'No-one can get through.'

'Ever again? Oh my God, Mr Pagnam, sir! That's Hornet Heaven completely… completely… excuse my language, Mr Pagnam, sir… buggered, Mr Pagnam, sir!'

'And what's worse is, Henry Grover's stuck on the other side somewhere.'

'Oh no, this is terrible, Mr Pagnam, sir!' Derek despaired.

He thought for a moment.

'But wait,' he said, 'I could help. I'm only small, so I might be able to squeeze through the turnstile. I could go to the aid of The Father Of The Club!'

The 13-year-old didn't hesitate. He asked Paggie

which game Henry was at, grabbed a programme, and rushed out of the programme hut.

He declared: 'I'm going to be the hero of Hornet Heaven!'

* * *

Meanwhile, at the Vetch Field, Henry and The Alderman trudged back to the ancient turnstile to see if it was working again.

After his shocking outburst, The Alderman was mumbling sadly: 'When I was Chairman, I had a clear picture of what I wanted for this club — and I achieved it. But ever since I died in 1929, I've been in Hornet Heaven watching an organisation without true direction. I want better for this club — but it won't happen while there's a bell-bottomed Friend Of Dorothy in charge.'

Henry was no happier. 'Well, we won't see *anything* happen unless the turnstile becomes unjammed,' he said. 'Let's hope someone's been working on it on the other side.'

At the same moment, on Occupation Road, Derek and Paggie edged through the large crowd surrounding the ancient turnstile. They saw Freddie Sargent supervising Neil McBain — who was lying on the pavement with his shirt sleeves rolled up and his hands deep in the mechanism of the ancient turnstile. McBain was staring up at a lot of complicated technology and hitting it with a wrench.

Derek called out: 'Stand back, Mr McBain, sir, I want to go to the aid of The Father Of The Club!'

Freddie Sargent put himself between Derek and the turnstile. He said menacingly: 'Don't try and steal my thunder, sunshine. Clear off.'

McBain called out: 'He's too late anyway. It's mended now.'

The Scotsman got to his feet. Freddie pushed the turnstile. It moved freely. He announced to the crowd: 'Ladies and Gentlemen, Freddie Sargent OBE has restored Hornet Heaven to its full working glory.'

'Hey, what about me?' McBain said. 'I was the one who—'

'The Father Of The Club and The Alderman were helplessly trapped,' Freddie continued regardless, 'but now, thanks to me, they can return.'

As the crowd cheered, McBain grumbled and young Derek stared miserably at his school shoes. The boy wasn't happy that he'd been denied his shot at being a hero.

Suddenly, though, Derek realised he could still grab a slice of glory: with the programme to the Swansea game in his hand, he could meet up with Henry and heroically lead The Father Of The Club home to a rapturous welcome from the Watford fans on Occupation Road. He fancied that.

He darted forward past Freddie Sargent.

Freddie shouted: 'Oi, where are you going, you little squirt?'

But Derek had already disappeared through the turnstile.

* * *

On the other side of the ancient turnstile, Henry and The Alderman were ready to exit the Swansea game. Henry gave the metal a tentative push. The turnstile moved.

'Aha!' he said. 'It's working again. Come on Alderman, we're in business.'

'The business of watching Watford go out of business,' The Alderman muttered.

Henry and The Alderman went through the turnstile onto Occupation Road. They were met by the

143

sight of Freddie Sargent, Neil McBain, and Fred Pagnam in front of a large crowd of Hornet Heaven residents. A huge cheer went up.

The woman in the 1960s skirt shouted: 'Welcome home, Henry!'

The Edwardian man shouted: 'Hoorah for the safe return of The Father Of The Club!'

Freddie shouted out in a pretend Welsh accent: 'And hoorah for Freddie Sargent — who made it happen!'

As Freddie stepped forward to greet Henry and take credit for his return, a disgruntled McBain accidentally on purpose let the wrench slip from his hand and drop onto Freddie's foot. Freddie collapsed to the pavement — as if he'd been tackled by Tom Walley. 'Owww!' he yelled. 'Buggeration! Owww!'

Meanwhile, Henry spoke to the crowd.

'Why, thank you!' he said. 'Thank you! How lovely! I must admit The Alderman and I were feeling a tiny bit sorry for ourselves in there. But it's wonderful to be back in the bosom of the Hornet Heaven family. Isn't it, Alderman?'

The Alderman didn't answer. To add to his misery about the way Elton John was running the club, he was feeling insulted that no-one had cheered for him. Over the years, he'd received such widespread flattery — as Club Chairman and as Mayor — that he'd come to expect it all the time. He felt strongly that he, personally, should have been given much more of a welcome.

Henry continued to address the crowd, warming to his role as The Father Of The Club.

'But this moment of celebration isn't just about me,' he said.

The Alderman looked up hopefully. So did Freddie, as he lay on the pavement.

Henry continued: 'The restoration of the ancient turnstile to full working order is vital to the happiness of *all of us* in Hornet Heaven — so we can take pride and pleasure in the past, and witness future glories.'

The Alderman and Freddie both fumed that they weren't getting a mention. The Alderman muttered: 'Huh! Future glories? Not until Elton John's sent packing!'

'And if there aren't future glories,' Henry carried on, 'well, it's the supporting, not the winning, that matters. I can't deny that I've been rather disinterested this season, but the prospect of everyone being deprived of access to the club we all love has focused my mind.

None of us could live — or whatever it is we do now we're dead — without Watford.'

The crowd murmured their appreciation of Henry's wise words.

'So, in a way,' Henry concluded happily, 'the malfunction of the ancient turnstile has been a good thing after all.'

On the pavement, furious that he was missing out on acclaim for his achievements, Freddie was about to shout out that he was responsible for the malfunction as well as the rescue — but he realised this probably wouldn't be smart. He got McBain to help him up and they skulked away.

After Henry had finished his speech, the crowd dispersed — relieved that Hornet Heaven would continue to be the Watford paradise it had always been. Everyone was happy again — except for Paggie, who realised something was amiss.

The former 1920s striker said to Henry and The Alderman: 'Here, you two. Didn't you bump into young Derek Garston in there?'

'No, old thing,' Henry replied. 'Why? Should we have done?'

'He went through the turnstile to look for you —

at the Swansea game, just two minutes ago.'

The Alderman grumbled. He felt he was above such trifling concerns. He said: 'I expect the child had the wrong programme.'

'He had the correct programme alright,' Paggie said. 'I saw him take it from the hut.'

'Oh, Lordy,' Henry said. 'This doesn't make sense. If he didn't arrive at the Swansea game, where did he go?'

The Alderman grunted with disgust: 'So. A boy has gone through the turnstile and gone missing. Why am I not surprised? Everything to do with Watford Football Club is malfunctioning — on Elton John's watch!'

THE END

THE STORY CONTINUES IN
'LIKE A CANDLE IN THE WIND

7

LIKE A CANDLE IN THE WIND

EARTH SEASON 1976/77

Thirteen-year-old Derek Garston frowned. The programme he'd brought through the ancient turnstile was for last Saturday's match — on May 7th 1977 — at the Vetch Field. But somehow he was at a game at Vicarage Road. He didn't understand.

He went and stood on the shallow covered terrace of the Rookery End — directly beneath the Watford Observer clock. As yet, he couldn't pinpoint which year he'd come to, but, looking to his right, he noticed the Main Stand extension didn't exist.

As soon as the teams came out, he recognised exactly which match he was at. It was Watford versus

Plymouth Argyle on the night of Tuesday April 15th 1969. He was about to watch Watford win promotion to Division Two for the first and only time in their history.

'Brilliant!' he said. 'I'll take this as a swap for 1977 any day of the week!'

* * *

Not long later, Henry and The Alderman — in search of Derek — arrived through the ancient turnstile with their programmes for the Swansea game. Henry came to an abrupt halt when he realised they weren't at the Vetch Field.

'I say,' Henry said. 'What's going on? This isn't right. The turnstile must be dicky.'

The Alderman muttered: 'Dicky? Under Elton John? No surprise there.'

They made their way into the Main Stand and saw they were at the Plymouth game.

'I don't understand,' Henry said. 'How can a Swansea programme from 1977 bring us to Vicarage Road in 1969? It seems completely random.'

The Alderman pondered this for a moment. He didn't like the thought that occurred to him.

'It had better not be random,' he said. 'That would be a disaster. We'd probably never see a new Watford game ever again.'

'Really? Why?'

'There must be over 3,000 past matches available in Hornet Heaven. So if the turnstile is working randomly, and you go through with the programme for, say, tomorrow's match at home to Darlington, there'll be only a 1 in 3,000 chance of finding yourself at the right game. You're bound to end up at a historic match instead.'

'You mean, we'd never see whether things get better after May 1977?'

'The chances are we wouldn't. Having a fancy-dressed fool for a Chairman would probably remain our freshest memory forever. We'd effectively be stuck in the past.'

Henry gazed down at the 1968/69 promotion side on the pitch below them. Keith Eddy was playing. Stewart Scullion and Barry Endean too.

'Well, on the positive side, at least everyone in Hornet Heaven would still have the past — which we didn't when the turnstile was stuck. This night against Plymouth was the pinnacle of success for the club.

'Huh! All we did was win Division Three, Henry William. I've got greater hopes for this club than that — provided, of course, that Elton John leaves the club. We need to get back and get the turnstile fixed so we can see the future glories you talked about. Come on, Henry William — we've got a lost boy to find.'

As the match moved into the second half, Henry found he was loving the experience far more than he'd loved anything during the 1976/77 season.

He joined in the chants: 'Na-na-na-na! Na-na-na-na! Hey-ey-ey! Watford FC!'

'He's up, he's down, he's in the Rose and Crown! Rodney Green, Rodney Green!'

The Alderman wasn't loving it, though. He was stomping up and down the Vicarage Road terrace, annoyed not to have found the boy. He came back to Henry and said impatiently: 'Where is the child? I'm in a hurry to see new Watford games. Even this one was a disappointment.'

'A disappointment? But this was the night the club achieved the level you were dreaming of when you became Chairman and recruited Johnny Allgood as our first manager in 1903. Watford Football Club finally reached the top two divisions of English football.'

'Huh! The problem was the Chairman. Jim Bonser took us up alright, but then he didn't know what to do. It was just like today under Elton John: no vision, no plan moving forwards.'

'There you go again, Alderman — criticising Elton John. I just don't understand what you've got against him. And you can't knock Jim Bonser — in 1969, at least. You have to credit him with—'

'Jim Bonser wasn't a benefactor like I was. He was a malefactor. In the end he let the club drop down into the bottom division — and sold it to a ludicrously-dressed pop star!'

'Well, that crosses a line, Alderman. I'm not having that. That's totally unfair.'

'Unfair to Jim Bonser?'

'Goodness, no. I'm glad that old Scrooge cleared off! Unfair to Elton John. Elton John isn't ludicrously dressed.'

'Yes, he is.'

'No, he isn't. Didn't you see those sparkly spectacles of his that spelt the word 'ZOOM!'? They were genius. And they'd have been even better if they'd been Watford-related. Imagine, last season, if he'd worn glasses that spelt "Goodeve".'

'Good grief, Henry William. You're obsessed with the dress-sense of a bizarre exhibitionist who will probably wreck our club — and I've had my fill of it. I have no wish to speak to you any more.'

'I say, that's a bit —'

Henry was suddenly distracted as the crowd went wild around them. Roy Sinclair had scored the game's only goal. Watford were going up.

Henry watched the crowd's celebrations. They were feeling the greatest joy they'd ever felt as Watford fans. Henry marvelled at it.

'Look at their faces,' he sighed. 'Just look at their faces.'

He turned to see what The Alderman thought but The Alderman had gone.

* * *

When the final whistle blew, Derek leapt over the Watford Observer hoarding behind the Rookery goal and rushed onto the playing area with hundreds of other fans. He loved the naughtiness of a pitch invasion.

The schoolboy hurdled a couple of hay bales and ran with the crowd towards the main stand — half-skipping, half-lolloping with excitement. He was momentarily distracted by the sight of a young man proposing to his girlfriend in the centre-circle, but carried on.

When he got to the paddock, he stopped, out of breath. He noticed the pure exhilaration on everyone's faces.

Someone shouted jubilantly: 'Next stop, Division Two!'

Derek beamed. With Watford currently in Division Four, and Elton John failing to create a positive impact, the youngster had forgotten how great it was, as a fan, to feel that your club was on an upward trajectory — on the crest of a rising wave. He hopped up and down excitedly, watching the Watford players drink champagne and smoke cigarettes in the Directors Box, until — suddenly — he felt someone grab his ear.

'Owwww!' he cried — and looked up to see The Alderman.

'Manners, boy!' The Alderman said.

'Owwww, your Worshipfulness, sir!' Derek corrected himself.

'That's better. Now, this is no time to be enjoying yourself. The ancient turnstile has developed a fault —

exactly like our club in 1977. They both need fixing. We're going back.

'But 1977 is awful, your Worshipfulness, sir!' Derek complained.

But The Alderman wasn't prepared to argue. He marched the boy back to the ancient turnstile.

* * *

Henry was already back on Occupation Road when The Alderman returned with Derek. It was clear that The Alderman still wasn't speaking to Henry. The former Chairman strode off up the slope, calling out: 'And tell The Father Of The Club he needs to get the turnstile mended — properly this time.'

Derek said to Henry: 'Actually, Mr Grover, sir, it's possible the fault is with the Swansea programme, not the turnstile. We need to run a test to find out.'

First, Derek took through a programme to one of his favourite matches: a 4-1 friendly win over Borussia Dortmund in 1954. But he didn't arrive at the floodlit European night he loved so much. He found himself in 1964 watching a 2-0 defeat at Workington.

'What a swiz!' he complained.

Next, Henry took through the programme to the club's first ever FA Cup tie — which he'd played in — at home to Swindon in 1886. He found himself at Kenilworth Road. He didn't wait to find out which year or match it was, he just ran back through the turnstile, appalled.

'This turnstile needs fixing immediately!' he insisted. 'No-one should ever be taken to that filthy hovel against their will!'

Freddie Sargent was passing by and saw Henry and Derek looking unhappy. He approached them. They didn't acknowledge him.

He said: 'What an ungrateful pair — after all I did to save Hornet Heaven.'

'Oh hello, Freddie,' Henry replied, downbeat.

'Great. Is that all the thanks I get?' Freddie complained.

'I'm afraid there's bad news, Mr Sargent, sir,' Derek said. 'The turnstile's taking us to random matches — which means we may never see a new Watford game again.'

Freddie was shocked. This hadn't been meant to happen. McBain must have messed up.

'Blimey,' he said, 'you mean, if a miracle happens

and we walk Division Four next season — somehow — we'd never know?'

'Exactly,' Henry said. 'This wretched 1976/77 season could be the last season we properly witness. For the rest of eternity.'

Derek added: 'And I'll have to abandon all hope of ever seeing Watford in Europe in future, Mr Sargent, sir.'

Freddie didn't like the sound of any of this — but he could see it was another opportunity to prove his superiority over The Alderman.

'Right,' he said. 'This is a proper crisis. But don't worry, I'll get the turnstile working correctly. I saved Hornet Heaven earlier today — and now I'll save it a second time. All in a day's work for Freddie Sargent OBE.'

* * *

Derek trudged back to the programme hut. He found Neil McBain and Fred Pagnam playing Soccerama. His spirits lifted when he saw that McBain had got his team into Europe.

'Wow!' he said. 'Europe! That's my absolute

dream, Mr McBain, sir!'

Paggie grumbled: 'I suspect match-fixing. Just like when McBain were manager in 1958 — and we threw that game against Brighton.'

'Hey!' McBain said. 'That was nothing to do with me.'

Derek explained to McBain and Paggie that the ancient turnstile wasn't working properly. He said: 'The cause is clearly faulty workmanship, I'm afraid, Mr McBain, sir.'

'Just like when McBain were manager in 1958,' Paggie repeated, 'and got us relegated.'

'Ach, shut up! Relegation wasn't my fault and neither is the turnstile.'

'But I haven't told you exactly what's wrong with the turnstile yet, Mr McBain, sir.'

'Whatever it is, it wasn't my fault. I don't get things wrong.'

Paggie said: 'You mean, like when you opposed the signing of Cliff Holton and called it "a tragedy" for the club?'

'Ach, that was—'

'Or when you went up the road to manage the filthy Hatters?'

'Oh God, shut up about that! Will you not just let it lie?'

Freddie Sargent entered the hut. He'd been looking for McBain. He came over to the table and said: 'McBain, I need you to fix the turnstile — properly this time. It's taking people to random games.'

McBain replied truculently: 'Well, I don't know that I want to fix the turnstile. Last time, you took all the credit. What am I going to get out of it?'

Freddie scooped up two handfuls of Soccerama bank notes. He stuffed them into a brown envelope and handed the envelope to McBain.

McBain said: 'Ah. That'll do nicely.'

When Freddie and McBain had gone, Derek and Paggie sat down to start a fresh game of Soccerama. Derek shook the dice.

'Ooh, this feels good, Mr Pagnam, sir. It's exactly the feeling the Watford fans had at the 1969 promotion game against Plymouth, Mr Pagnam, sir. In Soccerama, when it's your go, you're always moving forwards — you're always on the way up.'

'Aye, the total opposite of 1977.'

Derek threw the dice to start the game. After his second go, he'd had a win and a draw — so he landed on the fourth square up.

'Yes! I've won a penalty! Pass me a penalty card, Mr Pagnam, sir.'

Derek took the orange card Paggie gave him. He braced himself, then turned it over to see what it said.

'Hurrah!' he squeaked. '"Go To Division Three"!'

Paggie said: 'Well, that's as random as the ancient turnstile at the moment.'

'Ha! They're both like a Lucky Dip, Mr Pagnam, sir.'

'Ooh, I love a Lucky Dip at the fairground. You never know what you're going to get. Imagine if I went through the ancient turnstile — without a clue where I were going to end up — and found myself watching .. ooh, I don't know... a centre-forward in his prime — Charlie Livesey! — smashing in goals for fun in the Third Division in 1963/64!'

'Charlie Livesey! He was brilliant for half a season, Mr Pagnam, sir! Completely out of nowhere!'

'Aye, I love a bit of unpredictability, me. This season, you always knew what were coming: if we were playing away, we wouldn't be winning. As a football fan, you always want to be surprised.'

Derek suddenly slapped down his penalty card in

excitement.

'Crikey! I've had an idea, Mr Pagnam, sir! Instead of this being a programme hut, we could make it a Lucky Dip stall. There'd be a few duds hidden among the prizes, of course, but people might pick out an away game at Aberdare Athletic in 1921 and arrive at Old Trafford in 1969! The residents of Hornet Heaven would love it, Mr Pagnam, sir! Let's put up a sign saying "Lucky Dip Trips"!'

Paggie grinned and said: 'Ee, this has right cheered me up. Let's do it, lad! Let's do it!'

* * *

Half an hour later, Freddie Sargent was standing outside the ancient turnstile. He was supervising Neil McBain — who was lying under the mechanism, taking the only approach he knew. A loud clanging of metal on metal resounded down the road.

Freddie saw a group of Watford fans arriving to go through the turnstile. He stepped in front of them and said: 'You can't go through at the moment. The turnstile's taking people to random games.'

A woman in a Women's Royal Naval Service

uniform from the 1940s said: 'We know! It's genius!'

'Is it?' Freddie asked uncertainly.

'Absolutely,' she replied. 'We've got ourselves programmes for a "Lucky Dip Trip" from the new stall up the road. We can't wait to see where we randomly end up on the other side of the turnstile.'

Freddie hadn't seen such excitement on Watford fans' faces all season.

'Oh, that!' he said. 'Yes, the whole thing was my idea.'

He leaned down and muttered: 'Take a break, McBain. Get out of the way.'

Then Freddie stood aside and held out his hand so the fans could shake it in gratitude before they passed through the turnstile on their Lucky Dip Trips.

* * *

Meanwhile, Henry Grover was feeling unsettled that The Alderman wasn't speaking to him after the trip to the Plymouth game. He went back to the Supporters Club Bar, just off Occupation Road, to see if he could patch things up with his old friend.

In subterranean semi-darkness, a man called Jack

Gran was playing mood music on a piano in the corner. Gran had been a left-half for Watford in 1900 before becoming a music hall performer under the name Jack Cardiff.

Henry recognised the music immediately. It was an Elton John song and it seemed rather appropriate. In 1977, Watford's hopes of a successful future — and Hornet Heaven's hopes of seeing that future — were definitely flickering like a Candle In The Wind.

In the far corner, Henry saw The Alderman sitting in a chair, shrouded in mayoral robes and despair. With his eyes closed, the dignitary was gently swaying his head to the sad song.

Henry felt pity for his old friend. For most of his life and afterlife, The Alderman had been terrific company: "The Prince Of Good Fellows" had deserved his nickname in every way. But over the last few months — since Elton John had become Chairman — the demeanour of Alderman Ralph Thorpe had changed.

Henry went over and said gently: 'I say, are you OK, old chap?'

The Alderman opened his eyes. As Candle In The Wind played on, the former Chairman sighed and said: 'This music has brought out the melancholy in me. I was wishing I hadn't died. If I'd lived longer and gone back to run the club again, maybe it wouldn't be in its current state. After 1929, in the land of the living, all that was left was my legacy. My candle burned out long before my legend ever did.'

'Ha! Very clever!' Henry said.

'What? What was clever?'

'Using the words from—'

'Eh?'

'Oh well. Carry on.'

The Alderman's impatience with Henry suddenly returned. He said: 'I hope you're not having some kind of fun at my expense, Henry William. It's Elton John — the fashion hero you fetishise — who merits mockery and derision, not me. No-one can deny that I'm still the club's greatest-ever benefactor — in a way that a cheap musical entertainer could never be.'

Suddenly, the music stopped. Jack Gran, at the piano, got to his feet, huffed with indignation, and slammed the piano lid. He walked out.

Henry sat down opposite The Alderman — a little cautiously.

Henry said: 'To be fair to Elton, his dress sense is sublime.'

'Huh,' The Alderman grunted. 'Even if that were true, it's irrelevant, Henry William. The only thing that matters is that he's not the right Chairman for this club.'

'I don't agree,' Henry argued. 'He's leading by example — establishing the tone and style. Next season, I fully expect the team to trot out to play in yellow and black sailor boy outfits with matching matelot caps.'

'Elton John is damaging us: people think it's hilarious that a global pop star supports a bottom division club. It belittles us.'

'Nonsense. When our away kit is a red lace basque, with red fishnet stockings instead of shorts and socks, the world will admire us.'

The Alderman was getting increasingly cross. He said: 'What will fix things is proper investment. That new keeper of ours, Steve Sherwood, only cost £3,000. That's nothing. I gave £1,000 for Fred Pagnam more than 50 years ago.'

'If there's to be investment, it should go into shiny yellow matchday suits for the players — sparkling with glitter, and worn with red and black feather boas.'

The Alderman, infuriated, got out of his chair. He said: 'That's enough, Henry William. We shall have to agree to disagree.'

He marched towards the exit. Henry got up and followed.

'Wait,' Henry called out. 'I haven't told you about my idea for football boots with six-inch platform heels like Elton's. Imagine the free headers Ross Jenkins will get. Alderman! Alderman!'

* * *

The Alderman strode out of the bar onto Occupation Road. He saw the programme hut that Derek and Fred Pagnam had re-branded as "Lucky Dip Trips". He fumed: 'What the blazes is going on?'

He by-passed the long queue that snaked from the door, and went inside. He found Derek and Paggie handing out programmes to excited customers.

'Stop this at once,' he demanded. 'Hornet Heaven is in grave crisis and you're offering residents all the fun of the fair!'

'But they love it, your Worshipfulness, sir,' Derek piped up. 'Look at the queue.'

Paggie said: 'We've really struck a chord with people, Alderman. Nostalgia's brilliant when it takes you by surprise — it's like finding an old scarf you'd forgotten you'd kept.'

Suddenly Henry — who'd been following the Alderman — appeared through the door. He had a big grin on his face.

'Lucky Dip Trips!' he purred. 'I say! Well done on such a splendid idea, gentlemen!'

The Alderman growled. 'Not you too, Henry William. Does no-one in Hornet Heaven appreciate the seriousness of our situation?'

Derek squeaked: 'Don't be a spoilsport, your Worshipfulness, sir. Give it a go. You might re-discover an amazing goal you'd forgotten about — from a match you wouldn't have bothered to watch again.'

Paggie added: 'Or you might see a tiny incident you'd forgotten — like the Stockport County goalie chasing after Stewart Scullion to shake his hand after Scully had just rounded five players to score at the Rookery End in 1967.'

The Alderman remembered that moment. He felt his resistance starting to weaken. He steeled himself. Weakness was unbefitting for a man of his achievements and stature.

'No,' he said. 'Random is bad. Hornet Heaven and Watford Football Club need order and progress. Random is the behaviour of our risible pop-star Chairman when he's choosing what clothes to wear. The turnstile needs to be restored to its normal functioning.'

Henry ignored the insult about Elton John. He still wanted to make up with The Alderman — and saw a Lucky Dip Trip as an opportunity.

He said: 'But I don't quite see what the hurry is, old son. Freddie Sargent can get the mechanism fixed tomorrow — in time for the new game against Darlington. Honestly, Lucky Dip Trips are too jolly an idea to waste. And, if I may say so, you need jollying up. Come on, let's give it a go — you and me, old thing. It'll be amazing to arrive together somewhere completely unexpected.'

The Alderman's resistance broke. He hadn't enjoyed arguing with Henry about the current club Chairman. He hoped that sharing a wonderful football experience with Henry would renew their longstanding friendship.

'Alright. I suppose there's time,' he said. 'But just the once.'

Henry grinned. He wondered what game to choose. He deliberately plumped for an awful one.

'Derek,' he said, 'give us two programmes to last

season's defeat at Lincoln City. Our Lucky Dip Trip will take us to something far more cheering than a 5-1 thrashing.'

Derek quickly found the programmes. He said: 'I remember this game, Mr Grover, sir. Lincoln had a very good young manager called Graham Taylor. I wonder if he'd be interested in Watford's current vacancy.'

The Alderman couldn't resist saying: 'Huh! Fat chance he'd come to us with Elton John in charge!'

Henry let the jibe go. He smiled genially and took The Alderman by the arm. He said: 'Now, now, Aldie. Let's forget our differences and allow this experience to bring us together.'

He took the programmes from Derek. He couldn't wait to see where they'd end up.

* * *

On the other side of the turnstile, clutching their Lincoln programmes, Henry and The Alderman saw they weren't at Sincil Bank. They were at Vicarage Road.

'Aha,' Henry said. 'This is promising. This could be a *very* lucky dip.'

They went into the Main Stand. When they looked

out, they saw thousands and thousands of spectators in the ground. But the spectators weren't on the terraces or in the stands. They were on the pitch.

The Alderman said: 'This looks like the end of the Plymouth game again. But it's daytime. What in God's name is going on?'

Henry looked across to the far side of the ground. Along the front of the yellow Shrodells Stand was a low wide structure. Henry realised it was a stage. On the stage was a piano. At the piano was a man wearing a silky yellow-and-black hooped jacket. It was dotted with tiny yellow pom-poms that danced as he moved. It could only be one man.

Henry cried out in delight: 'Elton!'

On stage, Elton started to play his hit song 'Daniel'.

'This must be the fund-raising concert Elton John put on in May 1974.' Henry said.

'Good grief,' The Alderman said. 'This isn't just random — it's freakish. In every way. Look at what that bizarre little man is wearing.'

'Nonsense. Those tiny yellow pom-poms are a miracle of suavity and refinement! Why can't you appreciate Elton's splendour, old chap?'

'Well, maybe, in Hornet Heaven, my eyes have

died — and you see more than I.'

'Ha! I get you, old son! Very witty!'

'This is infuriating. You keep on saying I'm being clever or witty — why?'

'Don't worry. Let's just enjoy the show.'

'Enjoy this? How can I? This is a desecration of the stadium I acquired for this club. I can't believe I'm having to endure this.'

'Well, I can't believe I'm getting a chance to see an Elton John stage-costume first-hand!'

'Right. We need to leave. You said this trip would bring us together. It's clearly doing the opposite.'

'Leave? But I think I want to stay forever!'

The Alderman saw a gleam in Henry's eyes that he'd never seen before. Its intensity alarmed him.

'Staying forever is a bad idea, Henry William.'

'Nonsense, old thing! If I stay, I'll be able to spend eternity closely examining every outlandish detail of a silk hornet costume! What more could any Watford fan possibly want?'

'Personally, as a Watford fan, I'd start with not being stuck in 1977 forever, unable to see my team for the rest of time.'

The gleam in Henry's eyes intensified. 'Goodness,'

he said, slightly moistening his lips with his tongue, 'perhaps Elton will change costume mid-concert. Yes! Into yellow satin hot pants! With a sparkly yellow red and black garter, tight across the thighs! Oh my goodness! I'm going down the front!'

Henry dashed down to the front of the Main Stand.

'Henry William!' The Alderman called out. 'Don't!'

The Alderman watched Henry vault over the front of the stand.

'Henry William! Come back!'

Henry leapt over the hoardings and railings onto the pitch. He became submerged in the crowd — his Victorian suit disappearing into the sea of denim.

The Alderman stopped calling out. He stared out onto the pitch, wondering whether he would ever see The Father Of The Club again.

Then he clutched his head in his hands and uttered a primal scream of despair for what he felt had become of Henry Grover, Hornet Heaven and Watford Football Club.

* * *

The Alderman emerged through the ancient turnstile onto Occupation Road. He took a few steps across the pavement then lowered himself to sit on the kerb, submerged in his robes.

Before long, he heard footsteps approaching.

A voice he recognised as Freddie Sargent's said: 'Well, well, well. Look at this. How are the mighty fallen! Ha ha ha!'

* * *

A little later, on the other side of the turnstile, Henry had calmed down a little. Elton was off-stage for a while.

During the break, Henry noticed that a young woman near him was holding a programme. The front cover was bright yellow with nothing else on it apart from the club badge of the time — a red hornet — surrounded by a compact circle of text. Henry thought it looked supreme.

When the young woman opened the programme, Henry peered over her shoulder to read what it said. There was an introduction that started with two quotes from Elton himself.

Henry read Elton's first quote. It said: "Anyone can

join a club for 6 months and get fed up with it — but really you've got to be totally dedicated, and that's what I am."

Henry nodded with satisfaction. Here was proof that Elton John was totally committed to the club that Henry had started 96 years earlier. This was no pop star's passing phase. Elton was in it for the long haul.

Then Henry read the next sentence — Elton's second quote. It said: "I honestly think Watford have done more for me than I could possibly do for them."

Henry smiled. He thought this came across as suitably humble from a global superstar.

But then he frowned. The quote didn't make Elton sound very ambitious. In fact, Elton was talking down the extent to which he could actually help the club.

Henry read the sentence back to himself: "…more for me than I could possibly do for them."

Henry gasped. It was there in black and white: Elton John was telling everyone he was *unable* to help Watford Football Club. Henry was hit by a wave of shock.

'This is terrible!' he cried. 'He's saying it himself in the programme! Elton John can't possibly do anything for us! The Alderman was right about him all along!'

In that moment, Henry's priorities changed.

Suddenly he didn't care about the silk Hornet costume Elton had been wearing.

He didn't care about tiny yellow pom-poms.

The club he'd founded in 1881 was in the hands of a man who, by his own admission, was useless. This was what Henry now cared about.

Henry Grover wanted Elton John out.

* * *

As soon as Henry arrived back on Occupation Road, he saw The Alderman sitting on the kerb with his eyes closed.

Henry went up to him and announced: 'I'm back, old chap. And I've changed.'

The Alderman replied: 'If you're wearing one of Elton John's taffeta tutus, I'm never opening my eyes again.'

'I mean, I've changed my views on Elton John. I'm 100% with you now.'

The Alderman still didn't look up. He said: 'You won't be 100% with me until the day you agree it would be inappropriate for a football club Chairman to attend a board meeting in a lime green bathing suit, with miniature silver bells around the gentlemen's area. And that day's not any time soon.'

'Ah. Fair point,' Henry conceded. 'I'm not sure I could ever go quite that far.' Then he clarified: 'But I do agree that Elton John is definitely not the man to take Watford on a journey to football stardom.'

Henry explained what Elton had written in the concert programme.

The Alderman was delighted. He got to his feet and boomed: 'Ha! So he admits he couldn't possibly do anything for our club. I knew I was right about him.'

'I'm afraid you absolutely were, old son,' Henry said.

The Alderman instinctively spread his arms wide to hug his old friend. Then he remembered he was an important dignitary and just shook Henry's hand instead. He said: 'We stand united against Elton John, Henry William. Let us now restore Hornet Heaven to normality so we can see him gone as soon as possible. It's imperative he leaves the club.'

'Exactly. He's got to go. If Elton John stays in charge for the next five years, we could end up divisions away from where we are now.'

The two old friends finished shaking hands — and crossed Occupation Road to go and close down the Lucky Dip Trips stall.

*   *   *

The next morning, once they were sure all the Hornet Heaven residents who'd taken a Lucky Dip Trip had returned, Henry and The Alderman stood with Freddie Sargent by the ancient turnstile on Occupation Road. It was now Saturday May 14th 1977.

The Alderman said: 'Right, Mr Sargent. Time to get that turnstile fixed for good. Hornet Heaven needs restoring to full working order.'

'Oi!' Freddie replied. 'Don't you order me about. I'm the one in charge here.'

'Just get it done,' The Alderman demanded. 'I've had a proper bellyful of Elton John. I want to see him gone as soon as possible.'

'So do I,' Henry said. 'The randomness of the turnstile has had the happy effect of bringing The Alderman and myself together. There's a new programme due in this afternoon — for the final game of this dreadful season. The Alderman and I both sincerely hope the club will be announcing Elton John's departure.'

Freddie instructed McBain to crawl beneath the ancient turnstile — where the Scotsman got busy again with the same finesse that he'd brought to managing Watford in the 1930s and 1950s. Metal clanged on metal again.

Henry and The Alderman left Freddie and McBain to it — and went off to the Supporters Club Bar.

Soon, drawn by the sound of the hammering, Derek and Fred Pagnam strolled down from the programme hut. They watched solemnly as McBain struggled with the mechanism.

Derek said: 'It's a shame, really, Mr Pagnam, sir. Lots of people loved our Lucky Dip Trips. Do you think McBain will fix the turnstile correctly this time?'

'Will he heck!' Paggie replied. 'McBain wrecks everything he touches. If he buggers up Hornet Heaven even worse, I'll be wishing Watford Football Club had never existed.'

Derek gasped: 'What? You can't wish that, Mr Pagnam, sir! That's... ...treason, Mr Pagnam, sir!'

'Well, it's how I feel,' Paggie said sadly.

McBain manoeuvred himself out from under the

turnstile. He said: 'There. One turnstile properly mended.'

Freddie announced to Derek and Paggie: 'Freddie Sargent saves the day. Again. Meanwhile, certain other bigwigs — who clearly don't care — are living it up in the bar.'

Derek said: 'Can I be the first to test the turnstile, Mr Sargent, sir?'

Freddie had been planning to get The Alderman to test it — secretly hoping that, if McBain had messed up again, the turnstile would send The Alderman somewhere from which he could never return.

'Please, Mr Sargent, sir!' Derek asked again.

'Alright. I suppose so.'

Derek rushed away to fetch programmes. He returned with two — for himself and Paggie.

Freddie asked: 'Which match have you got?'

Derek replied: 'The home game against Exeter City on September 30th 1922, Mr Sargent, sir.'

'Why that one?'

'We scored our first-ever goals at Vicarage Road, Mr Sargent, sir. And a certain centre-forward called Fred Pagnam scored three of them.'

Paggie smiled — for the first time in a long while.

He said: 'Ee, thank you, youngster. That's a lovely gesture. Perhaps I am glad Watford Football Club exists after all.'

Derek and Paggie went through the ancient turnstile.

They arrived on the other side.

Paggie took one look and said: 'Bloomin 'eck! What's that clown McBain done to the turnstile now? We're not even in a football stadium!'

THE END

THE STORY CONTINUES IN
'LOSING EVERYTHING'

8

LOSING EVERYTHING

EARTH SEASON 1976/77

Derek Garston and Fred Pagnam were on a long, straight, wide road. The road surface was unpaved — churned up by cartwheels and the feet of livestock. Recent rain had made it a slurry of mud, cow pats and sheep droppings.

Old low buildings bordered the road, with courts and alleys between them. Signs for taverns and ale houses hung outside what seemed like every third building.

'Bleeargh!' Derek retched. 'The stench of alcohol is terrible, Mr Pagnam, sir!'

'Reminds me of the home dressing room before

matches in my day,' Paggie replied.

The road was busy. People in drab, filthy-looking clothes were hurrying out of their over-crowded houses and heading in one direction. Derek and Paggie followed the crowd to see what was happening.

'I reckon this is Watford town centre, lad,' Paggie said. 'What year do you think it is?'

'Some time in the first half of the nineteenth century, I would imagine, Mr Pagnam, sir.'

'Eh? But Henry didn't start up Watford Rovers until 1881. How come the ancient turnstile has brought us here? Does football even exist?'

Paggie got his answer a short distance down the muddy high street. Near St Mary's Church, the road was blocked by hundreds of people brawling. They were shoving and kicking each other, throwing each other to the ground.

Paggie said: 'Hooligans! Football must exist!'

'These aren't hooligans, Mr Pagnam, sir. They're players.'

Paggie saw a young man emerge from a pile-up of bodies holding a ball. The fellow was immediately hacked to the ground.

'Blimey,' Paggie said. 'Roger Joslyn would be in

his element.'

The young man, clinging tight to the ball, disappeared beneath a tide of boots and bodies.

Derek said: 'I think this is what we'd now call "folk football", Mr Pagnam, sir. It occasionally sprang up on public holidays. It doesn't bear much resemblance to what we've been seeing in 1977.'

'You can say that again,' Paggie replied. 'Steve Sherwood definitely wouldn't have hung onto the ball as well as that lad just did.'

Paggie and Derek watched for a little longer, but the ball didn't make any progress towards wherever the goals might be. Paggie observed that the game was as stuck in the mire as Watford Football Club was in 1977. They headed back the way they'd come. The turnstile still needed fixing.

* * *

Freddie Sargent was waiting on Occupation Road when Derek and Paggie emerged from the ancient turnstile.

'So,' Freddie said. 'Has McBain made a success of fixing things?'

Paggie asked: 'Are you seriously using the words

"McBain" and "success" in the same sentence?'

'Oh, Gawd!' Freddie groaned. 'What's the problem this time?'

To answer the question precisely, Derek fetched a selection of programmes from the hut. One programme at a time, he went back and forth through the turnstile. On each occasion, he spotted something that suggested to him the date of what he was seeing.

Eventually he said: 'Right. I think I've worked it out, Mr Sargent, sir. The turnstile now takes us to football that was happening 96 years before the date on the programme.'

Freddie did some quick mental arithmetic, subtracting 96 from 1977. He said: 'You mean we can only watch football from before 1881 — before Henry founded the club?'

'Correct, Mr Sargent, sir. It's almost as if Mr Pagnam's wish has come true.'

'Eh?' Paggie asked. 'What wish?'

'Don't you remember, Mr Pagnam, sir? You said that if Mr McBain buggered up Hornet Heaven even worse, you'd be wishing Watford Football Club had never existed.'

'Did I? Well, I didn't mean it.'

'But it's effectively come true, Mr Pagnam, sir. Right now, in terms of the games we can see in Hornet Heaven, there's no such thing as Watford Football Club.'

Freddie stared at Derek in horror at the revelation. Suddenly, he was feeling out of his depth. All he'd wanted to do, by getting McBain to tamper with the turnstile in the first place, was annoy The Alderman and take him down a peg or two. But the consequences were proving terrible — and getting worse with every attempted fix. Now — thanks to him — everyone in Hornet Heaven was completely cut off from their club.

Freddie hurried away up Occupation Road. He needed to make amends.

* * *

Not long later, Derek and Paggie arrived back at the programme hut.

Paggie sat down at the table and stared bleakly at the Soccerama board. The league system it represented was currently invisible to everyone in Hornet Heaven because the ancient turnstile was taking people too far back in time. Paggie sighed: 'I never thought I'd say this, but I'd be happy to see us in Division Four.'

As Derek put away the programmes he'd used for testing the turnstile, he saw the "Lucky Dip Trips" sign that they'd had to take down. A thought struck him.

'Ooh,' he said, 'what about this for an idea, Mr Pagnam, sir? We could take people on guided tours through the turnstile — to what was happening before 1881. You don't usually get that chance in Hornet Heaven. People would love it.'

Paggie dismissed the idea: 'But there weren't even a league in them days. The football will be absolute twod.'

'In which case it'll cheer everyone up, Mr Pagnam, sir.'

'What? How?'

'By making Watford's football this season seem better by comparison.'

'No thanks, lad. If there's a quality of football that makes our 1-0 defeat at Hartlepool this season look world-class, I really don't want to see it.'

But Derek wasn't to be deterred. He said: 'Come on, Mr Pagnam, sir. It'll be fun. Let's put up a sign advertising "Magical Ancient History Tours"!'

*   *   *

Freddie Sargent found Neil McBain and sacked him as his handyman.

McBain said: 'I'm sacked again? That's 1937, 1959 and 1977!'

'Each one fully deserved,' Freddie replied.

Freddie went looking for someone else who could solve the problem. On Occupation Road, he bumped into Johnny Allgood. Johnny was a man who'd been brilliant at many things at the highest level: football, cricket, bowls — even curling.

Freddie asked: 'I don't suppose you could fix a turnstile, could you?'

'I'm afraid not, Freddie. I was fine at sport, but I wasn't nearly so good at anything else. When I first left school, I became an iron turner and—'

'An iron turner? That's perfect! The turnstile's made of iron, and it turns! You'll be able to get it turning properly!'

'That's not what iron turning is, Freddie.'

'It doesn't matter. This is an emergency. Watford Football Club doesn't exist in Hornet Heaven.'

'What? What are you—'

'We need your skills. You've got to come with me.'

* * *

Down by the turnstile, Freddie watched as Johnny Allgood lay on his back beneath the high-tech mechanism and stared up at it.

Freddie said a little desperately: 'I remember when you made us invincible in your first season as manager: it was like you had a magic touch. Go on. Just lay your hands on the turnstile.'

Johnny slid out and stood up. He said: 'Sorry, Freddie. Not my talent. I daren't touch it.'

Freddie's brow knitted with worry. 'Have a go. Please,' he begged. 'It's like every single Watford game is behind closed doors at the moment. You've got to try.'

'It would be irresponsible of me.'

'Oh Gawd, I don't know what to do. I've ruined Hornet Heaven. It's all on me. I'm—'

Behind Freddie, Derek's voice rang out: 'Follow me, everyone! Follow your leader!'

Freddie turned to see Derek walking down Occupation Road, holding a programme high above his head. He was being followed by Paggie and a small group of Watford fans. The group stopped when they reached Freddie and Johnny.

'Hello, Mr Sargent, sir, and Mr Allgood, sir,' Derek said. 'Would you like to join us on our Magical Ancient History Tour?'

'Forget all that, boy,' Freddie said. 'I've got to find a way to fix the turnstile. I've got to get everyone their club back.'

Johnny Allgood saw the stress on Freddie's face and thought the OBE-winning organiser could probably do with a short break. He said: 'Sounds interesting, Derek. Where are you going?'

The teenager replied: 'This programme from April 1960 — at home to Gateshead, Mr Allgood, sir — will take us somewhere historically fascinating 96 years earlier.'

Freddie said: 'But what's the point, boy? It won't have anything to do with Watford Football Club! I've let everyone down! I've put Watford Football Club out of reach!'

Johnny decided Freddie definitely needed a break. He gently took Freddie's arm and said: 'Two please, Derek.'

* * *

Derek's tour group arrived on the other side of the turnstile. They found themselves on the edge of a meadow.

Paggie said: 'Ee, did you pack us a picnic, lad?'

Freddie Sargent said to Johnny Allgood in despair: 'Look what I've done to Hornet Heaven. The Gateshead game was a 5-0 win. Now it's just empty grass.'

Johnny put a consoling arm round Freddie.

Then Derek began the spiel he'd prepared for the guided tour: 'Right, Ladies and Gentlemen. If you look across the fields over there, you'll see Watford Junction station. The fact that the station recently opened in 1858 roughly dates what we're about to see.'

In the centre of the meadow, some men started to erect wooden posts for goals. Soon, an organised game of football began — though it didn't look much like the football the tour group knew. Derek pointed out that there were no pitch markings, no crossbars, no goalkeepers, no referee, and no punishments for infringements. Players were allowed to catch the ball with their hands.

'In these days,' Derek continued, 'the rules stated that any player ahead of the ball would be offside — resulting in kick-and-rush tactics.'

Freddie thought the football was much uglier than anything he'd seen in 1977. Even Pat Molloy was easier on the eye than this, he reckoned. He said: 'Sorry, everyone. It's my fault you're having to watch this kick-and-rush rubbish.'

A fan from the group replied: 'Well, I suppose it does make you appreciate the style of football we played under Mike Keen.'

Derek looked towards Paggie and winked. The tour was having the effect of making people appreciate 1977 more — just as he'd predicted. It was going to be a resounding success.

As they all headed back to the ancient turnstile, the fan said: 'Gawd! Imagine if the manager who replaces Mike Keen brings back kick-and-rush! Everyone will hate it!'

Soon, the group were moving onto the next game on the tour. They had programmes from December 1967. They arrived in a different meadow.

Derek said: 'This time we're just off Langley Road. It's 1871. There are goalkeepers now. And you'll notice that the goal-posts are joined by a length of string across the top.'

Freddie Sargent stood and stared. All of a sudden, he wasn't feeling stressed any more. He was feeling nostalgic. He said: 'Blimey, I remember playing in goals like this — for Clarendon in 1874. I'd forgotten the days before solid crossbars.'

The match kicked off. One of the players hit a long-range shot that went just over the goal — but only because the opponents' goalkeeper had pulled the string across the top a bit lower.

'Cheeky blighter!' Freddie said. 'I remember that happening in my own matches!'

Paggie pointed at the team in white shirts, white knickerbockers and black socks. He asked: 'Who's this team, then, Freddie? Do you recognise them?'

'I do, as a matter of fact,' Freddie replied. 'It's Hertfordshire Rangers.'

'Eh? What have they got to do with Watford?' Paggie asked. 'How come the ancient turnstile has brought us to see them?'

Derek had the answer. He said: 'Hertfordshire Rangers were based in Watford, Mr Pagnam, sir. They were the town's first major team — before Watford

Rovers were.'

Freddie added proudly: 'And I played for them —
from 1880 until they disbanded in 1882.'

'By heck,' Paggie said. 'You played for this
bunch? I never knew. Do you recognise any of the
players?'

'I do. That one over there was a great player —
Bob Barker.'

'Crikey, Mr Sargent, sir, I've read about him,'
Derek said. He played for England in the first ever
international football match in 1872.'

Derek felt pleased with himself for knowing this
fact. But announcing it got a reaction he wasn't
expecting.

Paggie said: 'What? You mean, Hertfordshire
Rangers had a player good enough to be chosen for
England, and Watford Football Club still never have —
more than a century later?'

Derek grimaced. This wasn't making people
appreciate 1977 more.

'Blooming heck,' Paggie moaned, 'that's so
depressing! We're useless! I'd love to see a Watford
player in an England shirt, but there's no chance!'

Derek didn't like where this was going. He knew it

was pushing things a bit, but he argued back: 'Don't speak too soon, Mr Pagnam, sir. For all we know, we might have a promising youngster on our books who could improve and play for England. I quite liked the look of that 18-year-old who scored on his full debut last season.'

'Luther Blissett?' Paggie scoffed. 'He hasn't started another game since! He can't even make the side in Division Four! Ha! Luther Blissett playing for England! Don't be daft, lad!'

Derek fell silent, disheartened.

Freddie, though, was remembering his playing days with the team they were all watching. He said: 'When I was with Hertfordshire Rangers we were one of the top teams in the country. We reached the 3rd Round of the FA Cup in 1881. We were only beaten by one of the eventual finalists.'

'Ha!' Paggie reacted. 'Well, you can't say the same for Watford. We're not a top team. This season we reached the 3rd Round of the FA Cup and got beaten by Northwich Victoria!'

The words "Northwich Victoria" cast a sudden chill on the occasion. The whole group stood in silence and cast their minds back to January's humiliation. It had been the lowest low of Watford's dreadful 1976/77 season.

Paggie shook his head and said: 'Northwich effing Victoria!'

Derek was upset his tour was ending on a low point. It didn't help when Freddie said: 'To be fair, joining Watford Rovers was a bit of a comedown for me. They weren't at the same level as Hertfordshire Rovers had been.'

Paggie added: 'And by my reckoning they still aren't! In 1977 Watford are doing worse than a team that played in the town when goals didn't have proper crossbars yet!'

The group stood in silence again, contemplating this thought.

Eventually Derek said miserably: 'I want to go home now.'

*   *   *

Meanwhile, Henry Grover and The Alderman were sitting together in the semi-darkness of the subterranean Supporters Club Bar. Jack Gran was playing mood music on the piano again.

The Alderman wasn't familiar with the Elton John song being played — Don't Let The Sun Go Down On Me — but he reflected that it was definitely easier on the ear than what he'd heard sung most often on the terraces during the 1976/77 season. That had been: "Keen Out! Keen Out!"

He stared at the sticky floor beneath his robes. Word had reached himself and Henry that the only football available behind the ancient turnstile was from before 1881. It felt as though Watford Football Club had been taken from him.

It hurt. It hurt because he was the man who'd saved the club from extinction in its early days. It hurt because he regarded a Football League club as his personal legacy to the town. And it hurt because, in Hornet Heaven, Watford Football Club was the only thing that mattered to him.

It was as if the sole reason for his afterlife had been extinguished.

In the gloom of the bar, as Jack Gran played the piano, The Alderman sat and imagined the eternal sunshine of Hornet Heaven fading to nothing. He muttered to himself: 'Losing everything is like the sun going down on me.'

Henry was feeling too down to bother commenting.

Soon, Henry and The Alderman weren't the only figures slumped in their chairs in the bar. The whole tour group joined them. For a long while they all sat with bleak thousand-mile stares.

Freddie Sargent felt particularly bad. It was his fault that no-one could watch Watford and that 1976/77 was their most recent memory. But he had no idea how to resolve the disastrous situation he'd created.

Eventually, Paggie said: 'So is this it, then? For the rest of eternity? Sitting around with no Watford to watch?'

Derek tried to look on the bright side. He said: 'In point of fact, Mr Pagnam, sir, things will improve — albeit slowly. As time progresses we'll start to see Watford games one by one, 96 years after they actually happened.'

Freddie picked up on this small crumb of comfort: 'So we will get to see next season — just a bit late?'

'Yes, Mr Sargent, sir,' Derek answered. 'If you call the year 2073 "a bit late", Mr Sargent, sir.'

Everyone slumped deeper into their chairs. Several of them whimpered.

The Alderman said: 'Good grief. You mean I've got to wait nearly a century to see Elton John turfed out of the club? We hoped we were going to see him gone this afternoon against Darlington, didn't we, Henry?'

Henry didn't answer. He had his head in his hands.

He said: 'I'm so sorry, everyone. This is all my fault. If I hadn't founded the club in the first place, none of us would be in this situation.'

Freddie stood up. He wasn't prepared to let The Father Of The Club assume any kind of blame. He said: 'No, Henry. I'm the one who's sorry. This is my mess. I'm to blame. We're all grateful you founded the club. What you did inspired—'

Freddie paused. He'd suddenly had a thought.

He rushed out of the bar.

A short while later, after a quick piece of research, he returned with an armful of programmes to the previous week's game at Swansea. He said: 'Come on, everyone. I want to show you something.'

* * *

Freddie Sargent led the group through the ancient turnstile.

Derek said: 'This is exciting. Where are we going, Mr Sargent, sir?'

They arrived on the other side. All they could see was rolling parkland.

'Where the hell is this?' Paggie asked.

Henry gazed at the verdant sweep of the vista before them. It was dotted with carefully placed clusters of trees. The Father Of The Club smiled and said: 'I recognise this place. It was designed in 1805 by the renowned landscape artist Humphry Repton. It was part of the Earl of Essex's estate.'

Paggie said: '1805? But that's not 96 years ago.'

'Ah,' Henry said, 'but the estate still looked like this at the back end of the nineteenth century, before it became a public space as Cassiobury Park.'

Freddie tried to whip up some enthusiasm. He said: 'It's Cassiobury Park, everyone. Surely you haven't forgotten what happened here?'

'I haven't,' Paggie said morosely. 'It's where Mike Keen held his training sessions this season — and turned decent players into rubbish ones.'

Henry said: 'Actually, Paggie, what Freddie means is that Cassiobury Park is where I first got a group of my pals together for a kick-about in 1881. In fact... I say!

Look! Here I come now!'

Everyone watched as a teenage version of Henry strolled up. He was carrying a brand new football he'd bought.

Derek said: 'Wow! Look at you, Mr Grover, sir! You're not much older than me!'

'Oh dear,' Henry said. 'That leather jerkin I'm wearing is frightfully dull. I really ought to have dressed more flamboyantly for such an auspicious occasion.'

'Auspicious?' Paggie asked. 'How is a kick-about in a park auspicious?'

Freddie was surprised Paggie didn't seem to know the club's origins story. He said: 'Because it's the start of the football club we know and love today. This is the 1881 kick-about that gave birth to Watford Rovers — which became Watford Football Club.'

Henry sounded rather moved as he said: 'Exactly, Freddie. This is it. The moment I founded the club.'

Freddie took the group closer to the kick-about. They sat beneath a tree. Freddie was pleased with how Henry was reacting to the trip, but The Alderman's mood didn't seem to have improved.

Henry remarked: 'Such innocent days, Alderman! Small boys… Jerkins for goalposts…'

The Alderman grunted. 'I'm not interested in nostalgia, Henry William. What I need to see is Elton John leaving our club in 1977.'

'…Rush goalie,' Henry continued. '…Arguing about whether the ball went in. …Slide-tackling into dog muck.'

'No thank you, Henry William. This isn't for me. I ran a professional club professionally. Frankly, it's embarrassing that the club I took into the Football League started as a lark in a park.'

Freddie said: 'But this was the start of absolutely everything, Alderman.'

The Alderman continued: 'What I'm watching is worse than amateur. It's a stain on my reputation to be associated with it. Under my leadership, we actually achieved something. Status. Respect.'

Freddie didn't want The Alderman's mood to affect the others, so he said: 'Here, Alderman — have you noticed? That young lad on the ball over there is Charlie Peacock.'

The ruse worked instantly.

'You mean that's Charlie as a teenager?' The Alderman said. 'Good old Charlie!'

The Alderman knew Charlie Peacock very well —

the teenager here in the park had gone on to play nearly 200 games for Watford Rovers and had later become an important figure in the town as the proprietor of The Watford Observer. The Alderman and Charlie Peacock had chinked sherry glasses at many a civic reception.

Freddie capitalised on his success by saying: 'Come on, everyone — let's go even closer.'

The visitors from Hornet Heaven walked across the grass all the way into the middle of the kick-about — which continued oblivious to their presence.

Soon there was a break in play and the teenaged Henry Grover went over to speak to Charlie. The Hornet Heaven contingent heard the young Henry say: 'Right then, Charlie. Next goal wins it.'

The young Charlie replied: 'Wins what, Henry?'

'Well, obviously I'd love to be playing for the FA Cup, old chum, but we'll have to leave that to Hertfordshire Rangers — for the moment, anyway.'

'For the moment? You mean, you think we could make ourselves good enough one day?'

'If we carry on getting together like this, and form a team — why not? Imagine it, Charlie — lifting the FA Cup high above our heads to a cheering crowd!'

'Count me in, Henry! Let's keep practicing and

improving!'

'Excellent. And, as for today's game, old thing — next goal wins an imaginary FA Cup!'

The visitors from Hornet Heaven stood back and watched the final moments of the 1881 kick-about. The young Henry was determined to score the final goal. Soon, he won possession, barged his way past two challenges, and smashed the ball between the jerkins on the ground. He jumped up and down with his arms aloft and shouted: 'Goal! Henry Grover has won the FA Cup for.... Oh, I don't know... Watford something... Watford... Rovers!'

The Victorian teenager clenched his fists in front of him — as if gripping something. Then he raised them into the air, lifting an imaginary FA Cup.

Immediately, the young Henry was joined by his friends and future Watford Rovers team-mates. They swarmed round him, cheering exuberantly. They all reached up to grab a shared handle of the imaginary trophy.

The Henry Grover from Hornet Heaven, watching all this, wiped a tear from his eye and said: 'This is what I started this football club for.'

Freddie Sargent saw that The Alderman, Derek

and Paggie were quite moved too. His plan to inspire them was working.

The Alderman said: 'I never knew you had such ambition at the start, Henry William. You've definitely shown far more there than Elton John ever has. Good for you. And, of course, your dream could still come true one day.'

Derek said: 'Yes! The Alderman's right, Mr Grover, sir. 1977/78 could be a whole new beginning. You never know what might happen.'

Paggie said: 'Well, we'll definitely never know if we stay here and don't get the turnstile fixed. Come on, Henry, let's go back and watch your club finally hit the heights!'

Henry had a new pep about him as he said: 'Absolutely, gentlemen. We've got unfinished business!'

The Father Of The Club clenched his fists in front of him — as if gripping something. He said: 'I want to see someone — anyone — even Elton John, Alderman — win my club…'

The 83-year-old raised his fists high in the air.

'…the FA Cup!'

* * *

Freddie led everyone back through the ancient turnstile. He was pleased he'd inspired everyone by taking them back to watch the original Watford Rovers kick-about, but he still wasn't sure how the turnstile would actually get fixed. Suddenly, Henry took off his Victorian coat and said: 'Right. It's time The Father Of The Club got his hands dirty.'

Henry clambered underneath the turnstile's mechanism. It looked very high-tech to someone born in the 1860s, but he gave it a few tweaks.

As Henry worked, Freddie said to the others: 'I'll be so relieved when we get our club back.'

Derek said: 'I can't wait, Mr Sargent sir. I want watching Watford to be just like Soccerama. I want to feel like every match is taking us forwards. I want us to race up the divisions. I want us to reach the two red squares at the top of Division One.'

Henry called out: 'Don't forget winning the FA Cup, young man.'

'Absolutely, Mr Grover, sir. I don't mind how we reach Europe, as long as we do!'

'Europe!' Freddie breathed in awe. 'Imagine!'

They all stood quietly in wondrous contemplation

of the notion that Watford Football Club might play even a single game in European competition. The Alderman, though, felt compelled to add a note of caution.

'That's all very well,' the former Chairman said. 'But our dream can only come true when Elton John has buggered off. Ideally this afternoon against Darlington.'

In time, Henry got back to his feet. 'There,' he said. 'I think I've finally fixed the turnstile. Derek, could you run and get some programmes to test the mechanism?'

Derek rushed to the hut and back.

'Here we are, Mr Grover, sir. In readiness for our glorious future, I've chosen the match where we beat the biggest team we've ever beaten. I've got programmes for Liverpool at home in the FA Cup in 1970!'

Derek ran to the turnstile. Freddie Sargent and Johnny Allgood decided to stay on Occupation Road — just in case things didn't turn out as planned — but Henry, Paggie and The Alderman followed Derek through.

On the other side they did indeed arrive at Watford versus Liverpool at Vicarage Road.

But none of them had seen this particular Watford

versus Liverpool before.

The Alderman said: 'What have you done, Henry William? This match isn't in Watford's history. What in heaven's name is going on?'

THE END

THE STORY CONCLUDES IN
'HOW WONDERFUL LIFE IS'

9

HOW WONDERFUL LIFE IS

EARTH SEASON 1976/77

Clutching their programmes for the 1970 FA Cup tie at home to Liverpool, Henry Grover, The Alderman, Derek Garston and Fred Pagnam stared down from the Main Stand.

'I don't understand what we're watching,' Paggie said. 'We've never worn this kit before.'

Henry gasped in awe: 'Red shorts! My word!'

Derek squealed in excitement: 'Look! There's a giant scoreboard at the Vicarage Road end! It says Watford *are* playing Liverpool!'

'Red shorts!' Henry sighed. 'I'm in love!'

The Alderman was irritated. 'What's going on?'

he demanded. 'There are seats in front of the Main Stand. And the Shrodells.'

'Red shorts!' Henry purred. 'Divine!'

'For goodness sake, shut up about the shorts, Henry William!' The Alderman ordered. 'The turnstile is still malfunctioning. We need to work out what's going on.'

As Watford kicked off against Liverpool in glorious sunshine, the visitors from Hornet Heaven saw that a fan in the land of the living was holding a programme. They went over to take a look. Paggie got there first. On the front cover was a photograph of Watford players wearing England kit.

Paggie said: 'Watford players playing for England? This is mad!'

Paggie remembered what he'd said at the Hertfordshire Rangers game earlier — that he'd love to see a Watford player in an England shirt. He said: 'It's like a dream come true!'

Derek asked: 'Can you see a date on the programme, Mr Pagnam, sir?'

'It says Saturday 14th May. Today's date.'

'But what year does it say, Mr Pagnam, sir?'

'1983.'

'Oh my God! That means we're six years into the future! First the turnstile took us way back into the past, and now it's brought us here. We're seeing the future!'

The Alderman said: 'Don't be silly, child. That would break the laws of time and space. This can't be the future.'

Paggie said: 'Hang on, here's something else the programme says: "Football League Division One". Blooming heck, we're playing at the highest level!'

'No,' The Alderman said firmly. 'That's out of the question. Look over there — Steve Sherwood is in goal. How could a £3,000 Division Four second-choice goalkeeper possibly play in goal for Watford in Division One?'

'Fair do's,' Paggie replied. 'He couldn't. Also, one of the players in the England kit on the programme cover looks like that Luther Blissett kid who can't get in our Division Four team. Ha! Never going to happen.'

The Alderman peered towards the front of the stand. He said: 'Aha. And if you want the ultimate proof that this isn't real — you only have to look down there in the Directors Box.'

Paggie and Derek turned and saw Elton John.

'For what we're seeing to be true,' The Alderman

said, 'Watford would need to have been promoted 3 times in 5 years with a pop star in charge. It simply isn't possible!'

Derek let out a sigh of disappointment. 'Then how do you explain where we are, then, your Worshipfulness, sir?'

'I'm not sure. Paggie said it was like a dream come true, so all I can think is that I'm watching someone's ridiculous fantasy.'

The Alderman turned to see Henry still gazing out at the pitch.

'Red shorts!' Henry sighed again.

The Alderman said: 'Which probably tells us exactly whose ridiculous fantasy it is.'

*   *   *

The following 90 minutes were incredible. Luther Blissett's goal meant that, according to a fan in the real-world crowd, he'd finish the season as top scorer in Division One. And in the end Watford beat Liverpool — the Champions, no less — 2-1.

But all this was literally incredible for the visitors from Hornet Heaven. When the final whistle blew, and the Vicarage Road crowd erupted with sheer joy, the visitors from Hornet Heaven weren't happy at all. What they'd witnessed was so unlikely to be true that they felt despondent. It only emphasised what a shambles of a club Watford was in 1977.

'Oh well,' Paggie said glumly. 'Shame it'll never happen.'

'It's not fair,' Derek squeaked. 'I thought fantasies were meant to inspire you — not depress you.'

Now they saw Elton John walking onto the sunlit pitch to congratulate the players.

The Alderman said: 'Huh! Watford Football Club in Division One under Elton John is so ludicrous it's like a fantasy having its own fantasy.'

Henry replied: 'Well, I've decided the fantasy can't be mine. Look — Elton's in a plain suit, topped off with a stetson. If it was anything to do with me, he'd probably be in a leopard-skin leotard.'

The four of them were just about to leave when, suddenly, there was a new outbreak of cheering around the ground.

A nearby fan shouted: 'They've said on the radio: we're runners-up! We're in Europe!'

Derek held up his hands and said: 'Sorry,

everyone. Must have been my fantasy all along.' Close to tears, he added: 'I blame Soccerama. Sorry.'

The Hornet Heaven contingent shook their heads sadly and trudged back to the ancient turnstile.

*   *   *

When they arrived back on Occupation Road, The Alderman and Henry retired to the Supporters Club Bar while Derek and Paggie returned to the programme hut.

Inside the hut, Derek walked straight up to the table and swept the Soccerama board game onto the floor with surprising force.

'I'm never playing that game again, Mr Pagnam, sir,' he said. 'It lured me into a foolish fantasy. Division Four clubs don't reach Europe in six seasons.'

He sat down and stared at the empty table, upset.

A moment later, Freddie Sargent entered. Freddie asked: 'Well? Is the turnstile working properly?'

Paggie explained to Freddie everything they'd seen.

'Oh Gawd,' Freddie said. 'Hornet Heaven's still broken.'

'It was awful, Mr Sargent, sir,' Derek said. 'Until I

actually witnessed it, I didn't realise how totally implausible my fantasy was. It was ridiculous: Steve Sherwood was playing in Division One, Mr Sargent, sir! I mean, he's a safe pair of hands, but—'

A look of great enlightenment suddenly flashed across Freddie Sargent's face.

Derek said: 'What, Mr Sargent, sir? What did I say?'

'A safe pair of hands! That's the answer!'

Freddie dashed away, excited. At last he'd be able to make good the damage he'd caused.

* * *

Henry and The Alderman sat in the subterranean Supporters Club Bar. A small band was playing an instrumental version of Rocket Man by Elton John.

Jack Gran was at the piano.

Jack Gran's team-mate from 1900 — Jack Cother — was on bass.

Freddie Sargent's brother and team-mate from the 1880s — Alf Sargent — was on drums.

And Freddie's other brother — Alec Sargent — was on synths.

The Alderman shouted: 'For crying out loud, can a former Chairman not get some peace and quiet when he's trying to have a conversation?!'

The music abruptly stopped.

'That's better,' The Alderman said.

The recent trip through the ancient turnstile seemed to have triggered him. 'As I was saying, Henry William,' he complained, 'the thing that really proved it was a fantasy was the presence of Elton John. Not in a million years — let alone six — could Elton John become the club's most successful benefactor.'

'No need to go on, old thing,' Henry replied. 'I've already told you I want him out — after I read his concert programme, remember?'

'The man's incompetent. If a 13-year-old child like Derek can have a vision of what they want Watford to achieve, why can't Elton John? He's never given any indication at all that he has a vision for Watford Football Club.'

'But what kind of thing are you expecting to see?'

'I expect to see a precisely stated 10-year objective for progressing the organisation towards a clearly envisioned future — with a fully-costed business plan attached.'

'Ah. Do you? To be fair, old chap, that doesn't sound the way a creative artist like Elton would express himself.'

'Creative artist! You make it sound as if someone could communicate a vision for a football club through a painting! Don't be ridiculous!'

Once again, Henry didn't feel comfortable that his old friend had such extreme antipathy towards Elton John. He wondered if there was a way to soften The Alderman's views. He said: 'I say, Aldie, do you remember how — when you brought Johnny Allgood to the club in 1903 — it was because you wanted to reach for the stars?'

'Of course I do. It was a mark of my own vision to hire the country's best-known footballer as our first ever manager.'

'Exactly. You believed a household name like Johnny could lead the club towards football's stratosphere. But here's the thing. Isn't the club hoping for exactly the same now — but with someone else as the household name?'

'Are you talking about the rumour that Bobby Moore is going to be our next manager? That would be a disastrous appointment.'

'No, I'm saying the Chairman himself is a household name. In time, Elton John could be the man to propel Watford Football Club on that journey to the stars. In time, he could be our rocket man.'

'Huh. I think it's going to be a long, long time.'

'Ha ha ha, very good.'

'Eh? What's very good?'

Henry sat quietly for a while and tried to work out why The Alderman was quite so vehemently against Elton John. He remembered the Alderman had also been critical of the previous Chairman, Jim Bonser. It was as if Alderman Ralph Thorpe had some kind of need to denigrate anyone who followed in his footsteps at the club.

Henry said sensitively: 'Listen, old chap, I really don't understand why you're so against Elton John.'

'Isn't it obvious? Because he knows nothing about how to run a football club.'

'But it seems as though there's more to it than that. You don't like his music, his clothing, his sexuality…'

'It's all disgusting.'

'But this is 1977. If you criticise him over that, it makes me wonder.'

'Wonder what?'

'What you're afraid of, old thing.'

'Well, if you think I'm scared of revealing that I'm a homosexualist, you're wrong.'

'Then are you afraid of something else? I just don't understand why you're always talking him down.'

The Alderman fell silent for a while.

'You can tell me,' Henry said.

The Alderman looked at his old friend. He seemed to shrink a little inside his robes as he contemplated revealing something he hadn't admitted to anyone else.

'Alright,' he said. 'Yes. I am afraid. I'm afraid of…'

'Go on, old son.'

'I'm afraid of… not being the greatest benefactor in the club's history any more.'

Henry nodded his understanding.

The Alderman avoided eye contact as he continued: 'Down on earth, all my adult life, I was an important man — in commerce, at the club, and in the town. In Hornet Heaven, I'm still important — but only because no-one else has yet had the impact on the club that I had. When someone does come along and transform the club, I'll be a nobody. That's what I'm afraid of. Everyone will forget Alderman Ralph Thorpe.'

'But the club really does need someone else to turn it around.'

'I know. But it's very hard to let go of who I am — and root for someone to become the new me.'

'I understand — especially if the new you is wearing pink platform shoes.'

The Alderman gave a gentle laugh — at Elton John, but also at himself. Now that he'd admitted his fear, he was regaining his sense of humour — and humility.

He looked back at Henry and said: 'For almost fifty years, I've flattered myself that I'm the biggest name in Hornet Heaven... But I need to be bigger than that.'

The Alderman sat silently for a few seconds. Then he said with new resolve: 'What I need to do is accept that Elton John could become Watford's greatest benefactor of all time.'

Henry nodded approvingly.

The Alderman lifted his robes and stood up. He said, even louder: 'Positively want Elton John to become Watford's greatest benefactor of all time.'

The Alderman clenched a fist and raised it. He

said: 'Actively spread the word that Elton John will become Watford's…'

The Alderman sat down again and said: 'No. I can't do it.'

*   *   *

A while later, Henry and The Alderman walked up the steps from the Supporters Club Bar onto Occupation Road.

The Alderman said: 'I'm sorry, Henry, but I can't come to terms with wanting Elton John to succeed. My vision for the future just doesn't include a Chairman who's a frilly-knickered exhibitionist.'

They stepped out into the eternal sunshine of Occupation Road and looked down the slope. They saw Freddie Sargent supervising a new attempt to repair the ancient turnstile. There was a new pair of legs extending out from under the mechanism. They went to take a look.

Henry said: 'Hello, Freddie. Who have you got under there?'

'It's taken a while,' Freddie replied, 'but at last I've found a man I can trust.'

Henry and The Alderman saw two huge hands grab the bottom rung of the turnstile and a man in a large flat cap slide himself out. It was Watford's pre-war goalkeeper Skilly Williams.

'Ah. Of course,' Henry said. 'The safest hands in Hornet Heaven.'

'Exactly,' Freddie said. 'I should have thought to get a goalkeeper on the job first time around.'

'To be fair, Freddie, you did,' Henry replied. 'Neil McBain played in goal for New Brighton.'

'Ha! It was only the once, and he let in three! He was as useless at goalkeeping as at everything else!'

Skilly Williams said: 'Anyway, Henry, what's been going on with this turnstile? Freddie told me you all ended up in Derek's fantasy or something.'

'Yes, but I don't know how. Have you worked it out, Alderman?'

'No,' The Alderman replied. 'It was as inexplicable as Elton John's dress-sense.'

Freddie thought he might have the answer. He said: 'Well, Paggie said the reason you saw Derek's fantasy was probably because Derek was the one carrying the programmes when you went through the turnstile.'

Suddenly, a thought flashed across The Alderman's mind. He said: 'You mean, if it had been me carrying the programmes, it would have been my fantasy?'

'I don't know,' Freddie said. 'You'd have to ask Paggie... Hey, where you are going?'

'I say, old top,' Henry called out to The Alderman. 'What are you doing?'

The Alderman was running across Occupation Road to the Programme Hut. He'd realised that, if Paggie was correct, taking a programme through the ancient turnstile would let him see his own personal vision of Watford's future — without Elton John.

'Stop fixing the turnstile,' The Alderman shouted over his shoulder. 'I'll be back in a moment.'

* * *

The Alderman, carrying the same 1970 Liverpool FA Cup programme as before, passed through the ancient turnstile. He couldn't wait to see his own fantasy. His vision was of a Watford that had developed fully as a club and a business — on and off the field. And the man responsible definitely wouldn't be Elton John.

When he arrived on the other side, he had to stop to get his bearings. He was behind a stand — but it didn't look anything like the 1977 main stand at Vicarage Road. He wasn't sure he was at Vicarage Road at all.

He went down some steps and found himself in a busy bar area full of Watford fans. Some were wearing Watford shirts he'd never seen before. One of the yellow shirts had horizontal black stripes of differing widths. The Alderman was pretty sure Henry Grover wouldn't have allowed such a rum design in one of his fantasies.

He walked on towards a large opening at ground level. Beyond it, he could see an astonishingly green pitch in front of a two-tier stand with an undulating roof. He smiled and congratulated himself on his vision. 'Outstanding work, Alderman,' he said to himself. 'Outstanding work.'

He kept walking and entered the arena at pitch level. He gasped as he saw stands on every side of the ground: 'An all-seater stadium! I'm a genius!'

A real-world fan was at the front of the stand holding a programme. The Alderman went up to her and took a look at the front cover of the programme. It told him he was at Watford versus Liverpool on December

20th 2015.

The Alderman said to himself: 'Ha! The space age! Well, it certainly looks a different planet from Watford in 1977!'

Awestruck by his surroundings, he stepped over an advertising hoarding and made his way onto the pristine pitch. The teams were coming out of the tunnel. He looked at Watford's goalkeeper — Heurelho Gomes — and muttered to himself: 'If that's still Steve Sherwood, he's lost a heck of a lot of hair.'

The tannoy was blaring out music and the stands were full of noise, colour and movement. The Alderman was thrilled with his vision — especially because there was a Directors Box in the two-tiered stand in which he could see no sign of Elton John. It felt to The Alderman like conclusive proof that Watford Football Club had an amazing future without the involvement of a strange little man pretending not to be Reginald Dwight from Pinner — a man whose only contribution to British life was polluting it with vulgar music and tawdry fashion.

In his red fur-trimmed robes, The Alderman arrived in the centre-circle — the perfect place for viewing the magnificence of the stadium. It was so greatly changed from 1977 that he still couldn't tell whether Watford had moved to an entirely new stadium or whether this was Vicarage Road. He looked for clues.

First he looked up at the two-tier stand. He noticed a sign saying 'The Graham Taylor Stand'. He had no idea who this Graham Taylor was.

Then he looked at the stand opposite — on the side he'd come in.

On the back wall, in flowing script, were what he guessed — from the phrasing of the words —were lyrics from a song. He didn't recognise them. He cast his gaze upwards.

Now he saw something meaningful. On the front of the roof, in the middle, it said 'Watford Football Club' in yellow lettering. The sight did his heart good.

Next, he moved his gaze slightly to the right.

Suddenly, he gasped. He thought he was going to choke. On the front of the roof, also in yellow lettering, it said 'The Sir Elton John Stand'.

The Alderman stared in disbelief. This was supposed to be his own personal fantasy. Elton John was meant to have nothing to do with any of this magnificence. He certainly shouldn't have a stand named in his honour.

And it wasn't just that. There was a particular

word up there that The Alderman just couldn't process in connection with Elton John. The word 'Sir'.

Sir Elton John.

Sir.

The Alderman stood in the centre-circle in shock. He looked down at his robes and mayoral chain. His own title was Alderman. He was an important man; a serious man. But he'd never received an honour. Not an even an OBE, let alone a knighthood.

He stared back up at the word 'Sir' and, for the first time he could remember, felt truly humbled.

His subconscious fantasy must be informing him that he'd always misjudged Elton John.

Completely. Horribly.

If Elton John — even in a fantasy — was the kind of person who could become a Knight of the British Empire, then Elton John deserved the eternal respect of an Alderman.

* * *

When The Alderman returned to Occupation Road, Henry and Freddie were still there.

Freddie asked: 'Can Skilly carry on fixing the

turnstile now?'

The Alderman sounded rather rattled as he replied: 'I, er… yes, of course… that trip was, er….'

Then he pulled himself together a little and said: 'Henry, I'd likc to speak to you. And Derek and Paggie. Can we meet in the Programme Hut?'

A little later, as the group assembled in the hut, Derek noticed that the programme for that afternoon's final game against Darlington had already arrived. The boy went over to the open window and shouted: 'Programme's in!'

But no-one came running. It had been that kind of season.

While the others sat at the table, The Alderman, in his robes, stood at one end of it. He began: 'I wish to apologise to you all. I've been gravely disrespectful to the Chairman of the team we all support. It was wrong of me. Selfish, arrogant, and wrong.'

Henry was relieved to hear this. His own desire to see the Chairman leave the club was a rational response to the historical document he'd discovered at the 1974 gig. He'd never shared the Alderman's vitriol for Elton John. His old friend's apology felt like a load being lifted.

The Alderman continued: 'From now on, I shall have an open mind. I shan't write off anyone because of my own deep-seated prejudices.'

'Ha!' Henry said jovially. 'Call yourself a football fan, old boy?'

Henry wanted to lighten the mood for his old friend, but The Alderman was too serious about making his apology to pick up on the interjection.

'To my shame,' The Alderman continued, 'ever since I died, I've never wanted anyone running the club to become a greater benefactor than I was. As a result I've denigrated and insulted Elton John purely to try and feel better about myself. But that won't happen any more. I'm going to support the club whole-heartedly even if there are aspects of a new benefactor that aren't to my personal taste.'

'Like a gorgeous silk hornet costume, you mean?' Henry asked. 'Or tiny yellow pom-poms?'

'Henry William! Please! So. From now on, before passing judgment, I'll wait to see what Elton John can do for this club. We can all fantasise about what the future may hold for Watford, but only Elton John is in a position to make an amazing future a reality.'

Derek was itching to ask a question. He had his

hand raised.

'Please, your Worshipfulness, sir,' he said. 'So do you now think that what we saw today could actually be the future — Watford actually getting into Europe?'

The Alderman thought about this for a moment. He raised his eyebrows and smiled at the idea. Then his eyebrows lowered themselves as he remembered the reality of Watford in 1977. He said: 'Well, I'd need to see a little more from Elton John to believe in it.'

'What kind of thing, your Worshipfulness, sir?'

'All along, I've wanted to see something visionary.'

Henry raised his hand too. The Alderman guessed what might be coming. He was feeling more his old self now — more "The Prince of Good Fellows" — so he smiled and said: 'And, no, Henry — when I say "visionary", I don't mean a space suit paired with a sumptuous fur stole and heart-shaped glasses.'

The others laughed.

The Alderman concluded: 'But if that's what he's wearing when he reveals his aspirations for the club, that's fine by me. Come on, let's take a few copies of the new programme and go and see if Skilly has fixed the turnstile yet.'

* * *

The Alderman, Henry, Derek and Paggie watched as Skilly Williams wiped his huge dextrous hands on his trouser legs.

Skilly said: 'The turnstile should be fine now. Freddie's just gone through to check.'

'There's bound to be something else wrong,' Paggie said, unable to shrug off his pessimism. 'We've seen random, we've seen ancient, we've seen fantasy…'

The Alderman said: 'Stay positive, Paggie. Like many people before me, I trust the safe hands of Skilly Williams. I'm confident that what we'll see will be the present day.'

'Great,' Paggie replied sarcastically. 'So we'll see Arthur Horsfield lumbering around at centre-half instead of centre-forward because his legs have gone. We'll see Keith Pritchett's right foot failing to reach the same level of education as his left. It'll be nothing like Derek's fantasy. We'll be watching the same old rubbish until 1983 and beyond.'

Henry was feeling bullish after The Alderman's speech in the hut. He said: 'But today feels like it could be a new beginning — for Hornet Heaven with a mended turnstile, and for Watford Football Club with this game against Darlington. It feels like the start of the future.'

'What a load of twod,' Paggie said. 'It's a meaningless game. The last of the season. There's nothing at stake.'

A moment later, Freddie Sargent appeared from the ancient turnstile. He had a huge smile on his face. He announced: 'Hornet Heaven is working again!'

He rushed up to Skilly and planted a huge bristly kiss on the former goalkeeper's forehead — relieved that, by putting a capable pair of hands to work on the job, he'd finally atoned for all the trouble he'd caused over the last two days.

'We're back to normal,' Freddie said.

'But that's exactly what we don't want,' Paggie moaned. 'This season, normal is dismal.'

The Alderman stepped forward and said with deference: 'Thank you, Freddie. You've done us proud by getting us out of our fix. You've proved why you're a man with an OBE and I'm not.'

Freddie was amazed to receive such praise from Alderman Ralph Thorpe, JP. But he knew he didn't deserve it because he'd caused the problem himself in the first place. He'd achieved what he'd set out to achieve — humbling the Alderman a little — but he wished he hadn't gone this way about it.

Freddie headed back up Occupation Road with Skilly, leaving the group to go through the turnstile with their programmes for the Darlington game. He heard Derek say: 'Come on, everybody. Let's see how 1976/77 ends!'

*   *   *

The game on the other side of the ancient turnstile was definitely the final game of the 1976/77 season because the 6,000 fans who'd bothered turning up were showing no sign of excitement, celebration, or anticipation. The atmosphere was as flat as Skilly Williams's cap.

The contingent from Hornet Heaven went and sat in the Main Stand extension — where there were plenty of empty seats.

Down on the pitch, a presentation was taking place: Keith Mercer was receiving the Player Of The Season trophy from Elton John. But the real-world crowd hardly seemed to be paying attention. The strongest emotional response came when someone stifled a yawn and apologised.

Henry said: 'Well, this is all a bit underwhelming.'

The Alderman replied: 'You may say that, Henry William, but Elton John's down there and I'm not saying anything against him. This is the new me.'

'Well, I hope this isn't the new Elton John. I adore the way his lapels reach all the way out to his shoulders, but the rest of his suit is awfully plain.'

The Alderman couldn't help thinking that this was good sign. Maybe Elton John was thinking less about his wardrobe and more about Watford's future. The former mayor carried on watching as the ceremony on the pitch was brought to a close.

Unexpectedly, there was one final presentation. Someone had carried onto the pitch something thin and quite large — perhaps three feet by three feet square. It was being presented to Elton John.

The Alderman was curious, but he couldn't quite see what this object was. He decided to take a closer look. He walked down through the stand — his robes flowing behind him — and went onto the pitch.

As he approached, he heard the man making the presentation — Oliver Phillips, from the Watford

Observer — explaining what the object was. It was a work of art, apparently. It had been painted by his colleague Terry Challis to depict, allegorically, Elton John's ambition for the club.

The Alderman was excited. Elton John's ambition was exactly what he'd been wanting to know. He ran up to Oli Phillips. But when he got there, he saw that the frame Oli was holding contained nothing but a large blank square.

The Alderman felt all his old prejudices returning.

'Huh!' he grunted. 'Of course it's bloody blank. Elton John has no ambition whatsoever, and the local paper is calling him out on it in front of the Watford public.'

The Alderman cursed himself. His subconscious must have deceived him by creating a fantasy in which the name of Sir Elton John was on a stand in a magnificent stadium hosting a game against Liverpool.

But then Oli Phillips turned the frame around. The Alderman had been looking at the back. The front was a colourful painting.

The Alderman realised he'd made a mistake. He stopped his negative thoughts and moved in for a closer look.

What he saw was that Terry Challis had captured the Chairman's ambition for the club by depicting Elton astride a giant airborne hornet, pointing the way forward. But it was the detail that drew The Alderman's attention. A player was shown emerging from a mire. Ahead of him was a new stand — with two tiers and an undulating roof. In the distance was the Eiffel Tower — presumably denoting Europe. And the player's destination was a summit occupied by the Liver Bird of Liverpool.

The Alderman stopped breathing. He couldn't believe what he was seeing. This was exactly what he'd seen in the two fantasies — Derek's and his own. Elton John's ambition was exactly what The Alderman had visited earlier today.

The Alderman started breathing again, but only as gasps. This couldn't be coincidence, he thought to himself. What he'd seen must actually be the future. The painting wasn't only a representation of Elton's vision — it was a prophecy. A 100% accurate prophecy of what would happen.

His eyes filled with tears. His gasps turned into sobs. This was what was going to happen to his club. Within six years.

He sank to his knees as Oli Phillips handed the

painting to Elton John — the man who would make it all come true. Elton John was going to propel this club from the doldrums to the very top in just six seasons.

Through his tears, The Alderman found himself laughing.

'I bloody love you, Elton John!' he said to the pop star in front of him. 'I bloody love you, Elton Hercules Bloody John!'

* * *

The Alderman made his way back into the stand to re-join the others. He was bursting to tell them the news that what they'd all seen earlier had been the future, not a fantasy.

But then he stopped to think. Wouldn't telling them spoil the wonderful experience they were about to have over the next six years? Wouldn't it be better if — like Watford fans in the real world — they watched the extraordinary story unfold gradually, step by amazing step?

When he arrived back at the seats, Derek asked him: 'What did you see, your Worshipfulness, sir? Anything promising?'

The Alderman quelled the excitement he was feeling inside and said: 'Nothing concrete, young man.'

'Right,' Paggie said, as pessimistic as ever. 'So our great future ain't starting today against Darlington after all.'

The Alderman shrugged and replied: 'I'm afraid I couldn't say, Paggie.'

The Alderman glanced down the row along the faces of his companions. Henry, Derek, and Paggie were looking bored. He particularly focused on the face of his old friend Henry — who'd spent so long totally disillusioned this season. The Alderman tried to picture Henry's face exactly six years into the future from today — on May 14th 1983, when Watford becoming runners-up in the top division would prove not to be a fantasy. The Alderman imagined Henry's pure and utter elation. It brought more tears to his eyes.

Henry looked up and asked: 'Goodness, are you alright, old son?'

The Alderman politely dismissed Henry's concerns and sat down.

As he waited for kick-off, he tried to let it sink in that, very soon, he'd no longer be the club's greatest-ever benefactor. Elton John would take his place and

Alderman Ralph Thorpe would become a distant footnote in history. It would be hard to take, but it would be worth it. As recompense, he'd see his club enjoy one of the greatest and swiftest transformations in football history.

He needed to prepare himself for this altered status, though. For years, he'd behaved as if he were the most important man in Watford's history. From today he'd need to adapt — fast. But how? Suddenly a thought struck him. He stood up.

Henry asked again: 'Are you absolutely sure you're alright, old thing?'

The Alderman hesitated before answering. With his new-found knowledge, he was going to have to spend the next six years being very careful what he did and said. He bluffed: 'I, er… it's a warm day. I think I may have over-heated a little.'

The Alderman slid his arms out of his mayoral gown. He lifted off the robes completely. He removed his chain of office from around his neck.

Derek squeaked: 'Crikey, your Worshipfulness, sir! What are you doing?'

The Alderman folded his fur-trimmed robes. Carefully, he placed them — along with his chain of office — beneath his seat. He'd leave them here at this game, he decided. He had no further use for them

He said to Derek: 'Call me Ralph, young man.'

*   *   *

At three o'clock on May 14th 1977, Ralph Thorpe — an ordinary man, not an Alderman — settled in for the match.

During the first half, he spent a lot of time gazing at the real-world fans around the stadium. Unlike him, they had no idea that Luther Blissett's reappearance in the starting line-up that day was a secret signal of a glorious future. Ralph smiled as he anticipated their happiness. He felt love for his fellow fans for the way they'd soon be paid back — unimaginably handsomely — for their loyalty during the lean years.

When half-time arrived, Ralph stayed in his seat and surveyed the ramshackle ground — enjoying his private knowledge of the magnificent stadium it would become. He felt as though he were in a daze of happiness.

After a while, he became aware of the music that was playing over the tannoy. He didn't know the music was written by Elton John; he didn't know it was called Your Song. But its rhythms were familiar and its uplifting nature brought a broad contented smile to his face, lifting his moustache at both ends.

After a while, his old friend Henry touched him on the shoulder and asked: 'I say, old chum. It's good to see you happy, but I don't get why. You can't be thinking about the current state of our club. What *are* you thinking?'

Ralph leaned back further in his seat and smiled even more broadly. He was recalling what he'd seen on the back wall of the Sir Elton John stand in 2015.

He said, knowingly: 'How wonderful life is, while Elton's in the world.'

THE END

10

MARKED FOR LIFE

EARTH SEASON 2018/19

'Hello! What's that sticking out from under the sleeve of your school blazer, my boy?'

'Nothing, sir.'

'It looks like cling film, young man. Let me—'

'Get off, sir!… Stop it, sir!'

'Hold still, my boy, while I unwrap it.'

'Unhand me, sir!'

'Now, let's see what… Oh no! Derek! You've got a tattoo!'

On July 27th 2018, Bill Mainwood — Hornet Heaven's 92-year-old Head Of Programmes — was horrified to discover that his young assistant Derek

Garston had got himself tattooed. They were in the programme office.

'Golly, young man! When did you get this done?'

'After we played Fortuna Dusseldorf in our pre-season friendly, sir. We beat a crack European side 3-1, sir!'

'And you got a tattoo to celebrate? Oh dear! This is terrible!'

'But I've done nothing wrong, sir!'

'It's illegal for a start, my boy! You're only 13!'

'That was when I died in 1921, sir. Technically, I'm 110 now. Which means I'm also old enough to have a girlfriend. Girls love tattoos, I've heard, sir.'

'But tattoos are so ugly!'

'This one isn't, sir. The man I've had inked is a Watford hero, sir. That makes him a vision of beauty in my eyes, sir!'

'Dear, oh dear. Tattoos are permanent, my boy. He's going to be on your forearm for eternity.'

'I know, sir. That's why I chose someone who would mean a lot to me for the rest of all time, sir.'

'But the player you've chosen is…'

'…What, sir? A wise selection, sir?'

'No, it's…'

'Someone we'll treasure forever, sir?'

'No, Derek. It's… It's… Abdoulaye Doucouré!'

'I'm not surprised you recognise him, sir. The artist has beautifully captured the quintessential character of Doucouré in a static image. Look at the way he's holding off an opponent while striding away with a burst of energetic athleticism, sir!'

'But why Doucouré? He's only been with us 5 minutes!'

'Why? Because in those 5 minutes, as you put it, sir, he's won Player Of The Season and Players' Player Of The Season, sir. Think how good he'll be when he's been with us for 20 minutes, sir!'

'Yes, but… but… I can't think how to break this gently… Don't you know he'll be leaving the club during this transfer window, my boy?'

Derek whimpered slightly. 'Wh-what, sir? What do you mean, sir?'

'He's been talking in public about moving on to a bigger club. He didn't play in either of our first two pre-season friendlies. He's obviously going.'

'Going? But… But that can't be allowed, sir.'

'Oh dear. This isn't good. Doucs is on his way after a couple of seasons, but you're going to be inked with a picture of him for thousands of years.'

Derek burst into tears.

'This isn't fair, sir! You've got to do something, sir!'

'Well, I don't really know what I can do.'

'You've got to get him off me, sir! Get him off me!'

* * *

Bill went in search of help. He made his way to the Gallery Restaurant in the south west corner of the stadium and found The Father Of The Club — Henry Grover — sitting with his old friend Ralph Thorpe, formerly known as The Alderman.

Bill said solemnly: 'Hello, Henry. Hello, Ralph.'

Henry replied cheerily: 'Ah, Bill! Come and sit down, old son.'

'Oh dear, William,' Ralph, the former Alderman, said. 'What seems to be the matter? You look as worried as a Watford fan at Christmas contemplating the rest of the season.'

'Young Derek has gone and got himself a Watford-related tattoo,' Bill replied. 'It's absolutely terrible news.'

'Ha! Marvellous!' Henry cried.

'What?'

'I'm absolutely delighted, old chap!'

'But why?'

'Because people marking themselves with their allegiance to the football club I founded in 1881 makes me feel proud.'

'But tattoos are horrible.'

'Nonsense, Bill,' Henry said. 'Body art is a beautiful thing. I've always wanted to get myself inked with Watford's wonderful 1995 away shirt. That sublime combination of burgundy and teal would look magnificent on my left bicep.'

'What?'

'And I'd love to get the 2013/14 away shirt on my right bicep. Do you remember that sumptuous port wine colour, Bill? Although, I suppose people might think the tattoo was just a birthmark.'

'But why would you want tattoos, Henry? You're an upstanding Victorian gentleman. Tattoos are for—'

'Careful what you say, old thing. Ralph has had one done — haven't you, Ralph?'

'I certainly have.'

The former Alderman rolled up his sleeve. On his forearm was an amazingly accurate and characteristic image of a young, balding pop-star with huge glasses. He said: 'Elton Hercules Bloody John. I still bloody love him.'

'I've had one done too, Bill.' Henry said. 'As soon as I heard that a high-class tattoo artist had arrived in Hornet Heaven, I rushed to see her. Let me show you, old pal. It's on my left thigh. I just need to drop my trousers and long johns for you. Hold on a moment.'

'No need, Henry,' Bill said. 'Really no need.'

'I insist, old chap. It's a depiction of a long-standing love of mine.'

'Oh no, it's going to be Almen Abdi, isn't it?'

'Goodness me, Bill. Now, there's an idea,' Henry said. 'I hadn't thought of him. Maybe I'll get inked with him somewhere else. Somewhere more intimate, perhaps.'

Henry took off his trousers, grunting with the effort. 'Hold on,' he said. 'My long johns are a bit stuck…. Let me just… Nearly there… Right. The grand reveal! Of the love that will stay with me for eternity…'

'Dear God,' Bill mumbled, 'please let it just say "Watford".'

'Ta-dah!' Henry announced.

Bill frowned. 'Eh? It's very good, but who's it a picture of?'

'Gladys Protheroe!' Henry said proudly.

'But you've never seen her. For that matter, no-one has ever seen her.'

'It's what I *imagine* she looks like, old chap. Ahhh, I'll never stop loving Gladys Protheroe, Bill. Especially when I finally get to meet her.'

'Yes, well,' Bill said, unimpressed. 'Thank you for your time, Henry. It's been, er, revealing.'

'Oh. Are you off again?'

'I think I'd better go and see the tattoo artist myself.'

'Ah. Of course. Good call, old thing.'

'Yes,' Ralph agreed. 'Excellent decision, William. She's quite brilliant. Go and get yourself inked with one of—'

'Get myself inked? Goodness, no,' Bill said, outraged. 'Never. What a dreadful thought. That's not why I'm going to see her.'

'Oh, for heaven's sake, William. Do lighten up,' Ralph said.

'Absolutely,' Henry agreed. 'Go for it, Bill. Get a

tatt that expresses your lifelong passion for Watford through the glorious medium of ink on plasma.'

As Bill left, Henry called out: 'But don't get Almen, Bill. Almen Abdi belongs to me.'

*   *   *

In the atrium, Bill had the tattoo artist pointed out to him. He recognised her from the orientation he'd recently given her. She was in her late 40s and had a sharply cut bob of dyed-black hair set off by red eye-shadow and bright red lipstick. She was dressed entirely in black. Her name was Kat.

Kat was sitting on one of the yellow leather sofas, sketching something. Bill looked closely and saw an amazing artistic depiction of a snarling Tommy Mooney clenching his fist in front of the Watford fans at Peterborough in 1994.

The image spoke to Bill, but he shut it out of his mind. He needed to confront the woman.

He said: 'Excuse me — are you Kat, the Watford fan who gives tattoos?'

Kat didn't look up from her sketch. She said: 'Do you mean, am I the Watford-supporting fine artist who inks discerning customers with works of lasting beauty?'

'Oh, er, I don't know. Do I mean that?'

Kat looked up and fixed Bill with a cold stare. 'What's your problem, flower?'

'Ah. Yes. Well, I'm afraid my young assistant Derek Garston regrets the tattoo of Abdoulaye Doucouré you gave him. You shouldn't have let him choose it.'

Kat looked down and carried on her sketching. She said flatly: 'I'm a tattoo artist, petal — not a nanny.'

'But surely you have a moral responsibility to ensure your customers make sensible choices.'

'If they want Jamie Moralee inked on their arses, they can have Jamie Moralee inked on their arses.'

'But a tattoo is a permanent commitment.'

'Same as supporting a football club, flower — as this heaven proves. I committed myself to Watford forever when my family moved here in 1976. You got a problem with that?'

'But—'

'And I ain't taking a lecture off of you, either. When I arrived in Hornet Heaven, did you warn me that if I wanted to change my mind at a later date, I couldn't?'

'No, but—'

'Right. Bye then, petal.'

'But—'

'I said "bye".'

* * *

Bill left the atrium and wondered how he could make Derek feel less upset about the tattoo. He had an idea. He rounded up an old friend and went back to the programme office.

In the office, he said to Derek: 'I'm sorry, my boy. I went to speak to the tattoo lady, but she wasn't very helpful.'

'Then I hate her!' Derek replied. 'Almost as much as I hate Abdoulaye Doucouré, sir!' Derek looked down at the floor in self-pity. 'He's played me for a fool, sir.'

Bill said: 'There, there, my boy. Maybe we're judging Doucs too soon. Think of The Big Fella — Cliff Holton. Think of The Great Man — Graham Taylor. They both left the club, but then they returned. They're two of the greatest figures in the club's history. Maybe it'll turn out to be the same with Doucs.'

'For God's sake, sir! Stop trying to make me feel better! I've got a total Judas inked into my flesh, sir! Or my plasma, or… whatever it is!'

'Look. I know how you feel, young man. You're not the only one to have something on your skin that's a bit embarrassing. An old friend of mine is in a very similar boat to you.'

Bill called out through the door: 'Eric! Come on in!'

An elderly man entered. Bill said: 'Derek, this is Eric. Eric, this is Derek.'

'Hello, Derek son,' Eric said. 'Bill told me about your tattoo. I thought it might help if I showed you—'

'Wow, Mr Eric, sir! Look at that beautiful club crest on the back of your hand. The detail's amazing! The blue shield! The letters W F C! The stag at the top!'

'Thank you, son. I got it done down on earth in 1958. Then, the next year, the club changed colours to yellow and black. I couldn't believe it!'

'But it's one of the great crests, Mr Eric, sir. And it shows how long you've supported the club. What's embarrassing about that?'

'Nothing. That's not what I came to show you, son. I've got something far worse on my belly.'

'Ewww, an embarrassing tattoo?'

'No, a hairy wart. Look, I'll show you. Here we

are. It looks just like…'

Derek squealed: 'Oh my god, sir! Get this man out of here, sir! That's hideous! I think I'm going to be sick, sir! That hairy wart looks exactly like David Pleat! Get this man out of here!'

Eric hurriedly left.

Derek said to Bill: 'How could you do that to me, sir? I can never un-see that, sir!'

'But I thought a wart that looks like David Pleat would put having Doucouré on your arm into perspective,' Bill said. 'Things wouldn't seem so bad.'

'Then you've completely missed the point, sir.'

'Missed the point? How?'

'Because I'm in pain, sir!'

'Really? From the needle, still?'

'No, sir. Spiritual pain.'

'Oh, my poor boy. How do you mean?'

Derek said sorrowfully: 'I mean I've marked myself out as someone who can't tell a true Horn from a passing mercenary, sir.'

Bill sighed as if his heart was breaking for his young friend. 'Oh, Derek.'

* * *

An hour or so later, Derek decided he needed to address the problem himself. He went to the atrium to see Kat.

At the yellow sofas, Derek noticed that Kat was finishing a beautifully detailed sketch of a floodlit Troy Deeney wheeling away after his successful penalty at home to Chelsea the previous season — with his middle-fingers raised. Derek desperately wanted the image inked onto his back. Then he imagined what Bill's reaction would be.

He said: 'Excuse me, Mrs Kat, missus.'

'You again, petal?' Kat replied. 'What's up? Didn't your girlfriend like your tattoo?'

'Girlfriend? I haven't got a girlfriend, Mrs Kat, missus.'

'But I saw you gazing from afar at a pretty young thing earlier.'

Derek blushed and changed the subject. 'I've come back because I've had second thoughts about my tattoo, Mrs Kat, missus.'

'Second thoughts, petal? About a permanent tattoo?'

'Yes. Apparently, Doucs has been talking about leaving the club, and I'm a bit worried that—'

'It's alright. Don't worry.'

'Don't worry?' Derek was suddenly excited. 'Has Doucs signed a new contract?'

'I mean, I can fix the problem. I can cover over the picture of Doucouré with someone else.'

Derek squeaked with relief: 'Oh my God, Mrs Kat, missus! That's brilliant news!'

Kat watched the 13-year-old boy hop up and down with excitement. She couldn't resist teasing him a little. She said: 'The only thing is, petal, it'll have to be someone larger.'

'Really? Why's that, Mrs Kat, missus?'

'So they properly cover up Doucouré. It'll have to be Stefano Okaka.'

Derek's eyes filled with consternation. 'What? Okaka? Inked into me for the rest of eternity?'

'Or you could have Troy Deeney from last season.'

'Oh my God! A fat Troy Deeney is the best I can hope for?'

Kat burst out laughing. 'Haaaa! Haaaa!'

'What?'

'Haaaa! I'm having a laugh, petal! I can cover over Doucs with anything at all.'

'Oh, thank goodness, Mrs Kat, missus,' Derek said, relieved again. 'Crikey. You properly bamboozled me there. I feel like… I feel like a Bournemouth full-back who's just been sat down by Richarlison.'

'Well, when you know what you want, just come and see me in my new parlour — and I'll get it onto you.'

'Actually, Mrs Kat, missus, can we go there now? I've just realised exactly what I want.'

'Oh. Right-o, petal. Follow me.'

*　*　*

Not long later, Bill Mainwood left the programme office and walked down Occupation Road. He was surprised to see a long queue. He spotted his friend Eric and asked what the queue was for.

Eric replied: 'Kat's opened a new tattoo facility. She's an incredible artist. I'm going to get her to change the appearance of my David Pleat wart. I'm hoping she'll be able to make it look like Nigel Callaghan's 1980s perm.'

In front of Eric in the queue was Neil McBain. McBain had been Watford's manager in both the 1930s and 1950s — separated by a spell up the road at the club that dare not speak its name.

Bill asked: 'And what tattoo are you getting, McBain?'

'Ach, I'm getting a nice simple one on my forearm,' McBain replied. 'Just to remove all doubt from people's minds. It's going to say "I hate Luton". With asterisks instead of the 'u' and the 'o', obviously.'

Bill couldn't help chuckling. 'You hate Luton? You? You managed them to 22 victories when any self-respecting Horn would have made sure they lost every game!' Bill chuckled some more. 'Just be honest, McBain. Get an "I love Luton" tattoo.'

'Oh, for God's sake!' McBain whined. 'Will no-one ever forgive me for a simple mistake!'

Next, Bill saw Ralph Thorpe, the former Alderman, further down the queue. Bill asked: 'After another one, are you, Ralph?'

'Very much so,' Ralph replied. 'I've fallen in love with Kat's action sketch of Paul Robinson. Have you seen it? It's amazing. She really does capture the true essence of Robbo — as he puts a Stockport County winger into the seats of the Lower Rous.'

Bill smiled and walked on down Occupation Road.

Soon he saw the parlour. Suddenly he wasn't smiling.

'Goodness me!' he exclaimed. 'This is outrageous!'

The parlour was a red portacabin — the red portacabin that had once been the The Bill Mainwood Programme Hut and had recently been The Bill Mainwood Man Cave.

To make things worse, there was an oblong yellow sign on the outside that said in red lettering: 'The Bill Mainwood Tattoo Parlour'.

'Not in my name!' Bill fumed — and marched past the queue into the hut.

* * *

Inside the hut, loud rock music meant the hut didn't feel at all like Bill's kind of place — despite his name on the sign outside.

On the walls, though, were sketches Kat had made of various iconic Watford moments. Bill's eye was caught by an image of Barry Endean, in mid-air, powering home his header against Liverpool in the FA Cup in 1970. Bill felt a deep urge to stop and look at

Kat's amazing artistry, but his outrage got the better of him. He marched on.

At the back of the hut, Bill saw the back of a large yellow, black and red reclining tattoo chair. Beside it, Kat was leaning forward from a stool, inking a customer.

Bill switched off the music system and said: 'We'll have no tattoos in Hornet Heaven! Stop this at once!'

Kat didn't look up. 'Great. You again,' she said.

'We don't need tattoos to prove our commitment to the club,' Bill said firmly. 'Just being here in Hornet Heaven proves our commitment.'

'Speak for yourself, petal. Some people want skin in the game.'

'Right. If you won't be dissuaded, I'll dissuade your customers.'

Bill stepped round to the front of the tattoo chair and said: 'Excuse me, but I don't think... ...Derek!'

'Hello, sir!'

Bill felt completely deflated at the sight of his young assistant in the chair. 'Oh no!' he sighed. 'You're getting another one.'

'It's alright, sir. Kat's altering my Doucouré tattoo, sir.'

'But… But what if it makes you as unhappy as last time, young man? I couldn't bear seeing you make another mistake that will last for eternity.'

'It's OK, sir. I realise I got it wrong choosing Doucouré, sir. That's why, this time, I've gone for someone who hasn't said he's leaving this summer, sir.'

'But that's hardly setting the bar very high, my boy.'

'What's more, he's played for us in pre-season already.'

'Well, at least that includes Deeney and Mariappa — two Hornets for life. Perhaps you've learned your lesson and made a good choice. Go on, then, show me who the tattoo is now.'

Kat had finished. She stood back.

'Look, sir,' Derek said proudly. 'Richarlison! Nut-megging a Bournemouth defender, sir!'

'Oh no,' Bill wailed.

'Richarlison won't be leaving any time soon, sir!'

Bill felt a bit off-colour. He said: 'But haven't you heard, my boy? Marco Silva has… Oh dear… I think I… I'm not feeling very…'

Derek continued regardless: 'The boy from Brazil is going to be a Hornet legend, sir!'

There was a thump on the floor.

Derek looked down. 'Sir?... Sir?... Oh.'

Derek said to Kat: 'Excuse me, Mrs Kat, missus. Could you help me pick Mr Mainwood off the floor, please?'

* * *

Quite a while later, in the atrium, laid out on one of the yellow leather sofas, Bill regained consciousness.

'Eurgh, he groaned. 'How long was I out?'

Derek was perched on the edge of the sofa opposite. He had his elbows on his knees. He was staring at the floor.

'Several hours, sir,' the boy said. He was sounding much more subdued than usual. 'You missed our friendly at Stevenage, sir.'

'Golly. Well, I'll go and watch later.'

'I went, sir. And I have disappointing news to report, sir.'

'Don't tell me, my boy. No spoilers, thank you.'

'I don't mean news about the match, sir.'

Derek started to weep a little. 'Sorry, sir,' he said. 'I'm not at my chirpiest at the moment.'

Bill sat himself up cautiously. He said: 'Oh dear. I'm sorry if I've made a drama of all this, my boy. I fainted because I was overwhelmed by the feeling that your new tattoo is, well, a calamity.'

'Yes, I thought that too, sir, when I first saw how big Kat had drawn Richarlison's nose. But it's actually very realistic, sir. In real life, Richarlison's got an absolutely gigantic hooter, sir.'

'No, the calamity is that you've made exactly the same mistake again — only worse. This time you've gone and got a tattoo of someone who's already in talks with another club. Richarlison played in our friendly against Cologne, but missed the Fortuna Dusseldorf game because he was discussing terms with Everton.'

'Well, he's not in talks with Everton any more, sir,' Derek said tearfully. 'That's what I found out at the Stevenage game tonight.'

'Oh. That could actually be good news. If he's still with us, he—'

'He's not, sir. He's not in talks with Everton because he's signed for them.'

'Ah. Whoops.'

Bill noticed Derek's head drop. The old man got to his feet gingerly and went across to his young assistant.

He sat down and put an arm around the boy's shoulder.

They sat like this for a while.

Eventually Derek said: 'I've been naive, sir. Again, sir.'

'Poor boy. Does it sting?'

'Do you mean the tattoo, sir? Or the humiliation?'

Bill could feel Derek's small shoulders start to heave as the boy broke into sobs.

Bill held him tighter. He said quietly: 'Don't cry, my boy. You're not alone. For the rest of eternity, all of us are going to keep discovering new ways that being a football fan hurts. But we'll cope, young man. We'll cope.'

* * *

The next day, during the away pre-season friendly at Brentford, Bill noticed that Derek kept nervously tugging the sleeve of his school blazer down over his wrist — terrified that other people might see the tattoo.

'Don't fret, my boy,' Bill said. 'I'm sure you'll think of an appropriate tattoo to replace Richarlison — all in good time.'

'Do you think the answer might be Andre Gray,

sir?' Derek asked brightly. 'He's scored his 3rd pre-season goal today, sir.'

'Last season, Andre Gray didn't look the answer to anything at all, my boy,' Bill replied. 'No. Take your time deciding. You don't want to rush into choosing the wrong person.'

A note of panic crept into Derek's voice. 'But I need a replacement urgently, sir! There's a big-nosed traitor on my arm, sir!'

'Patience, my boy. You need to consider things carefully — and identify someone who's made a huge and long-term contribution to Watford Football Club. I'd suggest The Great Man, but there's no need for a tattoo of him. They're unveiling a statue of GT next weekend outside The Hornets Shop. So there'll be a permanent commemoration visible to everyone everyday — down on earth and up here too.'

'Agh!' Derek squealed. 'This is no good, sir! I need someone to replace that dirty double-crosser Richarlison, sir! Now, sir!'

'But there's no hurry, young man. You just need to—'

'Right, sir! Things are so desperate, I'm going to close my eyes and point at a player. You tell me who it is and I'll get him tattooed.'

'Oh dear, I'm really not sure that's a—'

'Just do it, sir! Who am I pointing at… Now, sir!'

Bill looked onto the pitch. He said: 'That's Ashley Charles; academy lad; hasn't made a competitive start yet.'

'D'oh! How about… Now, sir!'

'That's Jack Rodwell; journeyman loser on trial with us; won't ever make a competitive start.'

'D'ohhhhh! How about… Now, sir!'

'That's the Brentford defender who shanked the ball into his own net for our equaliser.'

'D'oh— Wait! What? He's scored a goal for Watford? Perfect, sir!' Derek said enthusiastically. 'In my current situation, sir, I'm happy to accept an own goal as a huge and long-term contribution to Watford Football Club, sir!'

Derek kept up the enthusiasm in his voice even as he started crying again. 'Brilliant! He'll do for me, sir!'

* * *

During the week after Watford's win at Brentford, Bill managed to keep Derek calm — and away from Kat the tattoo artist. He spent the whole time feeling sorry for his young assistant, wishing there was a way he could stop the boy feeling so bad about the tattoo. But he couldn't work out how.

Then, on the Saturday, before the Graham Taylor Matchday game with Sampdoria, Bill and Derek went to the unveiling of the new statue of The Great Man.

Outside The Hornets Shop, the large real-world crowd was matched by the one watching from Hornet Heaven as Watford's Chairman Scott Duxbury made an introductory speech. 'The statue is to ensure,' Duxbury said, 'that, while we've lost a friend, he will never be forgotten.'

In the crowd, Bill and Derek found themselves next to Kat.

Bill felt a bit awkward after their last encounter — when he'd been cross with her and then fainted.

But Kat gave him a gentle smile. She wasn't nearly as cold with him as before. She said: 'I grew up with GT as manager. I can't wait to see his statue.'

Bill smiled back. He always immediately warmed to anyone who loved Graham.

'Nor can I, Kat,' he said. 'The Great Man was so great that he was honoured during his lifetime — with the re-naming of the stand. But, to me, that always felt a little impersonal. A statue will remind everyone what he was like as a human being. And he was a wonderful human being.'

They watched as Scott Duxbury gave way to the next speaker.

The MC, Jon Marks, announced: 'Now, to speak on behalf of the players and staff that worked with Graham, please welcome… Luther Blissett!'

Wearing a blue suit, white shirt and sunglasses, Luther Blissett stepped forward.

Kat sighed: 'Look. Luther's here. I love Luther.'

Bill sighed: 'Me too.'

Derek sighed: 'Me too.'

In the real world Luther began his speech: 'Fantastic. Thank you all very much for that welcome… Graham was obviously someone very dear to myself and all of you.'

In Hornet Heaven, Bill said to Kat and Derek: 'You know, after The Great Man's passing, it's like Luther has become the living embodiment down there of the values GT created at our club.'

Derek added: 'And don't forget, sir, he's our record appearance-maker and goal-scorer. He was a coach here for 5 years too, and still does loads of work in the community, sir.'

'Absolutely, my boy. And yet… it doesn't feel like he's ever been formally honoured during his lifetime.'

Kat said: 'He definitely ought to be. Luther's the biggest Hornet on earth.'

Derek turned to Kat. 'Wait, what?… What did you say, Mrs Kat, missus?'

'I said he's the biggest Hornet on earth.'

'You mean, bigger than a fat Troy Deeney? Big enough to cover over a tattoo of Richarlison?'

Kat grinned. 'Way big enough,' she said.

Derek's face lit up. 'Sir! Sir!' he cried. 'What do you think, sir? Should I get a tattoo of Luther Blissett, sir! What do you think, sir?'

Before he answered, Bill listened to Luther finish his speech in the real world.

'Thank you, Rita and family,' Luther said, 'for letting us — the players — have Graham on loan… And thank you GT for giving Watford more than great football — a club with a unique spirit and an inspired heart.'

Eventually, Bill turned to Derek. He'd thought about things and now he'd come to a decision.

He said: 'Hmm. A tattoo of Luther. You know what, young man? I'll join you.'

* * *

A week later, on the first day of the Premier League season, Bill and Derek went through the ancient turnstile to the home game against Brighton & Hove Albion.

As the match kicked off, Derek noticed that a certain player had returned to the team. He said: 'Look, sir! Doucouré's playing, sir! The transfer window has closed and he hasn't left after all! This is brilliant news, sir!'

'Marvellous,' Bill agreed. 'Keeping him could be the best bit of business we've done this summer.'

'Mind you, sir, keeping him means I could have stuck with my original tattoo, sir.'

'Oh. Oh dear. I hope this doesn't mean you regret the whole saga. You don't want to change what you've ended up with, do you?'

Derek pulled up the sleeve of his school blazer and then his shirt. He looked proudly at the wonderfully lifelike depiction on his arm of a smiling Luther Blissett wearing yellow and red, with both arms raised, celebrating yet another goal.

He said: 'I wouldn't change this in a million years, sir. In fact, I won't change it for more than a million years, sir — even when Luther's finally joined us up here.'

Bill smiled at Derek's certainty.

Derek asked: 'And what about you, sir? Any regrets?'

Bill wriggled his shoulders. His back was still feeling slightly hot. But when he thought of what he'd had tattooed there — a sketch by Kat of Luther Blissett rising to power home a header at Old Trafford in 1978 — he felt a warm glow all over.

He said: 'No regrets at all, young man. Supporting Watford marks us all forever — for better or worse. And my new tattoo makes sure I'm marked with with one of the very best moments I enjoyed down on earth.'

Derek smiled and looked up at his mentor. The 13-year-old said gently: 'Thank you, sir. I know you only got yourself tattooed to reassure me that I haven't made an eternal fool of myself again. You're a kind man, sir.'

Bill wriggled his shoulders again — to shrug off any sentimentality.

The old man pointed to the pitch and said: 'Right,

my boy. Now let's concentrate on the football. I can't wait to see what amazing moments Watford can produce this season. I've still got plenty of room on my arms and legs!'

THE END

11

TILL DEATH US DO JOIN

EARTH SEASON 2018/19

On Sunday August 26th 2018, Bill Mainwood — Hornet Heaven's Head of Programmes — was in the Rookery End, watching the second half of Watford's Premier League home game with Crystal Palace. The fan in the seat next to him — a chirpy blonde-haired 68-year-old called Sue — had got chatting to him.

Sue said: 'Forty two years we were married, down on earth.'

'That's nice,' Bill replied. 'It's a wonderful thing when a married couple are both Watford fans.'

'He promised to love and to cherish me — till death us do part. And he did exactly as he promised.'

'Ahh, that's really lovely.'

'Well, it was lovely until death didn't part us after all — and we ended up stuck together in Hornet Heaven for the rest of eternity,' Sue said chirpily, with a laugh. 'Now he can't stand the sight of me!'

Bill looked at Sue. He wasn't sure if she was joking or not. He suspected there was a painful truth behind her laughter.

'Oh dear. I'm very sorry if your marriage isn't what it was.'

'Oh, these things happen,' Sue said breezily. Then she said 'Oh, excuse me, sweetheart,' and shouted: 'Go on, Holebas... Sling a cross in... Wait!... Yesssss!'

The fans in the real-world and in Hornet Heaven yelled as Holebas's cross nestled in the far corner of the Palace net.

Sue turned to Bill in delight and shouted: 'It's two-nil to the Orns! We're level top of the Premier League! I've never been happier!'

Then she joined in the post-goal singing: 'La-la-la-la-la-la-la-la-la Watford FC! La-la-la-la-la-la-la-la-la Watford FC!'

When the celebrations were over, Bill returned to the subject. He never liked hearing of discord among

Watford fans in their afterlife paradise, but marital discord particularly saddened him. He asked Sue: 'Has your husband actually told you he can't stand the sight of you?'

Sue replied: 'A woman knows, sweetheart. It's the way Terry goes...' She raised her voice: 'Boooo! Boooo!'

'Golly,' Bill said. 'Things must be bad.'

'What? Oh. Sorry, darling — Wilfried Zaha just had the ball.'

'Oh, I see. So you were saying it's the way Terry goes...?'

'...goes to games on his own. Down on earth, we always went together.'

'That must have been nice.'

Sue said: 'It was lovely, sweetheart. But... Sorry, do you mind if we don't talk about it now? I've got bigger fish to fry.' She started chanting: 'Harry Hornet made you cry! Harry Hornet made you cry!'

Bill sat quietly for the rest of the game, wondering whether he should try and smooth things over between two Watford fans — or whether it was none of his business.

He had to admit Sue didn't seem hugely upset

about her relationship — on the surface, at least. In fact, by the time the game reached the end of added time, she was bouncing around repeating her claim that she'd never been happier.

But as the final whistle blew — and Watford completed the third win of their 100% start to the season — Bill still felt unsettled that a husband and wife had become estranged in Hornet Heaven. It wasn't the way things were meant to be in an afterlife paradise.

He got to his feet determined to find a way to reconcile Sue and Terry.

* * *

The next day, in search of ideas, Bill made his way to the south west corner of the stadium to talk to Henry Grover — the man who founded Watford Rovers in 1881. Henry was in The 1881 Movement's underground bunker where Hornet Heaven's many items of historic memorabilia were stored.

In the yellow-walled gloom, The Father Of The Club had surrounded himself with various types of leisurewear that had been sold in the Hornets Shop over the years. Today he was reminiscing over vintage replica shirts — lifting them to his face and breathing deeply — when he saw Bill enter.

'Ah,' Henry said, a little embarrassed. 'You probably think I was just... er... sniffing... er...' He decided to brazen it out: 'Bill! Good to see you, you splendid old thing! Were you at the game yesterday? We're third in the league after three wins from three games! I love winning!'

Bill replied: 'So do I, Henry. Even better, we actually won against Palace!'

'Crystal Palace! Those pustules on the buttocks of the Premier League! I tell you, Bill, these are special times. Such happy days for Hornets everywhere.'

'Ah. But that's why I came to see you. Unfortunately, not every Hornet is happy.'

'But that's impossible, old chap. Even José Holebas smiled yesterday.'

Bill explained to Henry that the marriage of two Watford fans — Sue and Terry — appeared to be in trouble. He finished by saying: 'I'd like to help them get back together again as a couple, but I can't think how.'

'Well, why don't you just do what you usually do, old sport?' Henry suggested. 'Take them through the ancient turnstile to a few old games.'

'One of my "Magical History Tours", you mean?

'Exactly, old thing. Up here in Hornet Heaven, going back to watch a carefully themed selection of historic Watford matches seems to solve anyone's deep-seated psychological problems — with remarkable consistency.'

'But what theme would I choose? I don't know what the problem is between Sue and Terry. I don't know them well enough.'

'I see. Well, do you know if they went to games together in the past?'

'Yes. Sue said they did.'

'Then maybe, to start out with, you could go and watch them at a few old games — to understand the background to their relationship. A fact-finding mission.'

'I see. But that wouldn't really be a Magical History Tour.'

'No. I suppose it would be more of a *Marital History Tour*!'

Henry burst into laughter. He said: 'By Jove, I'm rather pleased with that one, Bill. I'm really rather pleased with that one.'

Bill thought the idea of a fact-finding tour was a

good one. So he headed off to look for Sue again, leaving Henry to resume inhaling the memories that a 1982 IVECO home shirt held for him.

'Ahh!' Henry sighed. 'Such happy days then, such happy days now.'

* * *

Bill didn't see Sue again until the next day — Tuesday. She was in the atrium, chatting with a group of very happy Watford fans. Bill noticed she was leading the conversation and making most of the jokes.

He waited until the conversation had run its course. Sue gave everyone a hug before she moved away. Then Bill approached her and said: 'Excuse me, Sue…'

Sue said: 'Come here, darling! Give me a big Hornet hug!'

Bill quickly removed his glasses. 'Oh. I, er… Gahhh… Golly.'

'There,' Sue said, letting go. 'That didn't hurt, did it, gorgeous? You've got to share the love when the Horns are level top of the league.'

Bill sensed the mood of the moment wasn't quite

right to turn the conversation to matters of marital discord. But he felt he should. He said: 'Look, Sue. I just wanted to say, after our chat at the game on Sunday... You know, about you and Terry... If I can be of any help in any way...'

'No, sweetheart. I'm fine.'

'OK. But if—'

'If anyone needs help, darling, it's him. There he is — over there. That's the man I married.'

Bill looked where Sue was pointing. A stocky man in his late-sixties was sitting on one of the atrium's yellow leather sofas. He was scrutinising a programme very closely.

Bill turned back to Sue, but she had already gone. She was hugging someone else.

Bill went over to the sofa. He sat down and introduced himself to Terry.

Terry eyed up the programme he was holding and said: 'Perfect-bound, the programme these days. Impressive. But I've definitely got a soft spot for the twenty-page two-staple configuration of the 1960s.'

'Aha,' Bill said. 'A man who loves his programmes. A man after my own heart.'

'Mind you, the weight of the paper stock's an

improvement. I reckon it's about 150 grams per square metre.'

Bill felt he was in the presence of a man who was over-compensating for something. He said: 'You're Terry, aren't you? I was chatting to your wife Sue yesterday, and—'

'Sue? She don't appreciate programmes. She'll happily waltz through the ancient turnstile with one. But read it? Digest it? Savour it? No way.'

'Well, I'm sure you must have a lot else in common. You've been Watford fans together — as a married couple — for a great many years, I hear.'

'Yeah… well…'

Terry seemed unsettled by the subject matter. He started to blink erratically.

Bill took a careful approach. He said: 'You know, I always think that the friendships and relationships formed through a mutual love of Watford Football Club are very special. Did you and Sue originally meet at the football?'

Terry looked away from his programme for the first time. He looked down and said: 'Yeah… At home to Southport in 1958… Saturday August 23rd.'

'You remember the date? That's nice.'

'It was the first day of the season… The season we signed Cliff Holton… The start of something special.'

'In more ways than just the football, by the sound of it.'

Terry nodded his head.

Bill said: 'I'd love to see the moment you met. Would you take me?'

Terry sniffled slightly and nodded again.

* * *

Terry took Bill through the ancient turnstile to the August 1958 Southport game. They went to the south-west corner of the ground — The Bend, as it was known. Bill noticed blackberries ripening on bushes at the back of the cinder banking.

Terry said: 'That's us, there.'

Bill looked where Terry was pointing. Between two sets of parents, an eight-year-old boy and an eight-year-old girl were standing on milk crates, holding onto the railings that surrounded the dog track.

'Ah, sweet,' Bill said.

Bill watched the two children. At first, they ignored each other. But soon, bored of standing, they started playing chase over the cinder banking. They squealed with delight. The rest of the fans around them were enjoying watching Watford's 5-1 win, but little Terry and little Sue were in a whole world of happiness of their own.

Terry wanted to show Bill more. They left the Southport game and went to the 3-1 home win over Colchester United on Good Friday, March 27th 1964. Terry took Bill to The Bend again — where they saw 14-year-old Sue and Terry standing a few yards away from their parents.

Terry said: 'George Harris is about to score for us. Watch what happens. I'd been thinking about trying this for a long time.'

As George Harris's goal went in, the crowd roared. Teenage Sue jumped up and down. Teenage Terry jumped up and down next to her. He manoeuvred himself closer and put an arm around her shoulder.

Watching from Hornet Heaven, Terry said: 'I was worried I might get a slap.'

Teenage Sue turned towards Teenage Terry. She wrapped her arms around him and squeezed tight as they carried on bouncing.

The watching older Terry said: 'That's what got

my hopes up that we were more than just friends.'

Terry then took Bill to a home match against Scunthorpe on a floodlit Tuesday night in April 1966. He led Bill across The Bend, up the side of the Shrodells Stand, and into the passageway behind. Bill saw 16-year-old Terry and 16-year-old Sue kissing in the shadows. They briefly stopped and looked up when the crowd roared to greet Stewart Scullion's goal. Then they carried on kissing.

Bill was a bit flustered. He said: 'Well... There's no need to show me all that kissing and cuddling and stuff.'

Bill hadn't envisaged that a Marital History Tour might contain such sights. He worried about what else Terry might show him as the lovebirds got older. He said: 'I think that's probably enough now.'

'No,' Terry said. 'There's more to show you yet. You'll like the next one.'

Now Terry took Bill to the night Watford won promotion to Division Two, for the first time ever, on April 15th 1969 — at home to Plymouth Argyle.

At the final whistle, the two visitors from Hornet Heaven chased after 19-year-old Sue and Terry as the couple ran jubilantly onto the muddy pitch, holding hands. But while thousands of other fans ran over to the Main Stand, young Terry guided young Sue towards the centre-circle. On the centre-spot, young Terry got down on one knee. Young Sue clasped her hand over her mouth.

Terry asked.

Sue said yes.

Bill said: 'Ahh, that's wonderful.'

* * *

Back in the atrium, Bill and Terry returned their programmes to the shelves.

Bill said: 'You know, Terry, this tour really has struck a chord with me. For all the most significant events in my life — things like my wedding, or the birth of my children — I remember who Watford were playing that week.'

Terry replied: 'Probably true for a lot of fans, that is.'

'It's just like T.S. Eliot said about coffee spoons: "I have measured out my life with football matches."'

'T.S. Eliot? Who did he play for?'

'Never mind. And is your wife Sue the same?

Does she connect key moments of your relationship to Watford games?

When he heard the word 'wife', Terry started scrutinising the masthead on the front cover of the Plymouth programme he was still holding. He said: 'I love this typography. Serifs on upper case lettering. Beautiful.'

Bill tried again. He said: 'You looked such soul-mates at those games. I bet she is the same as you. I bet she dates significant events by Watford matches.'

Terry carried on staring at the typography on the programme masthead. He was blinking erratically again. He said: 'I wouldn't know... I ain't a significant event in her life anymore.'

Bill patted Terry's shoulder sympathetically. He could see it would be too painful for Terry to probe deeper into the problems that had developed in the marriage. He said: 'Let's take a break for now.'

Then he headed off to find Sue in the hope that she might show him more of their story.

* * *

Bill didn't see Sue until the Thursday — two days later.

She was on Occupation Road, and she greeted him with her usual hug. For a second or two, Bill wondered if your ribs can crack when you're not made of flesh and bone.

Sue said cheerily: 'Hello, sweetheart. I saw you met Terry earlier in the week.'

'Yes,' Bill replied, 'we went to some old games. He's good company.'

'Yes,' Sue said, pointedly. 'With *you*, maybe.'

'Ah… Look,' Bill said, 'I don't mean to pry or interfere, but I'm still wondering if I can be any help to the two of you… you know… iron out any problems…'

'It is what it is, darling. I've moved on. Times are too good as a Watford fan to dwell on the problems of the past. I don't want to think about Laurence Bassini while we're level top of the Premier League, and I don't want to think about Terry.'

Bill felt it was a little harsh to equate Terry with most helmet-headed owner in Watford Football Club's history, but he let it go.

He thought for a moment. He wanted to get Sue to take him to a game or two from later in her marriage to Terry, so he said: 'Maybe it's worth dwelling on the good times you shared. I mean, you were a married couple through the glory days under GT, weren't you? You must have enjoyed those together.'

'Well, yes. I suppose we—'

'Go on, what's your favourite match from that era?'

'That's an easy one, sweetheart. West Brom at home in 1982 — when we went top of the top division for the first time in our history. We were the best team in professional football. Now, *that* was a feeling.'

Bill saw his chance. He said: 'Golly, I love that match. In fact, why don't we go and watch it again right now — you and me. It's like you said to me the other day: you've got to share the love when the Horns are top of the league. Oh, yes. This is going to be great. Thanks for reminding me of such wonderful memories.'

Bill gave Sue a huge hug. It went against all his natural instincts, but he wanted to make her feel she couldn't refuse.

She didn't refuse.

He led her up the slope to fetch the programmes for the West Brom game.

* * *

'Here we are,' Bill said. 'September 11th 1982. I was on the north east terrace. Where were you watching from?'

'There was only one place to be, sweetheart,' Sue replied. 'Under the scoreboard.'

'Great,' Bill said. 'Let's watch again from there.'

They made their way across the Vicarage Road terrace. As they approached the scoreboard, Bill spotted 32-year-old Sue and Terry in the real-world crowd. They were wearing matching yellow Courtelle jumpers they'd bought for £10.99 each from the Hornet Shop on the Vicarage Road precinct. The jumpers had a motif on one breast that said 'Watford, Division One, 82/83'.

32-year-old Sue was chatting to other people around them on the terrace, laughing and joking. 32-year-old Terry was studying his programme. Apart from the 'his and hers' jumpers, Bill thought to himself, you wouldn't have known they were a couple.

Bill and 68-year-old Sue stood and watched the match kick off. Bill said: 'West Brom were second in the table, going into this game. They were no pushover.'

'That's what felt so good in 1982, wasn't it, sweetheart. We were playing big teams — good teams — and beating them. No-one expected us to be so high up in the league. But we totally deserved to be there.'

'Sounds like you're describing the start of 2018/19,' Bill said.

Sue nodded and smiled.

They watched Watford set about West Brom with energy and efficiency. Ian Bolton and Kenny Jackett held strong at the back. Les Taylor and Jan Lohman chased down every ball in midfield. Luther Blissett ran at the visitors' defence.

Sue said: 'You know, you're right. 1982 and 2018 really are the same. Brilliant spirit and brilliant effort — and a brilliant run of results.'

'Exactly,' Bill said. 'With everyone in football suddenly sitting up and taking notice of our little club.'

As the game continued, Bill kept an eye on 32-year-old Sue and Terry in the real world. He was interested to see they were standing closer together now — more like a couple.

They stayed like that, he observed, until six minutes before half-time — when Luther put Watford 1-0 up. Suddenly they hugged each other, full on — just like they'd hugged as 14-year-olds on The Bend in 1964. After that, for the rest of the half, and during half-time, they held hands.

Early in the second-half, Les Taylor scored

Watford's second. After more hugging, 32-year-old Terry pulled a transistor radio out of his bag and said to his wife: 'If other results go our way, we'll be top. We want Ipswich to stop Man United, and we want... Blimey, this hurts to say... We want the filthy Hatters to get something at Liverpool.'

32-year-old Sue said: 'Ha ha ha! Come on, the dirty scumbags!'

Terry held up the transistor radio to his shoulder and they leaned their heads together above it, hungry for news from Old Trafford and Anfield. The news sounded good.

On the pitch, Luther made it 3-0. Sue and Terry hugged again. When the final whistle went, they put their foreheads together, held each other's faces and kissed deeply.

After a few moments, Terry stopped and said: 'I know it's only football, but am I allowed to say this is the best day of my life?'

Sue nodded and kissed him again.

Moments later, the final scores came through. United hadn't scored enough goals against Ipswich, and the Scummers had managed a 3-3 draw at Anfield. Watford were officially top of the league on goal difference.

Terry yelled. He peeled off his yellow jumper and swung it around his head. Sue did the same with hers. The couple jumped up and down, swinging their sweaters in ecstasy.

In the parallel world of Hornet Heaven, Bill tapped 68-year-old Sue on the shoulder and pointed at the young husband and wife.

Sue watched for a while. Then she said, with a faint smile: 'Blimey. I'd forgotten.'

* * *

On the Friday, two days before the 2018 home match against Spurs, Bill was engrossed in work at his desk in the programme office. There was a knock on the door. In walked Sue and Terry.

Sue said to Bill: 'Hello, sweetheart. We've had a chat and we've come for your help. We both want to give our marriage another go, but our heads aren't in the right place.'

Terry added: 'Things have been wrong for too long. We need someone to help us talk through our issues. We think you're just the bloke.'

Bill was delighted. He was about to invite them to sit down on the chairs across from his desk when he remembered his 13-year-old assistant Derek Garston was also in the room.

Derek said: 'It's OK, sir. Don't mind me. I'll just sit quietly and listen, sir. It'll be good learning for me for when I get married myself, sir.'

Bill thought this was rather cute — a deceased 13-year-old expecting to find the girl of his dreams in an afterlife of mainly old men. But he decided a more private space was required for a counselling session. He asked Sue and Terry to bear with him while he found somewhere appropriate.

* * *

The following morning — the Saturday — Bill invited Sue and Terry to sit down on two easy chairs he'd placed side by side, opposite his own.

Sue said: 'Wasn't this place The Bill Mainwood Programme Hut?'

Terry replied: 'Yeah. Then it was The Bill Mainwood Man Cave for a while, I think. Last time I looked, it was the Bill Mainwood Tattoo Parlour.'

Bill said: 'Well, I've reclaimed it — for more important purposes.'

Bill pointed to an oblong yellow sign with red lettering that he hadn't yet had time to hang up on the outside of the hut. He said: 'Welcome to The Bill Mainwood Marriage Guidance Hut.'

The three of them settled into their chairs. Bill asked Sue to talk about what she saw as the main issue in their marriage.

Sue said brightly: 'Down on earth, Terry gave me the attention every wife wants from her husband. Oh, he was interested in programmes and badges and club crests, and all that, but he kept it in check — kept it away from me. He always made me feel special when we were together.' Then her tone became a little more bitter: 'Up here, though, he's become obsessed. He's got access to every Watford programme ever. When he sees me, he glazes over — he's too busy thinking about the bloody typeface on a 1950s Supporters Club badge, or something.'

Bill asked Terry to talk about how he saw things.

Terry said generously: 'Sue's always been an extrovert. She's great with people — and football brought that out in her when we went to matches. She's amazing — she must have known everyone's names on the terrace around us for decades. Down on earth, I didn't mind — it was only once a week, during the season, that she'd be hugging other men.' Then his tone changed to one of frustration: 'But up here, with non-stop football, she's hugging blokes all day, every day. It ain't right for a husband to have to watch his wife doing that.'

Bill listened. He noted that the problems had only started after Sue and Terry had died and entered a football-centric heaven — with no other aspects of life available to enrich their relationship.

He asked more questions. He kept the atmosphere polite, positive and supportive.

At the end of the session, he invited Sue and Terry to come back the next day for more discussion. As he showed them out of the hut, he said: 'Well, I don't know about you two, but I've definitely learned something from today. Different personalities get different things out of supporting a football club. For some people, sociability is important. Others engage with more intellectual or aesthetic aspects. Football fulfils fans in different ways. And that's fine. That's good.'

Sue said: 'But we're husband and wife,

sweetheart. We need to be compatible.'

Terry said: 'Yeah. What if we can't get past our differences?'

'Well, you did before — for 42 years,' Bill replied. 'It's Hornet Heaven where you've run into trouble. Tomorrow, we'll think about strategies for this particular environment. I'll see you back here in the morning.'

*   *   *

The next day — Sunday, the day of the Spurs game — Bill waited in the Bill Mainwood Marriage Guidance Hut.

He waited.

And he waited.

But Sue and Terry didn't turn up.

Bill went off to look for them. He found them in the atrium. They were arguing.

'You just can't stop hugging other men, can you?'

'I'm surprised you had your face out of a programme long enough to notice!'

Bill's marriage counselling seemed to have made things worse. He looked away. Apart from Sue and

Terry, all the other Watford fans in the atrium were extremely happy — chatting excitedly about the afternoon's upcoming match against Spurs.

Watford had started the season brilliantly — their best top-flight start since 1982 — and the winning run had brought a feel-good buzz to Hornet Heaven just as it had to the land of the living. But Sue and Terry definitely weren't in a good place. Bill wished they could be as happy as everyone else in 2018 — as happy as he'd seen them at the 1982 West Brom game.

He stood and thought. Since marital guidance didn't seem to be the answer, he wondered how else he could help the couple. Straightaway, he had an idea.

He left the atrium and went off to find Henry Grover.

* * *

That afternoon, Bill — from a distance — watched Sue and Terry walk separately down Occupation Road with their programmes for the Spurs game. Bill had with him a plastic Hornets Shop carrier bag, but he was keeping it concealed beneath his jacket in case its bright yellow colour drew Sue and Terry's attention to him.

He followed them through the ancient turnstile.

The couple went to the Vicarage Road end — the Family Stand. They both headed for the same spot until they saw each other. They exchanged glares and moved to separate parts of the stand.

Bill went and sat in the top row — where he could see them both.

During the first half, Watford played well enough to contain a Big Six team made up of internationals from the recent World Cup finals. But, eight minutes into the second half, the Horns conceded a scrappy own goal. Bill noticed Sue start chatting to fans around her and Terry get out his programme to read.

On the pitch, though, Watford stepped up a gear — with Troy Deeney leading the way. Watford were irresistible. First the ball hit the Spurs woodwork. Then, in the 69th minute, Troy equalised with a header from a Holebas free-kick.

The stadium erupted — and Bill seized the moment.

He walked down the gangway to see Terry. He said: 'Terry, you didn't turn up for counselling this morning. I was hoping to help.'

'Yeah. Sorry,' Terry replied. 'Things got a bit—'

'I want you to go and stand behind the goal over there, halfway up.'

'Eh? Why?'

Bill pulled the Hornets Shop bag out from under his jacket and lifted something from it.

'Just put this on and go and stand where I said.'

Terry did as he was told.

Bill hid the bag again and went to see Sue. When she'd finished hugging most of the breath out of him, he wheezed: 'Can I borrow you, Sue — over here?'

Bill led Sue towards the section of the stand directly behind the goal, at roughly the same height as the Vicarage Road scoreboard used to be. As they approached, Sue saw Terry was there. She saw what he was wearing.

'Eh?' she said. 'Where did Terry get *that*?'

'I got one for you too,' Bill said. 'Exactly the same.'

Bill reached into his Hornets Shop bag. He pulled out a yellow Courtelle jumper with a motif on one breast that said 'Watford, Division One, 82/83'.

Sue took the jumper. She smiled and said: 'Well, this brings it all back, darling. Thank you. You deserve an even bigger hug. Come here.'

Bill stepped back and said: 'Think about it, Sue. Terry's looking. Pop the jumper on and let's watch the match from where you two used to stand together.'

A minute later, Sue and Terry were standing next to each other behind the Vicarage Road goal in 'his and hers' jumpers — just like in 1982. Meanwhile, on the pitch, Watford were tearing into a big team — just like in 1982.

As the crowd roared Watford on, Bill noticed that, without taking their eyes off the football, Sue and Terry felt for each other's hand. He saw their fingers intertwine.

Another minute later, at the far end, Holebas sent over a corner. Craig Cathcart ran onto the ball and smashed home a header.

Bill watched Sue and Terry leap into each other's arms and hug — exactly the same way he'd seen them do it in the land of the living 58 years ago and 36 years ago.

Their differences — for now — were forgotten. They were united by the feeling that every Watford fan was feeling.

For the rest of the match, Sue and Terry — in their matching yellow jumpers — stood with linked arms and sang the Hornets home. Cathcart and Kabasele held strong at the back. Doucouré and Capoue chased down every ball in midfield. Success ran at the visitors' defence.

It really was like 1982 all over again.

At the final whistle, the Watford fans in the real world, and in Hornet Heaven, yelled and screamed in triumph. They punched the air and bounced up and down.

But not Sue and Terry. Sue and Terry did what they'd done at the West Brom game. They put their foreheads together, held each other's faces and kissed deeply.

After a few moments, Terry stopped and said: 'I know it's only football, but am I allowed to say this is the best day of my afterlife?'

Sue nodded and kissed him again.

* * *

The next day, Bill went back to his hut to tidy up.

Stepping inside the red portacabin, he saw the yellow sign for the Bill Mainwood Marriage Guidance Hut that he hadn't got around to hanging up. He smiled.

He wouldn't be needing it anymore. All he'd needed to help Sue and Terry were matching jumpers from Henry's stash of vintage leisurewear.

As he tidied up, he thought again about what he'd learned over the past week.

It was still true, he thought, that football fulfils fans of the same club in different ways.

But it was also true that watching a winning team unites fans of the same club, no matter their different personalities — especially when the team plays with the organisation, commitment, skill and passion on show at Watford at the start of the 2018/19 season.

Bill finished tidying. When he picked up the redundant yellow sign, he started to wonder what his hut should be used for next. But he couldn't think of any current problems in Hornet Heaven that his red portacabin could help solve because everything was going brilliantly for Watford fans at the moment — so brilliantly, in fact, that the winning start to the season had got some people wondering if the Horns could 'do a Leicester'.

Suddenly, a thought occurred to Bill as to how the hut could be used. He said to himself with a chuckle: 'No. Don't be a silly Billy.'

But he wanted to imagine it — just for a moment.

He turned the yellow sign over. Then he stared at its blank side and imagined, in red lettering, the name of a hut that in all probability wouldn't be needed in few months' time. But he didn't half enjoy, just for a moment, the possibility that it might. He said to himself: 'The Bill Mainwood Premier League Trophy Hut'. He chuckled with delight.

Then he closed the door and left the hut to go and enjoy the international break — two weeks during which Watford would be level top of the Premier League with a 100% record.

Bill smiled at the prospect. International breaks usually felt like they went on for eternity. But, with so many Watford fans so happy, he wouldn't mind at all if this one did.

THE END

12

NOTHING TO FEAR

EARTH SEASON 2015/16

'So. There you have it. That's your orientation finished. Welcome to Hornet Heaven — the afterlife reserved for people who love Watford Football Club with all their heart.'

'Wait. If that's who it's for, what's *he* doing up here?'

'Who?'

'Him in the red builder's helmet. Laurence Bassini.'

On October 31st 2015, in the atrium of Hornet Heaven, a newly arrived Watford fan had just spotted a chubby-faced man wearing a dark suit and a red builder's helmet. She said: 'Has Bankrupt Baz, like, actually died, babes? Or is he just looking for the keys to the Hornet Heaven safe?'

Daisy Meriden — a pretty, fair-haired 14-year-old — was with Bill Mainwood, Hornet Heaven's 92-year-old Head of Programmes.

Bill chuckled: 'Don't worry, young lady. That's not really Bassini. It's Halloween today — so everyone in Hornet Heaven is in costume. It's a tradition up here. We dress up as what has scared us the most as Watford supporters. Baz's time in charge was truly terrifying.'

'Oh. Alright. I get it,' Daisy replied. 'What else are people dressed up as?'

'There's another Chairman over there. Silver hair, pastel shirt and tie, cheesy grin… Jack Petchey. Horrific.'

'Before my time, babes. I know the guy with the beard, though, giving it the shark eyes. That's Jokanovic.'

'Yes. Last season, that murderous stare of his sent out a clear message: if we didn't get promoted, no-one would be safe in their beds. He'd kill us all. It still gives me the shivers.'

'And are you in costume, babes? Or is the

referee's kit and the mullet lid your usual get-up?'

'Today, Daisy, I'm Roger Milford. In the 1980s, he was everyone's nightmare. Look — there are actually fifteen Roger Milfords standing around the atrium. All preening themselves in case there are cameras.'

'Wait. I don't get that one over there. What's an Uncle Fester costume got to do with Watford?'

'That's Ray Wilkins.'

'And someone's in a Harriet Hornet costume. How's that meant to be scary?'

'Derek Garston's inside that costume — my young assistant. He's thirteen. He's not frightened of Harriet specifically — just girls in general.'

'Why's he frightened of girls?'

'Inexperience. He's been up here 97 years and not spoken to a girl his age in all that time.'

'What's he... Wait! Oh my God! Look at that zombie coming towards us! That costume's literally so realistic! Me nut just spun!'

There was a blood-curdling roar: 'Rrrrraaaahhhh!'

'Ah,' Bill said. 'That's not actually a costume. That's Hornet Heaven's chief steward — Lamper. Every Halloween, he stops being dead and becomes un-dead. Somehow. Just for the day.'

Lamper, the shaven-headed hooligan, had unseeing eyes as he roared again: 'Rrrrraaaahhhh!'

'Oh dear, he's trying to eat us,' Bill said to Daisy. 'Would you mind stepping aside for a moment? I've got a shovel here for our protection.'

There was a squelchy thump of shovel on flesh.

There were no more roars.

'There,' Bill said. 'He'll be fine again tomorrow. Now, Daisy. Let's go and get you a costume so you can join in the fun.'

*　*　*

Bill, in his Roger Milford outfit, took Daisy round behind the south west corner of the stadium to The 1881 Movement's underground bunker. It was where the Halloween costumes were kept in Hornet Heaven.

Inside the yellow-tinged gloom of the subterranean space, Bill spotted Neil McBain — Watford's manager when the club were relegated into Division Four in 1958.

'Ah, hello, McBain,' Bill said. 'I'd like you to meet Daisy.'

Daisy said: 'Hello, babes. You alright?'

Bill explained: 'Daisy's just arrived in Hornet

Heaven and—'

'I'd better stop you there, Bill,' came a voice with a Durham accent instead of McBain's Scottish accent. 'It's me — George Catleugh. I'm wearing a McBain mask.'

George Catleugh was a tough-tackling wing-half for Watford before, during and after McBain's wretched second spell at the club. He said: 'The idea that that man ever managed the club still terrifies me.'

'Well, yes,' Bill said sympathetically, 'who could blame you?'

Bill patted George Catleugh on the shoulder and took Daisy deeper into the dingy bunker.

The next person they met was wearing red mayoral robes trimmed with fur. It was Ralph Thorpe — formerly known as The Alderman. He'd given up wearing these robes at the final home game of the 1976/77 season — in deference to Elton John replacing him as the club's greatest ever benefactor. Ralph explained: 'I'm being me — the old me. It's scary how important I used to think I was.'

At the far end, Bill and Daisy found Henry Grover — the man who founded Watford Rovers in 1881. Each Halloween in Hornet Heaven, The Father Of The Club indulged his passion for clothing by taking charge of the costume cupboard. Bill introduced Daisy to Henry.

Henry said enthusiastically: 'Well, what a wonderful day for a young thing like you to arrive in Hornet Heaven! Halloween is such fun! We all wear things that scare us!'

Daisy asked: 'So which player are you being? I don't recognise that shirt.'

'Ah. I'm not being a player,' Henry replied. He was wearing a dark blue Hummel top smeared with white dashes and stripes. He couldn't conceal his raw emotion as he explained: 'This is Watford's 1994 away shirt. It's like a seagull has suffered the most appalling diarrhoea. A genuinely horrifying choice of kit.'

'Alright, calm down, babes.'

'Sorry. I still get rather worked up about it.'

Bill said: 'So, Daisy. What might you like Henry to get you from the cupboard?'

Henry pulled himself together again and said: 'Yes, young lady. What would you like to wear that's scary? Who would you like to be? Do join in, it really is such fun!'

'Well, there ain't a person that—

'I know!' Henry said. 'How about being Dave

Bassett for the day? I've got a mask here. Look at its cheeky-chappy grin — no wonder Elton fell for it. Poor Elton had no idea that pure evil was lurking behind.'

'Nah, I don't—'

'Actually, if you do want to be Bassett, I could arrange for a set of assistants to follow you everywhere. Just like in real life, back in 1987. Faceless ghouls with no apparent purpose.'

'Like I say, it ain't people that—'

'Or if you'd prefer something more recent, I've got a 2013/14 shirt with the name "Diakité" on the back. Imagine if we'd made his loan permanent. Truly terrifying.'

Daisy was a bit annoyed now. 'Stop it, babes,' she said. 'I mean, is this meant to be, like, a serious thing or what? I ain't gonna lie — there is something that scares me as a Watford fan. But it ain't a person.'

'Ugh,' Henry said. 'You're not talking about that despicable town up the road, are you? If I could find a costume with the wings of a sparrow and the arse of a crow, I'd fly over Luton tomorrow and—'

'Stop it!' Daisy shouted. 'I've got a real fear! You're acting like it's trivial! It ain't!'

A shocked silence hung in the bunker for a few

seconds.

Bill said: 'Don't worry about Henry, young lady. I'm listening. Go on.'

'The thing is,' Daisy said, 'we're new in the Premier League. Quique's done, like, an alright job so far. But I'm petrified we'll get relegated — like we always do.'

'Aha! I can help you there,' Henry said. 'For a general relegation fear I'd normally recommend the McBain outfit. But Premier League relegation is on a much greater scale of horror. I've got an Aidy Boothroyd outfit somewhere here. Originally, it came with a ball — but whenever people dress up as Aidy they're never interested in keeping hold of the ball.'

Bill said: 'Henry! Please! Daisy has just confessed a genuine fear that's afflicting many Watford fans now we're in the Premier League. We should be offering her proper help — not just immature costumes and low quality jokes. Come on, Daisy. This isn't the place for you.'

Bill led Daisy back out of the bunker.

Henry called out after them: 'Ah, what about this Allan Nyom shirt? His defending strikes terror into the hearts of everyone… Bill?… Daisy?…'

*   *   *

Bill and Daisy returned to the atrium.

Near the programme shelves, they saw Harriet Hornet — with Derek Garston inside the suit. He was trick-or-treating. The boy had a bucket in which he was collecting pin badges, Panini stickers and several other knick-knacks of Watford memorabilia that people had given him.

Bill said: 'Derek, my boy, can I introduce you to a new arrival?'

The 13-year-old turned and saw the pretty 14-year-old girl. He yelled: 'Aggh! Oh my God, sir! Help, sir!'

The giant furry insect dropped the bucket and ran away in terror.

'What's that about?' Daisy asked Bill. 'Is he, like, calling me ugly?'

'No, no — quite the opposite. You're a very lovely-looking young lady and, as I said, Derek hasn't met a girl since he died in 1921. Golly, look at him go. At that speed, he'd outpace Victor Ibarbo.'

Bill took Daisy to the yellow leather sofas to meet

some more people. One of them was Neil McBain — the real one, this time. He was wearing a Luton scarf.

Bill immediately forgot the niceties of introducing Daisy to McBain. He hissed: 'You dirty scummer!'

'Ach, not you too,' McBain moaned. 'This whole dressing up malarkey has backfired. What scares me is the thought that I might deep down be a Luton fan, and—'

'You blooming are one!' Bill said furiously. 'You cleared off up the road to manage them, you filthy Judas!'

'Ach! Will you not let it lie? I'm trying to confront my fear by *pretending* to support Luton. Where's your compassion, man? You need to be sensitive to my deep-seated psychological issues.'

Bill spat: 'Piss off and take your scummy scarf with you, you disgusting brown-hatter!'

McBain walked away, hurt.

Bill said to Daisy: 'Goodness. Sorry, young lady. I'm not quite sure what came over me there. Let me introduce you to this gentleman instead. Daisy, meet one of Watford's former managers.'

'Hello, Daisy. I'm Mike Keen,' said Graham Taylor's immediate predecessor.

'Whoa, babes,' Daisy said. 'That costume's, like, definitely over the top. Why are you got up like that?'

Mike Keen was wearing a skin-tight silver jump-suit that was sparkling with sequins. Sprouting from the shoulders were two huge plumes of silver feathers.

Mike explained: 'I was sacked by Elton John in 1977. It still haunts me.'

'Aw, you poor thing. Does wearing that help?'

'I think it does more for Henry Grover than it does for me. He watched me change into it. He couldn't stop licking his lips.'

Mike moved off. Bill and Daisy sat down on one of the sofas.

Daisy said: 'I tell you what. Some of these Halloween costumes are definitely a bit, like, unusual.'

Bill adjusted his Roger Milford mullet and said: 'Yes. Actually, I've never been terribly comfortable with the whole dressing up thing. It's a bit childish, if you ask me. More to the point, though, it won't properly help you tackle your fear of Premier League relegation. Perhaps it would be more therapeutic for you just to sit and talk things through.'

'Talking won't help, babes. I've been scared ever since we arrived in the Premier League in the summer.

We started off with four games without a win. That, like, totally panicked me. Then we lost at home to Palace a month ago and I had a meltdown on Twitter. The worst was when we lost to Arsenal two weeks ago. I ain't gonna lie — I ended up phoning the club to tell them they had to sack Quique. It was awful. I don't want to be that person.'

'Yes. Fear makes a lot of football fans behave like that. But maybe this trip up to the Premier League will be different.'

'But it won't be, will it? We always go straight back down.'

'In the past, we have done, yes. But Gino Pozzo does things differently from before.'

'It ain't just Watford it happens to, though. Most teams that get promoted go straight back down through the hatch.'

'Gino knows what he's doing. I can explain, if you like. You see, Gino's business model is—'

'Don't. You're wasting your breath. It ain't something you can argue me out of. Supporting a Premier League club that ain't one of the Big Four is, like, pure terror. It's like sitting in the dark watching Paranormal Activity over and over.'

Bill reflected that he himself had never felt this terror. It seemed to be a modern affliction, felt by younger fans. Was this because younger fans been exposed to the shrieking hype of the Premier League for the whole of their lives, he wondered? If Daisy had grown up with it, she might never grow out of it.

'Oh dear,' he said. 'Well, if sitting and talking isn't going to help, we'd better try something else to calm your fears. Ah. I know. I know exactly what you need.'

'Go on, then. What do I need?'

'You need one of my "Magical History Tours". Come along, young lady. Follow me.

* * *

Bill — in his Roger Milford outfit — took two programmes from the atrium shelves and led Daisy through the ancient turnstile on Occupation Road to a game from Watford's past.

'Recognise where we are, young lady?' he asked.

'Oh my God. Anfield,' she replied. 'This is amazing.'

'I've brought you to our first spell in the Premier

League — before you were born. This game took place in August 1999.'

'Wait. My dad said this season was, like, totally miserable. He said it wrecked the club, and that. For the next five years. Watching this won't stop me being paranoid of relegation.'

'But it'll make you realise that, despite the awfulness, there were wonderful moments we'll treasure forever. This was the first time Watford Football Club won at Liverpool. It's still the only time.'

Bill and Daisy settled down and watched the match. What she saw on the pitch was glorious. A totally committed Watford team set about Liverpool from the start. Pagey, Robbo, Mooney and Johnno piled in. Liverpool didn't know what had hit them.

Before long, Peter Kennedy's free-kick from the right took a couple of deflections in the Liverpool box and fell to a defender. Two Watford players slid in at his feet, hurling themselves hungrily at the ball. It came free to Mooney. He tucked it into the net.

Daisy and Bill leapt to their feet and roared. Bill's mullet wig slipped down over his eyes. Daisy helped him adjust it. Then they roared again and sang their hearts out.

Daisy said: 'This is brilliant!'

They carried on watching an extraordinary performance of grit and determination. At the end, the 1-0 victory was rounded off with a moment that perfectly captured the entire afternoon. On Watford's left, Robbo threw himself into a sliding tackle. He won the ball and the Liverpool forward went flying. The final whistle blew and Robbo punched the air.

In the Anfield Road end, Daisy did the same.

She said to Bill: 'Best. Trip. Ever!'

* * *

Back on Occupation Road, Daisy and Bill walked up the slope towards the atrium.

Bill said: 'You see, being in the Premier League isn't scary. The big time always provides big moments — regardless of how your season ends. We'll always have Liverpool away. It's ours for the rest of eternity.'

Daisy said: 'That was proper brilliant. I want to go to more away games from that season. What have you got?'

'Well, the game at Middlesbrough on the last day of the season was very special. Watford fans were all in fancy dress — just like we are today. It was great fun.'

'Did we win?'

Before he could answer, Bill was distracted by a crowd of more people in costumes coming towards them. The programmes for that afternoon's home game against West Ham United had just arrived in Hornet Heaven and residents were on their way to the game. Bill spotted a couple of people kitted out as skinheads from a previous home game against West Ham — the one in 1979 when the Inter City Firm infiltrated the Vicarage Road end.

Seeing the hooligans gave Bill the chills. It made him forget to maintain the Spirit of Anfield '99 with Daisy. Slightly rattled, he replied: 'What? Er…. Liverpool was our only away win that season. And we lost 16 of the other 18 away games.'

Daisy stopped. She said: 'Oh my God. The season really was a total horror show. Worse than a horror show. Away games must have been, like, Saw 1, Saw 2 — all the way through to Saw 16.'

Bill realised his mistake. The Liverpool exception had proved the rule. By taking her to the only away high spot that season, Bill had reinforced her fear of Premier League relegation here in 2015.

'Hmmm. OK, let's forget that season,' he said. 'I've got plenty of other games planned for the rest of the Magical History Tour. They'll help you put your fear into perspective.'

Daisy didn't move. She shook her head and said sadly: 'Thanks, babes — but no thanks.'

'But I'm going to take you to games that wouldn't have happened if we hadn't been relegated from the Premier League. The Leicester play-off semi. Winning promotion at Brighton. Wonderful life-affirming moments. Or afterlife-affirming — depending on where you were at the time.'

'No, babes. I've got to face it. I'll always be frightened of the Horns dropping out of the Premier League. There ain't nothing you can do.'

'But those games are the ultimate proof that no-one should be scared of relegation.'

Daisy wasn't to be persuaded. She gazed despondently into the approaching crowd.

Amongst the revellers, she saw someone covered head-to-toe in a white sheet with two posts and a crossbar crudely drawn onto it. She guessed it was meant to be the ghost goal from the home game against Reading in 2008 — when the club had been back down in the Championship with financial trouble looming again, all because of Premier League relegation.

But the childishness of the costume made her giggle. Her dad had always said the last days of Boothroyd were a horrific time, but now someone was making a joke of it. She felt a bit better.

She said to Bill: 'OK. Change of plan, babes. I need to forget about relegation — and have a laugh about something else that's scary. I'm going to get myself a silly costume like everyone else.'

'Oh. Good,' Bill replied. 'Anyone or anything in mind?'

'Yeah. He's in the current squad. His tackles scare the living daylights out of me.'

'That sounds very appropriate.'

'And I've always wanted peroxide streaks.'

'Aha! Valon Behrami! The horror!'

'I ain't too keen on having a stubbly beard, to be fair, though.'

'It's an excellent choice, young lady. Come on, let's go back to the 1881 bunker and get you kitted out.'

* * *

Not long later, Bill (as Roger Milford) and Daisy (as Valon Behrami, with blood-stained fangs for good measure) went through the turnstile for the game against West Ham.

They joined up with a group of various Halloween characters including the Laurence Bassini, the Jack Petchey, Harriet Hornet, six other Roger Milfords, and two Gianluca Viallis.

Before kick-off, in the Rookery End, Harriet Hornet came close to Bill and Daisy. Bill was amused that Derek — inside the Harriet outfit — obviously hadn't recognised Daisy beneath her Behrami get-up. Otherwise, the boy would have a run a mile.

Or would he? Because Bill now heard Derek whispering through the Harriet Hornet head: 'Excuse me, sir, but purely out of academic interest, sir, who was that girl I saw you with earlier, sir?'

Bill smiled at the idea that Derek's interest was 'academic'. He couldn't stop himself teasing the boy a little. He said: 'Pretty, isn't she?'

Derek squeaked and pulled Harriet's head down tightly to make sure no-one could see how red his face had gone. He moved away.

A few moments later, Bill asked Daisy quietly:

'Are you OK, young lady? How are you feeling about today's game?'

'Not great, babes,' Daisy replied. 'West Ham have won all their away games so far this season — at Arsenal, Liverpool and Man City. We're going to get stuffed. It's going to make me panic about relegation and do something I'll regret.'

'Well, now you're in Hornet Heaven, at least you won't be able to phone up the club.'

The match started. Even though Watford hadn't beaten West Ham at home for 30 years, they were much less cautious than they had been previously under Quique Sanchez Flores. Nathan Aké and Miguel Britos had early headed chances, and the Hornets dominated. In the 39th minute, West Ham's Andy Carroll dithered in his own penalty area. Aké dispossessed him and Odion Ighalo squeezed the ball over the line. The fans from Hornet Heaven went crazy. The Laurence Bassini threw his red helmet into the air. The two Gianluca Viallis kissed each other's bald heads.

Just after half-time, Ighalo struck again. Anya squared the ball. Ighalo, fifteen yards out, controlled it and curled it into the top corner. The fans from Hornet Heaven went even crazier. Bill watched the other six

Roger Milfords swing their mullet wigs round and round in celebration. Then he saw Harriet Hornet hugging Valon Behrami in jubilation.

Bill smiled to himself that Derek had no idea who he was hugging. Bill wondered if it might be the start of a beautiful relationship. Young love might blossom.

After the second goal, Watford played strong, positive football. Nathan Aké was a colossus at the back. Ben Watson commanded the midfield. Up top, Deeney and Ighalo caused havoc in the West Ham defence. It felt like a Premier League team coming of age.

When the final whistle blew, the fancy dress characters from Hornet Heaven bounced, clapped and chanted. Watford had won comfortably — 2-0. All seven Roger Milfords linked arms. They turned round — so their mullets were facing the pitch — and did a Poznan.

Once the celebrations were over, Bill and Daisy headed back to the ancient turnstile.

Bill asked: 'And how are you feeling about today's game now?'

Daisy grinned through her Valon Behrami stubble.

'It's changed everything, babes,' she said. 'We've won before, but it's always felt like we've got away with it a little bit. Not today, though. We totally deserved that.

We played like a team that belongs in the Premier League.'

'Maybe we do belong now,' Bill said. 'Maybe Gino Pozzo really does know what he's doing.'

Daisy beamed with happiness. She said: 'Definitely. It's Halloween today, but I tell you, babes… After a Watford performance like that, I've got nothing to fear.'

* * *

After the match, Derek Garston — still suited up as Harriet Hornet — paid a visit to Henry Grover in the 1881 bunker.

Derek said: 'Excuse me, Mr Grover, sir, but I was wondering… have you seen the girl who's just arrived in Hornet Heaven?'

Henry, like Bill at the match, couldn't resist teasing the boy. He said: 'Pretty, isn't she?'

Inside the suit, Derek's face went as red as Harriet's face was yellow.

But this time he plucked up enough courage to ask Henry another question: 'Please can you tell me which costume you gave her, Mr Grover, sir?'

Henry told Derek what Daisy was wearing.

Derek thanked Henry and headed straight off to the annual Hornet Heaven Halloween party.

*   *   *

In the Sir Elton John Suite, a band made up of former Watford players was providing the music at the party. Jack Gran, Jack Cother, Alf Sargent and Alec Sargent were rocking out in Roger Joslyn wildman wigs with matching straggly beards.

Bill and Daisy entered the room, still in their costumes. Bill glanced around. He saw Mike Keen, in his spangly Elton John jump-suit, jiving with Uncle Fester. He saw the real McBain cavorting with a fake McBain. Everyone looked happy — carefree, even.

The only exception seemed to be Harriet Hornet — who was standing on the far side of the room alone. Derek's body language inside the suit suggested a great deal of nervousness. But Harriet soon disappeared from view behind twelve Roger Milfords doing a conga.

Bill glanced around the room some more. He said to Daisy: 'Golly. Look at that.'

The Laurence Bassini was attempting to

breakdance — spinning upside down on his red builder's helmet. The chubby businessman crashed into the sound system.

Daisy remarked: 'He dances the way he runs businesses.'

Bill laughed and carried on watching everyone party into the night.

It had been a good day, he reflected. October 31st 2015 had moved things on rather nicely in the land of the living and Hornet Heaven. Down there, Watford seemed to have matured into a proper Premier League side. And, up here, young Daisy had conquered her young person's fear of relegation. He liked to think she might be feeling a little older and wiser underneath.

On stage, the band finished the rock song they were playing. Now the mood of the music changed. Jack Gran continued at the piano. He began an instrumental version of Elton John's Can You Feel The Love Tonight. He was accompanied by Alec and Alf's brother — Freddie Sargent — on cello.

Bill stood with Daisy and watched as the dancing couples moved in closer together for the slow song. It unsettled him slightly to see Uncle Fester and 1970s Elton John holding hands. And real McBain and fake

McBain resting their hands on each other's hips — looking as though they were about to smooch — was genuinely the most horrific thing he'd seen all day. He turned away.

When he did so, he saw that Harriet Hornet — or, rather, Derek Garston — was now striding purposefully towards him. He wondered what the boy wanted with him.

But the boy didn't want anything with Bill. Thirteen-year-old Derek, dressed as a brightly coloured furry insect, stopped nervously in front of fourteen-year-old Daisy, dressed as Watford's midfield hatchet man.

Derek asked nervously: 'Excuse me, Mr Behrami, sir. Would you like to dance?'

Daisy put a finger to the designer stubble on her chin for a moment. She smiled and replied: 'Love to, babes.'

Beneath the furry head he was wearing, Derek gasped. He'd never asked a girl to dance before — not down on earth, not in Hornet Heaven. The moment felt like a rite of passage, 97 years late. On the outside of the costume, Harriet Hornet's eyes were static and glued-on, but — inside — Derek's eyes sparkled with amazement and delight.

The teenagers took each other's hands. They stepped close to one another. They began to dance to the music.

Bill Mainwood, watching, smiled his broadest smile yet.

For Watford Football Club in the Premier League, Daisy Meriden in Hornet Heaven, and now Derek Garston too, Halloween 2015 had been a great day for growing up.

THE END

13

THE POWER OF LOVE

EARTH SEASON 2018/19

Halfway through September 2018, Watford Football Club were undefeated, having won their first four Premier League games of the season. The international break was over and Watford fans had actually enjoyed it for once.

On the morning of Saturday 15th, Bill Mainwood was with 13-year-old Derek Garston in the Rookery End. They were re-watching the most recent game — Watford's home win over Tottenham.

Bill said: 'I love beating Spurs, my boy.'

'So do I, sir,' Derek replied.

'I love hearing their fans whine,' Bill continued.

The 92-year-old put on a moany voice and said: 'It's not fair! Little Watford are meant to be little! It's not fair!'

Derek grinned and said: 'They don't like it up 'em, sir.'

'Exactly, my boy. Whenever we take the game to the big teams we—'

Suddenly everything in the stadium became still and silent.

'Eh? What's going on?' Bill said.

'Look, sir! The ball's frozen in mid-air, sir!

'Golly, my boy. The players have stopped. They're like statues. The whole crowd too.'

'The match has got stuck, sir!'

Just as suddenly, the noise and movement returned.

Derek said: 'Ah. That's better, sir. Everything's moving again.'

Now the match juddered and stopped once more.

'Oh. No it's not,' Bill said. 'Oh dear.'

The matched glitched a couple of times, then resumed as normal.

Derek said, alarmed: 'What's going on, sir? This is terrible, sir! Hornet Heaven is on the blink, sir!'

*   *   *

Bill and Derek returned to the atrium. In the real world, Watford Football Club were level top of the Premier League with a perfect record. But in the afterlife paradise of Hornet Heaven things definitely weren't perfect.

In the atrium, they found Henry Grover — the man who founded Watford Rovers in 1881. The Father Of The Club was reclining blissfully on one of the yellow sofas.

Henry said: 'Ah, there you are. You know, I've been thinking, chaps. This season has started so well, I can't help wondering if now is the time to stop being a Watford fan. You know, bow out at the top with a 100% record for the season intact. Retire undefeated. Before we play United this evening.'

Derek replied: 'What are you talking about, Mr Grover, sir? You can't stop now. This might be the season we win a serious trophy, Mr Grover, sir — for the first time ever. This is the time to step up your support, Mr Grover, sir. We can beat United, Mr Grover, sir.'

Bill said: 'I tend to agree with Derek, Henry, but

I'm afraid there are more pressing matters to discuss. We have worrying news. We've just been back to watch the win over Spurs from two weekends ago and—'

'It was the fourth time we've watched it, Mr Grover, sir,' Derek interrupted. He added pointedly: 'We went because Mr Mainwood and I can't get enough, Mr Grover, sir — unlike you, Mr Grover, sir.'

Henry didn't mind the jibe. He said: 'I don't blame you, young man. Beating Spurs is rather more-ish.'

Bill brought them back to the point. He said: 'Henry, you need to hear this news. We were at the game and... Derek, what minute of the game was it?... Derek?... Derek!'

Derek was gazing distractedly across the atrium at Daisy Meriden — the fair-haired 14-year-old with whom he'd danced at Halloween parties for the last three years. Since 2015, he hadn't plucked up the courage to go near her unless they were both wearing costumes.

'Derek!' Bill said. 'Pay attention, boy!'

'What, sir? Oh. Sorry, sir.'

Bill and Derek described to The Father Of The Club how there had been a glitch in the Spurs match — causing it to stop and start fitfully like one of those dodgy internet streams they'd heard about. The news shattered Henry's bliss.

'Good golly,' he said. 'We've had this happen in Hornet Heaven before.'

'May 27th 2013, Mr Grover, sir. Shortly before the Play-Off Final against Palace, Mr Grover, sir. The day the atrium suddenly appeared in Hornet Heaven, Mr Grover, sir.'

'Ah yes. The time of the upgrade. If I remember rightly, wasn't the glitch something to do with the software that runs this whole place?'

'Correct, Henry,' Bill said. 'A Chief Executive took charge of Hornet Heaven and—'

'Ugh! I remember him. Pony tail. Ghastly man.'

'—and the glitches occurred when he was uploading changes to match footage. He was falsifying the games we were watching so we thought that Watford were winning every game.'

'Ha!' Henry cried out jovially. 'Just like we're winning every game now — in actual reality!'

He paused.

He continued: 'Er… why are you looking at me like that, Bill?… Derek?… Have I missed something?'

Derek said in a rather patronising way: 'It's nearly a century since I did arithmetic at school, Mr Grover, sir, but even I can still put two and two together.'

'What? What haven't I worked out?'

Bill said: 'If the Chief Executive was tampering with games back then, Henry, he may be tampering with them now. Derek and I are worried that in the real world, we might not have a 100% record after all.'

'Good Lord!' Henry exclaimed. 'My word, by Jove, and good Lord!... Right! This won't do! We need to find the pony-tailed charlatan!'

* * *

Bill asked around. He learned that, after disappearing in May 2013, the former Chief Executive had moved into a hospitality suite in the Upper Graham Taylor Stand. Bill went to confront him.

He made his way through the sparkling white-walled reception of the Executive Club. He climbed the spacious and spotless staircase to the third floor. He passed through the swanky Gallery restaurant and down the sleek white corridor. He knocked on the door of the FX Pro Suite and went in.

The former chief executive was reclining with his feet up on a black leather Chesterfield in front of a window overlooking the Vicarage Road pitch. The man was exactly as Bill remembered him — in his early forties, wearing a sharp suit, with dark hair tied back in a pony tail. The appropriate word to describe the man, Bill thought, was 'oily'.

Nor had the former Chief Executive forgotten Bill from the events of May 2013.

'Well, well, well,' the man sneered. 'If it isn't the soppy old fool who ran that ramshackle programme hut. Good God, I enjoyed sacking you.'

'Oh. That's not very nice.'

'There you go. "Nice." As if anyone gets anywhere by being nice. Use your eyes, old man. Do you really think Gino Pozzo has transformed this stadium and this whole club by being nice?'

'Well, I—'

'He's doing what I wanted to do to Hornet Heaven. Do you remember my vision? "A Premier Paradise." Gino's creating one down on earth. All he's needed to do is get the on-field results to match. And this season he's started. We're winning every game! Winning! Winning!'

As well as the clothes and the pony tail, Bill recognised the slightly crazed look in the former Chief

Executive's eye.

'Well, I have to admit — we are all enjoying it,' Bill conceded.

'See? I was right all along. Yes, I was cheating things a bit, but the end fully justified the means. It was a disgrace that mob rule won the day and I was hounded out of my job by the residents. Football fans are stupid and ignorant. Always have been, always will be.'

Bill wanted to stay in this man's presence for as short a time as possible. He saw the opportunity to ask the question he'd come to ask.

'So you've never wanted to take power again?'

The former Chief Executive put his hands behind his head and stretched out further on the settee.

'Look at me — happily holed up in hospitality. Gino Pozzo is doing all the work for me. I don't need to lift a finger.'

Normally, every ounce of plasma in Bill's body would have told him not to trust a chancer like this. But he believed the man. The former Chief Executive was so oily — so unctuous, so oleaginous — that schmoozing in a suite for the rest of eternity was completely in character.

Bill turned on his heel and left.

The glitches in the Spurs game must have been caused by something or someone else.

* * *

Bill went back to the atrium. This time he went up the grand staircase. He climbed to the top floor, knocked on the door of the IT department and went in.

Roy from IT was there. He nudged his glasses higher and said: 'Hello, Bill. Got a problem?'

Bill told Roy about the glitches he'd seen when re-visiting the Spurs game from two Sundays ago.

Roy turned to his computer screen. Rapid-fire, he tapped the keys on his keyboard.

'Hmm,' he said. 'Could be all kinds of things. Probably a fuel problem.'

'A fuel problem?' Bill replied, surprised. 'What's fuel got to do with anything?'

'Ha! You think Hornet Heaven runs on thin air, do you?'

'I don't know. It's a heaven. Does it need an energy source? I've never thought about it.'

'Tsk! Typical! No-one ever thinks about the technical side. But as soon as something goes wrong, it's

"Roy, fix this! Roy, you're useless! Roy, I'm going to stick those spectacles so far up your—'

'Yes, I get the picture, Roy. So do you think it is a fuel problem?'

'I'd be very surprised if we're running low at the moment.'

Roy stopped tapping his keyboard. He nudged his spectacles again and put his nose close to the screen.

'Cripes!' he said.

'What?'

'We certainly have got a fuel problem. A massive fuel problem.'

'Too little of it? But you said—'

'Too much of it. Far too much. Those glitches you saw will be the system choking. You know, like car engines used to do — back in our day down on earth.'

'I see. Well, you just need to reduce the flow of fuel, then.'

'Easier said than done.'

'Why?'

'Because of what the fuel is.'

'What is it? Diesel? Unleaded?'

'Love,' Roy said.

'I beg your pardon?' Bill said.

'Love,' Roy repeated. 'The same thing that brings every resident of Hornet Heaven here in the first place. Love for Watford Football Club. Hornet Love.'

'Golly. I never knew. But I suppose it makes sense.'

'Love powers the games. It powers the atrium. It powers Occupation Road. It powers you and me. Our entire afterlife depends on it — but it needs to be flowing within certain margins.'

'Gosh. I see. Have there been problems before?'

'Well, Hornet Heaven has been extremely low on love in the past—'

'Golly, I bet we were running on fumes when Jack Petchey was Chairman of the club.'

'—but we've never had too much love before. It must be because of our 100% record in the Premier League. People are loving our start to this season at highly dangerous levels.'

'Dangerous? How do you mean?'

Roy peered even closer at the screen. He wrinkled his nose. He said: 'System-critical. I reckon if Watford carry on winning like this, the whole of Hornet Heaven will crash.'

'What? That sounds terrible,' Bill said. 'Would

you be able to reboot it?'

Roy laughed: 'Re-boot it? Really, Bill! From inside the system that's crashed? Of course not. If we do well against Man United later, there'll be so much love flooding Watford's way that Hornet Heaven will go down forever.'

* * *

Bill staggered out of the IT office. He felt numb with shock. Shakily, he reached for the bannister and made his way back down the grand staircase.

He was finding it hard to process the enormity of what he'd just been told. The Manchester United game could be the last one he — or anyone in Hornet Heaven — would see. There would be no more afterlife for the generations of Watford souls already in this paradise. No afterlife in future for the generations down on earth. There would be no more Hornet Heaven.

The thought brought Bill to a halt. A few steps down the staircase, he stopped and gripped the bannister with both hands to steady himself.

Trying to deal with the news, he peered down over the rail into the main part of the atrium several floors

below. It was teeming with deceased Watford fans —
happy deceased Watford fans — fetching programmes
for old games and chatting excitedly about the season so
far. These people all assumed what Bill himself had been
assuming until a moment ago. They believed the bliss of
being in Hornet Heaven was eternal.

But it wasn't, Bill now knew.

They were all going to die again.

* * *

At the bottom of the staircase, Bill found Henry and
solemnly ushered him into the programme office behind
the atrium's programme shelves so that they were out of
everyone else's earshot.

Henry said in his usual cheery manner: 'I say.
What's up, old thing? You look like you've seen a ghost.
Ha! See what I did there? We're *all* ghosts because
we're all dead!'

Bill turned even paler than he already was. He
asked Henry to sit down. He said: 'I'm afraid you need
to compose yourself to receive some terrible news.'

Henry sat down.

Bill continued: 'I don't quite know how to break

this gently, Henry, so I'll just say it. It looks like our afterlife is about to come to an end.'

Henry replied breezily: 'Golly. We've reached the end of eternity? That was quick. How time flies when you're having fun! Oh, well. At least we're finishing with a flourish. It's like I was saying before — we can retire undefeated this season.'

Over the years, Bill had often marvelled at Henry's ability to take a positive approach to truly awful news. But Bill wasn't marvelling now. He took off his spectacles and rubbed his eyes, wondering how to get Henry to comprehend the true gravity of the situation. As he rubbed, he didn't notice Derek enter the room.

Bill looked up and tried again with Henry. He said: 'Henry, we haven't reached the end of eternity, but our afterlife is ending. Probably tonight. The real world will continue, but Hornet Heaven won't exist. *We* won't exist.'

A shrill voice exclaimed: 'What!'

Bill turned and saw his 13-year-old assistant.

Derek burst into tears. He sobbed: 'It's not fair, sir. I'm only young, sir!'

Derek had been young in Hornet Heaven for 97 years, but Bill didn't feel the moment was right to point this out.

'There's so much I haven't done yet, sir!'

Bill wasn't quite sure what Derek meant. In Hornet Heaven, the 13-year-old had been to every single match Watford had played since the club was founded in 1881. To Bill's mind, the boy had led the fullest and richest afterlife possible.

Derek continued with rising panic: 'It's so not fair, sir! No football fan wants to die mid-season because it means they won't find out what happens. But it happened to me last time and now it's going to happen again! With Watford level top of the Premier League! We can't die now, sir! You've got to do something, sir! You've got to do something!'

Henry tried to help. He asked tentatively: 'Is this one of those problems you could fix with one of your Magical History Tours, Bill?'

Bill looked at Henry. He looked at Derek. Sometimes, in a crisis, they were totally useless. He was going to have to shoulder the burden of trying to save Hornet Heaven himself.

He left the office with a firm instruction to the others: 'What I've told you must stay within these four walls.'

* * *

Bill cleared his mind and returned to the IT department. If he was going to save Hornet Heaven before the United game started, he needed more information on the nature of the fuel problem.

He sat down next to Roy and said: 'There must be a way we can control the supply of Hornet Love to the system — surely.'

'It was all set up long before I arrived,' Roy replied. 'No-one provided a manual — as always. But I can try and explain how it works.'

Roy leaned forward towards his computer screen and tilted his head. He said: 'These blooming varifocal glasses. I've never got used to them.'

He pointed to two digital dials.

'Look,' he said, 'there are two sources of Hornet Love. This dial shows the levels of love in Hornet Heaven, and this dial shows the love in the land of the living.'

'I see,' Bill said. 'Internal and external, if you like.'

'Quite. In the early days of Hornet Heaven, when

there weren't so many matches to visit, the love we generated up here ourselves could sustain everything. But as time went on, and the number of matches grew, the system needed more Hornet Love than the residents could provide. We reached crisis point about a decade ago when the internal supply nearly dried up.'

'Because the club was totally unloveable? Don't tell me — the last days of Boothroyd!'

'Exactly. That was when the external supply was added to keep us going.'

Bill tried to read the dials. There was a lot of gobbledegook data surrounding them, and buttons with words he didn't understand. 'There's an awful lot of computery language,' he said. 'We need Steve Palmer up here.'

But the colours on the display told Bill everything he needed to know. The internal dial had reached a medium red danger level, but the external dial was in the dark red — with virtually no headroom left.

Roy pointed to the external dial and said: 'This is an amazingly high reading. There must be more Watford fans than ever out there — all around the world, perhaps. Plus a fair bit of extra love from fans of other clubs when they see Watford competing with the Big Six clubs this season.'

'So if the love coming from the real world is what could kill us, can we control its flow in any way?' Bill asked.

'It'll reduce if we start losing, I suppose. But that means we're at the mercy of external events.'

'Surely there must be a shut-off facility. Some kind of stop-cock.'

'Good luck finding that. You'd have to locate the pipes, or whatever. I've never found any. Like I say, it was all set up long before I arrived. There's probably some ancient plumbing somewhere.'

Bill thought for a while.

'Wait,' he said. 'What if I could dramatically reduce the flow of love coming from people inside Hornet Heaven — the internal source. Would that save the system from being flooded?'

Roy replied: 'In theory, yes.'

'Then that's the way forward. I wouldn't need to locate any pipes.'

'But how would you reduce the flow?'

'I don't know. Maybe I could just say or do something here in Hornet Heaven that makes people love Watford less.'

'I see. Any idea what?'

Bill hurriedly got up from his chair and headed for the door.

He said: 'Not yet. But at least I now know what I have to do. I have to find a way to get the residents of Hornet Heaven to love Watford less. In the next hour or so.'

* * *

Bill hurried back to the programme office, expecting to find Derek and Henry still there.

Instead, he found Derek with Daisy Meriden. The teenagers were standing awkwardly, a yard apart. The boy was blushing. Bill had the distinct impression he might have interrupted something. He said: 'Ah. Hello, Daisy.'

'Hello, babes. You alright?'

Bill knew that Derek had held a torch for Daisy since she'd arrived in Hornet Heaven three years earlier. He wondered if impending doom was finally prompting the boy to act on his long-suppressed romantic impulses. But there wasn't time for any of that now.

Bill replied: 'If I'm totally honest, I've had better

days, young lady. Look, could you do me a big favour? Could you go and find Henry and ask him to join us?'

'Sure. No problem, babes.'

When Daisy had gone, Bill cautiously approached Derek. The news that today was probably the last day that they'd be Watford fans — that their souls were about to be cast into an oblivion of eternal nothingness — understandably seemed to have hit the boy hard.

Bill said gently: 'Are you alright, my boy?'

Derek started tidying some programmes. He said falteringly: 'Not really, sir.'

'I expect you're feeling a little bit frightened.'

Derek nodded.

Bill looked at the boy who'd been his assistant for the last sixteen years in Hornet Heaven. His friend and companion. His son — as good as.

Bill said: 'Do you, er… Would you feel better for a hug, my boy?'

Derek nodded again. He said: 'But I was hoping it wouldn't be from you, if I'm honest, sir.'

Bill was wondering how to take this when Henry arrived through the door.

He closed the door and they all sat down together.

Bill explained as quickly as he could what he'd

discovered from looking at Roy's computer.

He concluded: 'The upshot is this: we need to make Hornet Heaven residents love Watford less. So I need ideas. What could I tell people to make them instantly fall out of love with Watford? Hit me…'

Henry said: 'Ah! Super! What fun! I love banter like this. We should get Ray-Bans and Hipster involved. Right, I know — I'd tell people Walter Mazzarri was coming back! Ha! Wasn't he terrible? Ha!'

Bill said: 'Henry — please! This is deadly serious. Let me rephrase the question. What could the club actually do in real life that would make you genuinely stop supporting Watford?'

Derek and Henry gave this some proper thought.

Derek said: 'Relocate to Udine and become Udinese B for real, sir?'

'Aha, I get it now,' Henry said. 'Or relocate to Milton Keynes?'

Bill said: 'Both of those are good. What else?'

'I know, sir. Merge with another team, sir. Merge with…' Derek gasped at the thought that had just occurred to him. 'Merge with them from up the—'

'Good Lord!' Henry said. 'Don't you dare even say it, young man.'

'Brilliant, my boy,' Bill said. 'Hearing that news would definitely be a deal-breaker for Watford fans. The Hornet Love dial would hang limply at zero.'

Henry disagreed crossly: 'No. This is going too far. We couldn't tell people that. This is a heaven, not a hell.'

'But it would be for people's own good, Mr Grover, sir. We'd be saving their lives — or rather their afterlives, obviously.'

'No. I'm The Father Of The Club, and I simply couldn't countenance—'

Bill said: 'This is an emergency, Henry. We have to be pragmatic.'

'No,' Henry insisted. 'We have to uphold standards.'

Derek squeaked back: 'But we're in a life-or-death situation, Mr Grover, sir... Or, "afterlife-or-death"... Wait — or is it "death-or-death"?' The teenager grunted in frustration. 'Whatever! I just want to still exist tomorrow!'

Derek's voice juddered on the word 'tomorrow', repeating and wobbling.

The boy cried out: 'Oh my God! I just glitched. I'm about to die!'

Derek jumped out of his chair and ran out of the office in panic.

Henry looked rather shaken by the glitch. The Father Of The Club said to Bill: 'Look, er... maybe we shouldn't get too worked up, old thing. This might all have blown over by later tonight. We're bound to lose to United, so the world will lose interest in Watford and Hornet Heaven will survive to live another day... Plenty more days... Forevermore. I'm sure this is all a false alarm. Everything's going to be fine.'

At that moment, Roy from IT burst through the door.

'Bill!' Roy said in alarm. 'The levels have hit absolute maximum! There must have been a flattering pre-match preview in the papers or on the telly! The people out there love Watford more than ever! Hornet Heaven could crash out of existence at any moment!'

Henry stared at Roy.

He turned and stared at Bill.

Then he, too, ran out of the office.

* * *

Back in the atrium, Henry rushed to the yellow leather

sofas.

He clambered up onto one. The situation was now so urgently critical that he had to take matters into his own hands as The Father Of The Club. He had to do whatever it took.

He shouted: 'Everyone! Listen to me! I've got terrible news! Watford Football Club is merging with Luton!'

A few fans turned round and looked at him.

One said: 'Cobblers!'

'It's true,' Henry insisted. 'We're merging. I've heard.'

'How have you heard? In Hornet Heaven we don't have any contact with the land of the living between matches.'

'Erm… It says so in the programme. Today's United programme.'

'The programme ain't in yet. You're making it up.'

Henry hesitated.

'Bugger!' he said. 'Right. In that case, I'll tell you something I definitely know… Um… Yes. This. I've always been a secret Luton fan. I founded the club as an offshoot of Luton Town. I tricked you all by calling it

Watford Rovers. This club is actually Luton in disguise… Hey, come back… It's the truth!… You've got to believe me! You've got to despise me! You've got to hate our club!'

Another fan called out: 'Give it a rest, mate. We're about to beat United and make it five wins on the trot. How could anyone hate Watford right now?'

Henry climbed off the sofa. He mumbled to himself, distraught: 'This is the end. This is actually it.'

* * *

At the same moment, Derek was at the other end of the atrium, hiding between two rows of programme shelves. He was about to die again. Everyone he knew and loved was about to die again. Deep, terrified sobs leaped out of him.

Daisy heard him and found him. She approached him.

Despite their three Halloween dances, it was only today that Derek had been brave enough to actually start talking to Daisy. But she was aware he had feelings for her.

She stood in front of him and put a hand on his

shoulder as he cried. His shoulders heaved as he sobbed.

She lifted a hand and touched his cheek.

Derek looked her in the eye. He blurted: 'I'm going to die! Any moment now!'

Daisy had no idea what had brought on this extreme behaviour. She said nothing. With her forefinger she gently stroked away one of the streams of tears.

'I'm going to die!' he cried. 'And I've never even been kissed!'

Daisy moved her forefinger to his lips — to hush him.

Then she leaned forward.

Derek looked at her lips. He held his breath. He was trembling.

Daisy leaned further forward.

Then…

'Programme's in!' shouted a voice.

Suddenly there was a rush of footsteps towards the shelves. Dozens of Watford fans appeared at the end of the row to fetch themselves the United programme. One said: ''Scuse us, young lovers! We've got a game to go to!'

Daisy stepped away from Derek.

Derek bowed his head.

* * *

In the centre of the atrium, Derek and Daisy arrived from the programme shelves. Bill arrived from the programme office. They gathered around Henry — who was sitting on one of the yellow sofas with his head in his hands.

Henry looked up. Bill, Derek and Henry looked at each other with the unspoken knowledge that if Watford beat Manchester United, it was the last time they'd see each other.

Daisy was holding four programmes for the game. She said: 'I don't know what's going on with you guys, but we've got a game to go to.'

Bill, Henry and Derek didn't move.

'Come on, guys!' Daisy said. 'It'll feel amazing if we beat United. We'll be so loved up!'

Bill shuddered at Daisy's choice of phrase. He said: 'I'm sorry, Daisy, but I'm afraid that — today — I don't want Watford to win.'

'What?'

Derek said: 'Me too, Miss Daisy, miss.'

Henry said: 'Me too, old girl.'

'Whoa! Me nut just spun!' Daisy said. 'You want

us to lose our 100% record?'

Henry said: 'It feels terrible, but for the first time in 137 years, since I founded the club, I want us to lose.'

'But why?'

Bill said: 'To be honest, Daisy, we're being selfish. Really, we should sacrifice our own interests and want the right thing for the club — for the community of fans in the land of the living. But...'

'But what?'

Bill continued: 'But... Come on, United!'

'You what?'

'Come on, United!' Derek said.

'Come on, United!' Henry said.

* * *

Bill, Derek and Henry sat in the Sir Elton John stand behind the dug-outs. Daisy had refused to sit with them if they were supporting United. She'd gone elsewhere in the stadium.

From his seat, Bill noticed there were several TV cameras around the pitch. The game was being shown live all over the world. There was an audience of millions waiting to love Watford. Bill tried to put this out of his mind.

Watford started the game well. Derek said: 'All three of us have watched every single Watford match in history, sir and Mr Grover, sir. But this is looking like the last game we'll ever see. It's the end of our own 100% record.'

Bill and Henry nodded gravely. Henry said: 'It's my last game and I'm having to support a team wearing shirts the colour of baby sick. There couldn't be a worse way to go.'

Troy Deeney had a shot from the edge of the box at the Vicarage Road end. United's keeper, De Gea, tipped it over the bar. Suddenly the match froze.

Bill said: 'Oh golly. The system's flooding. The watching world must be loving what they're seeing.'

Henry said: 'We're done for.'

Suddenly the match re-started.

Bill shouted: 'Come on, United!'

Derek shouted: 'Come on, United!'

Henry shouted: 'Come on, United!'

In the 35th minute, Romelu Lukaku scored for United, brushing the ball home at the far post. Bill, Derek and Henry instinctively got to their feet. But they managed to hold back any raucous cheers. They looked around discreetly before fist-bumping.

Three minutes later, Chris Smalling hooked the ball into Watford's net for United's second. Bill, Derek and Henry began to feel a little safer. It allowed their natural loyalty to Watford to resurface.

Derek asked Bill: 'Do you think it's alright to hope that Watford pull one back, sir? Or would it bring about our catastrophic demise, sir?'

'Well, there haven't been any glitches for a while, I suppose, my boy.'

'Good,' Derek said. He squawked loudly: 'Come on you, Horns!'

'Derek!' Bill said. 'Careful, young man!'

In the second half, after 65 minutes, Watford did pull one back: Andre Gray scored from an Abdoulaye Doucouré cut-back. The real world crowd around them roared. But then all the celebrations glitched and stopped.

'Oh golly,' Bill said. 'The worldwide love for Watford is back.'

'Be brave, my friends,' Henry said. 'We're on the edge of destruction.'

The crowd and the action resumed.

'Crikey,' Derek said, 'that was a close thing!'

For the next half hour, Watford had the best of the game. They gave it everything. The crowd were right behind the Horns.

Derek said: 'I'm sorry, sir. I can't do this anymore. The club I love deserves my full support. Look at the way we're playing.'

'I know what you mean, my boy, but—'

Bill's voice juddered and wobbled for a few seconds. Then he said: 'Oh Golly. I've just glitched!'

'I don't care, sir,' Derek said. 'If we've got to go, we should go in the right way, sir — supporting Watford to the absolute end.'

The Father Of The Club looked at Derek. He said: 'The boy's absolutely right. I can't finish my afterlife supporting another team. I'm Watford till I die — again.'

Henry stood up and said: 'Do not go gentle into that good night / Old age should burn and rave at close of day / Rage, rage against the dying of the light… You Orns!'

Bill stood up and said: 'Though wise men at their end know dark is right / Because their words had forked no lightning they / Do not go gentle into that good night… You Orns!'

Derek stood up and said: 'Grave men, near death, who see with blinding sight / Blind eyes could blaze like meteors and be gay / Rage, rage against the dying of the light… Youuuuu Orrrrrns!'

Watford continued to give it everything. In the last minute of added time, United's Nemanja Matic was sent off for a foul on Will Hughes not far outside the area in front of the Graham Taylor Stand. Hughes readied himself to swing the free-kick into the box.

Derek said: 'Oh my God, sir! This is amazing! We could equalise here!'

Bill said: 'Yes, but… grabbing a last-minute point against United will make the world adore Watford. This could be the last thing we ever see.'

Henry said solemnly: 'Gentlemen…'

The Father Of The Club, in the middle of the three, took Derek's hand. He took Bill's hand.

Henry continued: '…It's been wonderful knowing you.'

They watched as Hughes's free-kick curved into the box. Christian Kabasele climbed high and got in a header. The ball flew towards the top corner and…

…The match froze.

When the match didn't start again, Bill, Derek and

Henry looked at each other in the silence.

Henry said: 'I say, what's going on. Is that it? Has Hornet Heaven crashed?'

Bill replied: 'Golly, I don't know.'

Derek said: 'You didn't say it would be like this, sir. Are we going to be trapped in this frozen game forever, sir — not knowing what happened next? Are we going to spend eternity here — wondering what might have been?'

The three of them waited — surrounded by the silent, static, real-world crowd — but the action didn't re-start.

After a while, teenaged Derek got bored. He went on to the pitch to have a wander round. Bill and Henry decided to do the same.

Many other Hornet Heaven residents came onto the pitch too. They had no idea what was going on. They asked Bill. Bill informed them calmly: 'There's a technical problem. Roy from IT will find a fix for it soon, with a bit of luck.'

Bill, Henry and Derek went to the Rookery End penalty area where the players were posed like figures in a tableau. Kabasele was staring at the ball he'd just headed, mouth agape in hope. Deeney, Gray and Success were fiercely fixated on the ball, seemingly willing it into the net. A trio of United defenders — Fellaini, Smalling and Bailly — were half-turned, staring back at their goal in what looked like terror. It was like a Spot The Ball photograph — except that the ball was visible, suspended in mid-air on its way towards goal.

Henry said with a sigh: 'You know, I could probably live with this.'

Bill was taken aback. He said: 'Being trapped at a frozen game for the rest of all time, you mean?'

'No, this scene in the goalmouth,' Henry clarified. He explained serenely: 'I could live with it as a memento of having supported Watford. I mean, look what's here: a magnificently developed stadium; rather splendid striped shirts; a team with a 100% record to date; a performance that's been full of fight and character; and Manchester United terrified that we're about to prove we're their equals. I'll take all that as a permanent souvenir of the love I've had.'

Bill looked at the scene. He saw what Henry meant. Throughout their afterlives, they'd enjoyed the ability to go and watch any Watford game they wanted — re-live every game, feel every game. But if they could only have one still image, this might do.

Bill said: 'Well, I guess this is it, then. This is us. For all time.'

Henry nodded solemnly. A tear slipped down Derek's cheek.

Suddenly, though, there was a noise.

Bill, Derek and Henry turned to watch as the match action re-started — in slow motion at first.

The ball continued towards goal.

United's keeper De Gea took off to his left.

De Gea stretched.

De Gea finger-tipped the ball past the post.

As the match action resumed normal speed, Derek shouted: 'Saved!'

* * *

After the United defeat, Derek scampered off to look for Daisy.

Meanwhile, Bill and Henry climbed up the grand atrium staircase to the IT department.

They weren't as bullish as Derek had been at the match that they were out of peril. They wanted to know if the levels of Hornet Love flowing into Hornet Heaven were still dangerously high.

Roy welcomed them in. He pushed his spectacles higher and peered at his computer screen. It wasn't good news.

'Oh,' Roy said. 'Both dials are still at maximum, I'm afraid.'

Bill said: 'You mean, the external flow hasn't gone down at all?'

'People down in the real world must have loved how the team played in defeat,' Roy said.

'Oh no.'

'And they'll probably feel even more love after the match,' Roy continued. 'There'll be glowing match reports; Javi Gracia will smile modestly and charmingly.'

Bill said: 'Oh golly. A Troy Deeney post-match interview could be the thing that finishes us off.'

Henry sighed heavily. He said: 'Fair play, I suppose. If you have to lose a game, that's how you should lose it. Gentlemen, I was proud to be a Horn today. Today — and always.'

Henry left the room and went and stood outside.

Bill followed.

They stood together at a balcony rail, looking down on the main part of the atrium several floors below.

Bill said: 'You sound as if you've reached some kind of closure, Henry.'

Henry replied: 'I think I have, old thing. If my story has to end here, it's ending in a good place.'

They gazed at the deceased Watford fans and former players milling about happily down below — despite the defeat to United. They saw Johnny Allgood, Ralph Thorpe (the former Alderman), Fred Pagnam, Freddie Sargent, Lamper. No-one down there knew what Bill and Henry knew about the continuing danger levels in Hornet Heaven; it was probably best they didn't know.

Henry spotted Derek — with Daisy — chatting by the programme shelves on the ground floor.

Henry asked Bill: 'And what about your young assistant, old chap? I'm not sure he's reached any kind of closure.'

Bill saw the teenagers step closer to each other.

They moved closer still.

Briefly, tenderly, Derek and Daisy kissed.

Bill could see the smile on Derek's face from several floors above.

But Bill had a far bigger smile himself.

Henry said: 'And you, old sport, you loveliest of all old things. How are you feeling?'

Bill looked down and reflected for a moment. Then he said: 'I'm think I'm ready, Henry. Watford was a big part of my life down on earth, and all of my afterlife up here. But being a Watford fan isn't about the individual. It's not about whether I was personally at a game, or how I felt about a result. It's about enjoying being part of a special community of people, with special values — a diverse group unified by the love of one thing. And, golly, have I enjoyed being part of that group, Henry. If my time's at an end, it's at an end. The club — the group — will go on.'

Henry was silent for a while. Then he managed to say: 'And what would you miss, old pal — if our souls end up elsewhere, far from Watford, in some other kind of afterlife?'

Bill replied: 'The programmes, obviously. You. Derek. Everyone in the group, really. And the match days. Oh, the match days, Henry. The excitement, the noise, the colour — the yellow shirts and the black shorts.'

Henry said affectionately: 'Red shorts, Bill — surely. Red shorts.'

Bill smiled. He wrapped an arm around his old friend's shoulder. Together they laughed, looking down from on high at the ghosts of Watford-lovers below, until their laughter juddered, glitched and faded into silence.

THE END

WANT MORE?

This volume contains the stories that were broadcast in Series 6, 7 and 8 of the Hornet Heaven podcast (plus one special out-of-series episode).

You can listen to audio versions of the stories by visiting www.HornetHeaven.com or by searching for 'Hornet Heaven' in Apple Podcasts, Google Podcasts, Spotify, or any other good podcasting app.

Printed in Poland
by Amazon Fulfillment
Poland Sp. z o.o., Wrocław